Praise for EART

"When you find yourself thinking of certain characters long after you've finished the book, you know the author has done her job. Patricia Hickman has certainly 'done her job' in EARTHLY VOWS—the charming ending to a charming series."

— Sylvia Bambola, author of *Refiner's Fire* and *Return to Appleton*

"Patricia Hickman's EARTHLY VOWS, the finale to her popular Millwood Hollow series, presents a deeply emotional voyage into human hearts—the good, the wandering, and the misguided. Truth shimmers in every phrase."

—Lyn Cote, author of the Women of Ivy Manor series

"EARTHLY VOWS is the perfect ending to the Millwood Hollow series. Patricia Hickman's spare, unvarnished prose is well suited to her Depression-era tale."

—Deanna Julie Dodson, author of *In Honor Bound*, *By Love Redeemed*, and *To Grace Surrendered*

"Patty Hickman's EARTHLY VOWS is a sepia portrait of life in the 1930s. Her characters step alive off the pages and walk straight into your imagination."

—Eric Wiggin, author of the Rebecca of Sunnybrook Farm series

EARTHLY VOWS

THE MILLWOOD HOLLOW SERIES

PATRICIA HICKMAN

NEW YORK   BOSTON   NASHVILLE

This book is a work of fiction. Names, characters, places, and incidents are the product of the author's imagination or are used fictitiously. Any resemblance to actual events, locales, or persons, living or dead, is coincidental.

Copyright © 2006 Patricia Hickman
All rights reserved.

FaithWords
Hachette Book Group USA
1271 Avenue of the Americas, New York, NY 10020

Visit our Web site at www.faithwords.com.

The FaithWords name and logo are trademarks of Hachette Book Group USA.

Printed in the United States of America

First Edition: November 2006
10 9 8 7 6 5 4 3 2 1

Library of Congress Cataloging-in-Publication Data

Hickman, Patricia.
  Earthly vows / Patricia Hickman.— 1st ed.
      p. cm. — (The Millwood Hollow series)
  Summary: "The fourth and final novel of the Millwood Hollow series finds Jeb Nubey and Fern Coulter finally setting a wedding date, but visiting Fern's family in Oklahoma proves unexpectedly rocky"—Provided by the publisher.
   ISBN-13: 978-0-446-69235-9
   ISBN-10: 0-446-69235-2
  1. Clergy—Fiction. 2. Arkansas—Fiction. 3. Depression—Fiction. I. Title.
  PS3558.I2296E17 2006
   813'.54—dc22   *2006007621*

To Randy

If ever two were one, then surely we.
If ever man were loved by wife, then thee.

ANN BRADSTREET

Acknowledgments

A special thank-you to Jim Gabbert of the State Historical Society, for providing me with the facts about Oklahoma City, Ardmore, and Norman during the 1930s.

Thanks to the Warner team for your faith and confidence in the Millwood Hollow series.

Thanks to my peers and the fantastic faculty at Queens University for your input and comments.

EARTHLY
VOWS

I

THE AIR WAS STIFLING HOT, INSULATED BY the hard blue Oklahoma sky. The meeting in the campus president's office convened beneath the shade of the oldest oak tree on the Bible school campus. Jeb loosened his tie. The summer of 1936 was breaking all heat records. A student strummed a hymn on an oversized guitar, not far from where Jeb stood with Jonathan Flauvert, the school's president. It was agitating, but he didn't let on. It was hard to keep his composure, what with the heat. But Flauvert was long in description, and what he had to say left Jeb stunned.

Abigail Coulter, his fiancée's mother, arranged for all of them to meet two of Fern's brothers and their wives for lunch, to tell them of their engagement. That was all that had been made of the trip to Ardmore. Jeb did not tell Fern of the small detail in Gracie's letter from Cincinnati. There was no need. It was probably nothing.

His introduction to Jonathan Flauvert was through a mutual friend, his former mentor Reverend Philemon Gracie, the preacher who penned the letter tucked in his coat pocket. Jonathan walked him into the shade of the oak that centered the Bible school campus. "I won't beat around the bush. Our church committee has read your letter of recommendation from Philemon Gracie. We want to offer you a church here in Oklahoma."

Jeb had not misread Gracie's hint about a new pulpit opportunity. Maybe he should have mentioned it to Fern after all. But if it amounted to nothing, then why trouble her?

Philemon retired a few years ago from the Church in the Dell in Nazareth. He was nursing an ulcer but kept close contact with Jeb, whom he had trained to assume his post. When Jeb wrote and told him of their upcoming trip to Ardmore, Gracie must have sent a letter of introduction at once to the dean of the school. "Gracie told me he was finagling a deal," said Jeb. He was astonished. "This is what he meant. My only scholastic background was gotten under his tutelage, Dr. Flauvert. Did he tell you that?" he asked.

"Gracie is highly respected here on our campus. Your credentials are respectable."

There was no harm in asking, so Jeb said, "I'd like to know more about the church, Reverend. The work in Nazareth has come through a lot of fires, so to speak. But

I'll admit that the thought of a change has crossed my mind lately." He and Fern had known the best and worst of times at Church in the Dell. "My fiancée has settled in Nazareth. I don't know what she'll say."

"Your engagement is recent?"

"A few months," said Jeb.

"I hear your fiancée is a connoisseur of antiquities," said Reverend Flauvert. He was a short man with hair so blond that the rest of him looked as pink as a salmon. He walked with toes out, black shoes worn at the heels, but polished.

Gracie evidently said more about Fern and him than he admitted. "She not only collects them, but reads every book in her library and the town's library," said Jeb. "You've not seen a library like Fern's. Fern buys books before she buys food."

"Maybe a gift will help to soften her up." The president smiled. "Fern sounds the intelligent type." He opened a small box that held a book, an old copy of *Jane Eyre*.

"You know her mother lives in Ardmore. Dad's buried right on the family estate." That didn't mean she'd jump at the chance to move back here. Her trips to Ardmore were slow in coming.

"Give her the book first, just in case." Flauvert was sober, much like Gracie. "Allow me to walk you out to your automobile," he said. He opened up the book and showed him the title page and the scrawled ink beneath the title. He kept pushing his eyeglasses up the bridge of his nose. "There's another matter, a matter of a dinner party Friday night. My wife, Rachel, has no use for parties. One of the parishioners is a businessman in Oklahoma City and he and his wife throw lavish dinner parties. When the Oakleys heard of you, they wanted you in their pulpit on Sunday. They insisted that you come into the city Friday evening and bring your Fern."

Jeb was reluctant. Fern would wonder why they were attending a party with strangers. "Can you tell me more about the Oakleys?"

"Somehow my name made it onto the dinner lists when I became the school president. I always believed that if Henry and Marion Oakley saw the smallness of the school, they'd drop me. But they have, and they didn't," said Flauvert. "When this Depression hit, the school would have floundered had it not been for people like the Oakleys. So when their invitation arrived, Rachel felt some culture in Oklahoma City might soften you and your fiancée to the idea of moving." He held out the invitation.

She'd raise objections. Fern could not be rushed. "Fern's always saying that I need a better suit for special occasions."

"My suit is fifteen years old. But we're clergymen. It's expected, it's expected." He kept talking as he walked Jeb out to Fern's car. "Gracie mentioned that you have three children. Are you a widower?"

"I take care of three kids not my own. The Welbys were abandoned and took up with me in Nazareth. Angel is the oldest and she has a younger brother and sister, Willie and Ida May. They're back at the house with Fern's mother. She's quite taken with them, especially Ida May."

"So you and Fern will come with a ready-made family. That's a challenge for a newlywed couple."

"To tell you the truth, I tried to find the Welby kids' family, but it never worked out. I held off proposing to Fern, thinking someday we'd be free to marry." He tucked the party invitation into a pocket. "She said yes anyway."

"Fern sounds special."

"There's no woman like Fern. In my old skirt-chasing days, I never met anyone with Fern's character. I'm lucky she'll have me."

"That copy of *Jane Eyre* belonged to our daughter, Ellie. She died of typhoid."

"It's a twice-blessed gift, Jon. Are you sure your wife wants to part with it?"

"When I told Rachel about you, that you might come and shepherd our city flock, she wanted you to have it." Flauvert handed the box to Jeb, a small, lidded container covered with violet fabric.

"That was one of Rachel's old jewelry boxes. She keeps a lot of Ellie's things tucked in all kinds of places."

"Fern will be grateful, Reverend Flauvert. Would it be a good idea to bring Fern by to meet you?"

"Rachel's hosting a luncheon tomorrow at our place for the faculty. Nothing fancy, but two of our domestics will be preparing a banquet. I'd love it if you dropped in with Fern. Join us for lunch and I'll give her the details of the city church. First Community is the name."

He couldn't let Flauvert be the one to spring things on Fern. Who was he kidding? Hadn't she mentioned more than once how happy she was to leave Oklahoma behind? She was the teacher who'd brought the Stanton School in Nazareth up to her higher standards. She attacked it like a missionary. Several towns benefited from Stanton's ability to thrive in a Depression.

"You'll pass our little house on your way back into Ardmore. Redbud House is in the middle of a pecan grove on your right before you take Moor Road back into town." Flauvert opened the car door for Jeb. "Best pecans in the county, by the way, grow in that grove." Jeb read the school's history in a pamphlet. The president's house was a new work some of the college students started a few years back, before the Depression hit. So when they found that grove on school property, they decided to build the house right smack in the middle of the pecan trees. He wrote down the time and address and handed it to Jeb. "The faculty reception is a modest gathering, good food. I'll introduce you around."

Fern would come to a reception. "I'll bring her by tomorrow."

࿂

"Nazareth has taken its toll on you, Jeb. That's why we came to Ardmore, so you could take some time off. No other reason than that." Fern buttoned up the laundered shirts brought in from the clothesline by her mother's housemaid.

"So many churches have floundered under the weight of this Depression. Think what we could do to help," said Jeb.

Fern lifted a half-dozen shirts by the coat hanger crooks.

The maid appeared. "Miss Coulter, I'll take care of the wash." She took the shirts out of Fern's hands.

"I'm making myself useful, Myrna. Heaven knows why my mother continues to knock around in this big old place all alone."

The maid smiled and then left them alone in Fern's bedroom.

"Did you tell him you would take the Oklahoma City church? Or that you might? What exactly did you say?" She was as irritable as he had seen her.

"Only that we would drop by tomorrow to discuss the matter further."

She folded her arms. "Did you want to tell him that you would do it?"

There was the word that she always managed to slip into the conversation, "want." Jeb sat on the edge of her bed, the one she slept in as a girl.

"Tell me what you're thinking, Jeb. You're scaring me."

"I'll admit that I was interested. I don't know why, though, other than the fact that I've been feeling weary lately. You're right, Nazareth is weighing on me."

"Do you think Oklahoma City would be any different?"

"My past followed me into Nazareth, Fern."

"Everybody has a past."

Everyone except Fern, he thought. "Can we visit the church first, and then condemn it?"

"This isn't like you, to try and uproot us without talking to me."

"Isn't that what we're doing now, talking?"

"If I would have known—is that what Gracie's letter was about? Did you know that we were coming here to size up a new parish?"

"I'm as surprised as you. But, yes, Gracie hinted in his letter. Didn't I show you his letter?" The minute he said it, she had him pegged.

"You didn't show it to me."

"I only met with Dr. Flauvert today because Gracie asked me to meet him." He put the lavender box between them on the bed. "Dr. Flauvert asked me to give this to you. It belonged to his daughter, Ellie."

"I have *Jane Eyre*." She turned the book over, glanced at the cover.

"It's signed by the author, Fern. And his daughter has passed away."

Fern opened the book to the title page. "He gave this to me?"

"Gracie told him what a fan you are of antiquities."

Fern wiped her eyes. "This must have meant a lot to the Flauverts. I'm sorry I've been so emotional." Her voice softened and she leaned back into her bed pillow, more relaxed.

"There's more. We're invited to a dinner party this Friday at a hotel in Oklahoma City." He sat next to her on the bed.

"You don't have a good suit, not one you could wear to an evening affair."

He was ready for that objection. "I'll manage. You dress me. With you on my arm, who will notice the suit anyway?" She was moving ahead with him. He could feel the momentum.

"Jeb, when I left Ardmore, I left behind all of those superficial people."

"What people did you leave behind, Fern?" Fern's mother, Abigail, appeared in the doorway.

"Are you ready for lunch, Mother?" asked Fern.

"Fern and I have been invited to a dinner party in Oklahoma City, Abigail."

"You'll need a new dress. This is thrilling, Fern. A dinner party is always a good idea. Summer parties are almost as good as autumn, a little warm, but after the sun sets, it's all about the music and the costumes anyway. We'll have to buy it ready-made," said Abigail.

"I didn't say I'd go," said Fern. Her face lost all color.

"Are you sick?" asked Abigail.

"I'm not in a dinner party mood. As a matter of fact, I'd like to head back to Nazareth Friday."

Jeb pursed his lips and then said, "I've got a pastor friend taking my pulpit Sunday, remember, Fern? So I can rest? The ball is perfect. We need a night out and the invitation is a gift from a great friend of Gracie's. It would be an insult to turn them down."

Fern wouldn't look at him.

Jeb's confidence faltered.

"You know that Angel and I can handle Willie and Ida May," said Abigail.

"Mother, don't get involved."

"Well, I only came in to tell you I'm dressed to go out. I'll be waiting in the den. That is, if we're still in the mood for lunch." Abigail left, but pushed the bedroom door back open behind her.

"Jeb, you ought to know I never include my mother in my plans."

"She's not really in your plans, Fern. She happened to walk in, and you can't blame her curiosity. But I agree with her. You saying that a party wouldn't lift your spirits?"

She lay back on the white coverlet and turned her face toward the window.

"Fern, we've been living hand-to-mouth, mending our lives back together only to have them come unraveled again. We need this—I need this."

"You don't know anything about these kind of people. Their decorum, Jeb."

"Is that it? Are you afraid I'll embarrass you?"

"That's not it, and you know it. I don't know how everything got so out of focus. This was supposed to be a simple trip to my family's house to get some rest and tell them we're getting married."

A laugh came from down the hall.

"You just told your mother, Fern."

"Don't tell Buddy and Lewis, Mother! I'll tell them today over lunch," Fern yelled. "Jeb, the people who go to these balls, they don't understand us. We're the proletarians, they're the blue bloods." She never saw herself that way, even though he did.

"Would you let me experience blue bloods for myself, Fern? I like the sound of my water glass being filled by someone else for a change."

"What I've always liked about you is that you don't

mind serving the down-and-outer, and during this godawful Depression, there are more of them than there are those
who only give to have their name printed in the society
pages."

"You asked me to take a leave from the pulpit so that
we could finally know one another in a different light. No
church around my neck. So here we are without shackles
and there you go slapping them back on."

"Do you really want to go, Jeb?"

"Only if you go with me." Jeb looked toward the open
door and then kissed her. "You look good lying here in the
afternoon sun."

She faked a smile, her eyes looking away from him.
He was going to kiss her again until she pursed her lips in
a patently obligatory kiss. Her head dropped back onto the
pillow. "Are you sure you're ready to meet my family?
They're not like what you think. Coulters come from wild
stock." She rolled off the bed and the white coverlet,
dipped to straighten her stockings, and left Jeb alone on
the bed.

"I'm from wild stock too," he said. She knew that. But
she had never told him anything of the sort about the
Coulters. "Tell me more about this wild stock." But she had
already walked out of the room.

❧

Angel ran her fingers across the collar of a tailored dress
that hung in the back of Marshella's Dry Goods and
Clothiers. She moved her drawstring purse up her arm and
over her shoulder.

"So you live with my aunt Fern?" a teenaged girl asked Angel. She was a short fifteen-year-old named Phoebe, slightly younger than Angel.

"I live with Jeb, along with my brother and sister, Willie and Ida May." Angel pulled out the dress, as though she were seriously considering shelling out the five dollars to buy it.

"Jeb's good-looking, but his shoes look worn out. If a man can't keep a good pair of shoes, he can't buy you the things you need," said Phoebe.

Phoebe's mother, Betty, had offered to take them window-shopping before meeting up with Jeb and Fern for a noon meal downtown. Angel stopped short of referring to Jeb as Fern's fiancé. She was sworn to secrecy.

"Are you an orphan?"

"My mother got sick, so my father sent me to live with my sister in Nazareth." She no longer had to explain her story back in Nazareth, so to rehash it made her irritable. "But Claudia had moved away, so we stayed with Jeb. You met him this morning. He's the minister in our town."

"Where does Claudia live?"

"My aunt Kate sent me a letter a few weeks ago about Claudia. She said that she had finally gotten word that Claudia settled in Norman." Angel pulled off her hat. "Miz Abigail says Ardmore's not far from Norman." Abigail was Phoebe's grandma.

"Would you look at this dress? I look good in purple," said Phoebe.

Angel backed away from Phoebe. "Is it stuffy in here?" She put the dress back on the rack and said, "You keep looking and I'll go out for some air." She left Phoebe holding the purple dress in front of her. Phoebe was not Fern's best niece.

The sun bore down. Shimmers of heat danced over the downtown road, but a breeze cooled Angel's skin. She breathed in the fresh air.

"Aren't you the pretty thing?" A youth sat behind the wheel of a deep blue Studebaker parked out in front of Marshella's. His blond hair was cropped short on top, a patch of bangs hanging over his left brow.

Angel glanced back inside Marshella's. Phoebe was marching her momma to the rear of the store. Angel wanted to see inside the Studebaker. "I've never seen one of these before."

"Have a look then," he said.

"No one would drive this back home."

"Where's back home?" he asked.

"Nazareth. It's close to Hot Springs."

"Is that in Oklahoma?"

"Who are you?"

The youth shifted in the driver's seat and glanced down the street. "I'm Nash."

"You don't talk like you're from Oklahoma," said Angel.

"I'm from Boston."

Angel rubbed the chrome on the door.

"Open her up. Have a look." Nash smiled at Angel. He had good teeth, straight and shining out from a tanned face. He had combed in a good deal of male hair ointment, which darkened his hair.

Angel opened the door. She touched the leather and he was smiling, so she said, "I'm going to have a car like this one day. Is it yours?"

"I can't lie. I'm the driver for the owner. He's not around at the present, though. Want a ride around the block?"

Angel stepped away and backed under the shade of the faded store awning. Nash kept smiling out at her through the opened car door.

"How old are you?" he asked.

"Seventeen. You?"

"Older than you. Not much, though. You look older, kind of like a girl I knew back in Boston. Her name was Ethel Fox. Is that your name too?"

She smiled. Inside the store, Phoebe and her mother were looking over the tops of the store racks. "I have to go. I'm shopping with . . . an aunt." She didn't want to explain her life all over again. If Jeb and Fern married, Betty and Phoebe would be like family soon enough. She came out into the sunlight and closed the car door.

Betty stuck her head out the store door. "Angel, we're trying to decide on this dress. Want to help us?"

"I got faint, need some air. I should stay out here," said Angel.

Betty stepped from the doorway and felt her forehead, so Angel kept saying she was fine. Finally Betty went back inside.

"Your name suits you," said Nash.

"There's a drugstore around the corner. I could use a

cold drink, what with the heat and all." Angel pulled out the neck of her dress and fanned.

"How convenient! I can drive you." Nash jumped out of the car and ran around to open the door for her. She sunk into the hot leather seat. "You have a nickel for the soda?" she asked.

"Don't worry about money. Tab's on me," he said.

She would have to meet Jeb and Fern in a half hour at the Blue Moon Diner. "I can't stay long," she told him.

Nash checked his watch. "I got a minute I can spare for a girl like you."

⟋⟍

Jeb cranked up the Coulter Packard. Abigail never drove, not since Francis had died. Fern and her mother, Abigail, climbed inside. Abigail complained of the heat, but Fern didn't say a lot, and hadn't since Jeb brought up the church offer.

"Ida May and Willie want to stay here at the house, Jeb," said Abigail. "My niece likes doing for them, you know, making up lunch and all."

Jeb said, "Your brothers are coming to lunch today, as I understand it, right, Fern?"

Fern nodded and then let out a breath.

"My guess is that I could cook chicken out on the brick walk. Fern, roll down your window before I faint." Abigail laughed. "Now that'd be a memory here on the announcement of your engagement. I wish your father were here." She stared out the window. "Fern, you'll have to get Buddy to give you away. Jeb, I don't believe you've met

Fern's oldest brother, Lewis, have you? I hope you marry in the winter. Oklahoma's too hot this time of year."

"I've not met any of her brothers, Mrs. Coulter."

"That's right. The last time Fern was here was for her father's funeral. You stayed back home and sent Angel in your place. I wanted so many times to take her aside and talk to her about her family. But what with the funeral and all, it never seemed the right time."

"Angel doesn't open up too well with me," said Jeb.

"You're a man, though, Jeb. No offense," said Abigail.

Jeb drove them off the Coulter estate and toward town. "Looks like some clouds moving in," he said.

"It hasn't rained since I can't remember. Fern, you remember the summer we prayed for rain and you ran out on the lawn and did an Indian dance?"

"Did it work?" asked Jeb.

"I don't think I did that, Mother," said Fern.

"I know that had to be you. Your sisters were all too fussy to do such a thing," said Abigail.

Fern sighed. She hadn't ever described her sisters as fussy.

"There's a drop of rain on the glass. Want me to stop the car and let you out to dance, Fern?" asked Jeb.

"I'd do a dance if I thought it would help." Abigail rolled up the window glass before the road dust seeped inside.

"Angel sure likes your hospitality, Abigail. She says she'd rather be at your house than anyplace else," said Jeb.

"I wonder if those girls have shopped out all the

downtown stores," Abigail asked. "You'd think they had a bag of money the way they ran out of here this morning."

"Angel can't resist a new dress," said Fern. "She has a little money from a job she took back home."

"Not anymore. She bought Ida May some new shoes," said Jeb. "I should have given her some spending money." He had never seen Angel hang on to what money she made for long. She acted guilty about Willie and Ida May and thought it her duty to see to them when her mother and father hadn't.

"Maybe Betty can buy her something, just anything. I hate to see her empty-handed," said Abigail.

"Angel finds ways to get the things she needs. She's, how do I put this, resourceful." Jeb slowed for a rabbit.

Abigail guided Jeb all the way into downtown Ardmore. "As you pull into town, you'll drive past the Ardmore Savings and Loan and then drive for four more blocks." Her manicured fingers pointed, directing Jeb as though she were leading a choir. "See, yonder there's the bank. The first street on your right is Ashton. Take that and then park beside the drugstore. The Blue Moon is directly across the street."

"Lively town," said Jeb, only so Fern would give him a look.

Cars lined most of the streets outside the storefronts. A group of men smoked out on a bench near the bank. Some women and children formed a commodities line out the door of the courthouse and down the marble steps.

"I think they're passing out milk today. Such a shame to see so many families hit so hard." Abigail fell quiet for a moment and then said, "I feel helpless when I see the children in rags."

"Is that Gary Hayes?" Fern asked, looking toward the courthouse.

Abigail pushed her glasses up higher on her nose. "It is."

"He was the groundskeeper at our high school. I hate seeing him standing in the milk line," said Fern.

"At least he's got milk to get. The teachers have all kept their jobs for the most part, but some of the staff was let go. They could use a teacher like you."

"Here's the Blue Moon." Jeb parked across the street. He opened the car door and walked around to open both doors for Fern and Abigail.

"I see Betty and Phoebe inside already." Abigail led them across the street. She waved at the girls.

The aroma of the noon special—fried chicken, biscuits, and black-eyed peas—floated out to the street. Jeb opened the door for the women. He didn't see Angel. Fern had introduced him that morning to Betty and Phoebe. "Afternoon," he said. "Angel still buying out the store?"

"I was hoping to find her here with you, Reverend. The last time Phoebe and I saw her, she was standing out in front of Marshella's," said Betty.

"She was talking to a boy." Phoebe blew a large gum bubble.

"I didn't see that." Betty sounded disgusted with her, like she didn't believe her. "I'll go back and see if I can find her." She turned to leave.

"Why don't you ladies secure us a table? The rest of

the Coulters haven't arrived yet. I'll go and look for Angel."
Jeb saw the look Fern gave him. "Don't worry. She's close
by, I'm sure."

"Marshella's is down Ashton Street and then around
the corner, about a block and a half, if you want to start
there." Betty asked a waitress if she could help them find a
table for nine.

"Yonder she is," said Abigail. "Coming out of the
J&M Drug."

"Is she with a boy? He was really good-looking," said
Phoebe. "Nice car."

Angel walked out of the drugstore adjusting her hat,
dabbing her mouth like she'd eaten.

"She went for cold refreshment, that's all." Abigail
sounded relieved. "In this heat, who can blame her?"

Jeb hated to believe Phoebe, but he knew Angel well
enough too. He didn't see anyone follow Angel out of the
drugstore. He opened the door for her and she smiled.
"You finally made it, Biggest," he said.

"I bought a soda. I was burning up hot in this dress. I
should have dressed in something lighter."

She must have had enough money. He didn't ask.

The waitress seated them all right as Fern's brothers
appeared. Jeb got up and shook hands with the Coulters.

"Jeb, these are my brothers, Buddy and Lewis. Betty
is Edward's wife and Phoebe is their daughter," said Fern.

Angel lit up. "I met you, didn't I, at the funeral?" She
was putting a folded piece of paper in her pocketbook.

"Angel was with us when I came home for Daddy's
funeral," Fern told her brothers. "You remember, don't you?"

Buddy gave her a pat. "You've gotten taller and prettier, though, while I just seem to keep getting older."

Angel laughed.

A pretty woman with dark hair and a dotted red dress joined them. Buddy introduced her as his wife, Esther. "Our daughter, Fawn, is back at Mother's watching your youngest children, Reverend."

Jeb thanked them. They all took a seat and started placing their lunch orders.

Angel took off her hat and placed it in her lap.

Jeb leaned over and whispered, "I hope you're behaving yourself."

Abigail said directly to Angel, "When Fern told me your family might be living in Oklahoma, I told her I'd check into it. Did I understand you, Fern?"

"Oh, yes, ma'am, you did," said Angel. "In a letter I got last week from my aunt Kate, she says that she has heard for sure that my sister Claudia is living in Oklahoma. She called it Norman."

"When was the last time you saw your sister?" asked Abigail.

"It's been a while, ma'am. Claudia left Snow Hill long before my momma went off to Little Rock and Daddy sent us away," said Angel. "Her husband had a good job, but he lost it. At least that's what Aunt Kate says."

"I know a family who owns a little café in Norman. I'll see if they know anything about—what is your sister's name again?"

"Claudia Drake. She's married and has kids, maybe two by now."

Abigail wrote it down and slipped it into her handbag.

Angel was smiling. "I miss Claudia more than life. I wish she'd write. Aunt Kate says she sent her our address in Nazareth."

"That does it! We're taking this child to Norman," said Abigail.

"I'm afraid we're running out of time, Mother. We've got golf all day tomorrow and then that party on Friday," said Fern.

There she was using that tone again, showing her irritation.

"Fern, you can't miss that," said Abigail. "I'll think of something."

A siren sounded out in the street. One face after another appeared in the shop windows along the street as people craned their necks to look up Ashton Street.

"Curtis Flannigan's calf must have gotten loose," said Buddy.

Everyone laughed.

"That's about as exciting as it gets here in Ardmore," said Abigail.

A man in overalls rushed into the Blue Moon. His face was ashen. He yelled, "The Savings and Loan, it just got robbed!"

"This never happens here," said Buddy. "It's a rumor."

Angel looked out the window. All was quiet on the street. A squad car roared past a minute later.

The Coulters went back to their eating.

"Did you see them?" Buddy asked the man in overalls.

"My neighbor, he got a good look at the driver and

one of the gunmen. Said they were driving a Studebaker. But another man gave a different story entirely."

Phoebe cast a curious glance at Angel. "That good-looking boy you were talking to out in front of Marshella's, he drove a Studebaker, didn't he?"

Angel shrugged. "I don't know what you're talking about."

"You want to tell me what Phoebe means?" asked Jeb.

"I only talked to him. Let's eat."

Fern and Jeb exchanged glances.

"The girl's right. Let's eat before we faint," said Abigail.

2

*F*ERN SAID SHE WOULD BUY JEB A NEW SUIT
of clothes. But Abigail took one of her husband's
suits and fitted it to him. Myrna was brought in on the fitting and Jeb elevated on a stool in the parlor, where the
light of morning poured into the room. The black suit
jacket's broad shoulders were drawn in, measured soberly
by Abigail and Myrna.

He smelled the leftover chicken being warmed for the
noon hour and either collards or turnip greens boiling, the
green, pungent smell hanging in the air. Myrna put it on to
cook straight after breakfast, to clear away some time for
the alteration. The women kept pinning the trousers until
the waistband tucked snugly next to his stomach and the

seat of the pants were tailored close-fitting but leaving some give for the times he might want to sit.

Fern sat in her father's old reading chair frowning down at the pages of Dr. Flauvert's gift of *Jane Eyre*. The two bookcases behind her converged in a dark corner displaying a red leather-bound set of medical journals, several three- or four-pound books, a dried sponge from Tarpon Springs, Florida, two hundred or so books lettered in fading gold and the books' binding tattering, and numerous framed photographs of Francis Coulter in golf attire posing with golfing friends. Fern turned another page and cocked her head. She had let down her hair from beneath the beret she wore on her morning walk. The tendrils shone next to the flame of a tapered candle lit by Myrna and left on the end table.

Abigail lifted Jeb's right arm to confirm that the sleeve length was exactly as she said it would be—"perfect." She kept swabbing her forehead with a handkerchief. "You best go check on the greens, Myrna, before they boil over," her Southern accent allowing for every vowel due to her eastern education.

Myrna unfastened the pincushion from her wrist and slid it into her smock pocket, Hooverettes, the ladies called them. "If the reverend can leave his trousers with me this morning, I'll have them sewn and done up by Thursday latest."

Fern looked up from her book. Her eyes were darkened by the shadow of the bookcase.

"The coat's a good fit. I'm glad to see this suit in use again," said Abigail. She glanced at Fern, who was still buried in *Jane Eyre.* "I don't know what's gotten into her," she said to Jeb.

Fern closed the book and laid it next to the melting candle.

Jeb slid off the dinner jacket and handed it to Abigail. "Your husband had good taste, Mrs. Coulter. I like the feel of good cloth."

Myrna turned on the radio, but turned it down before Abigail complained about the throbbing swing music.

"We'd better get on our way, Fern. Reverend Flauvert will be waiting for us at his home."

Abigail folded the jacket over her arm. "Fern, I thought you would want to be married here in our church."

"This isn't that kind of meeting. Dr. Flauvert is a friend of our former minister of Church in the Dell. You and Dad met Reverend Gracie years ago. Jeb's made Dr. Flauvert's acquaintance through Gracie's introduction is all."

Abigail said, "You-all have a good meeting then," and then followed Myrna into the kitchen.

"I'll only be a minute. I'll get these pants to Myrna and then we can leave," said Jeb.

Fern nodded and leaned against the windowsill that looked out over the eastern acreage of her family's estate.

There was a brown haze on the windowpanes from a July dust storm.

"I'm not going to drag you to meet Flauvert, Fern."

"You're irritable today. Why don't you go and change?" She slid on a white jacket and hat, along with a pair of gloves. "I'll wait in the car."

Jeb intercepted her at the parlor door, placing his

hands on her shoulders. "I want you to tell me what you're thinking."

Fern lifted her face to say, "I said I'd go and talk to Dr. Flauvert with you. What else do you want?"

"I want to offer you a better life," said Jeb.

"Define 'better.'"

"You live like a missionary in Nazareth. I see how different things are for you here, Fern. Everyone in town knows you; your family has political ties. You've done your part for Nazareth, and Stanton School is a better place because of you. But here in Oklahoma, you're a Coulter."

"So your definition of better is being a Coulter?"

"Is that a bad thing?"

Fern clasped Jeb's forearms and backed out of his grasp. "Myrna's waiting for your pants. I'll go and meet this Dr. Flauvert, Jeb. I said I would."

Jeb reclaimed her wrists. He didn't like it when she moved away from him. "I know that when you meet Flauvert, you'll want to know him better. There's a grand scheme to all of this, Fern, I can feel myself fitting into something bigger than Nazareth, Arkansas."

"I said I'd go, didn't I?" She pulled away.

Jeb changed out of the pants and took them to Myrna. He could hear the Coulters' car idling outside the kitchen door. Fern sat out in the car brooding, staring out the window toward Nazareth.

ૐ

What bothered Jeb the most was Fern's silence. A rabbit crossing the road caused her to lift and point in time for

Jeb to slow the car, but then she settled back into a world that had somehow been closed off to him. She pulled out a notepad to make a note to herself, took great interest in staring into a compact mirror—she never did that—and kept sighing until Jeb said, "If there's something you want to say, you ought to say it."

"Nothing I can think of."

"I never realized how much you hated it here."

She sat up. "I don't hate Ardmore. Ardmore is as good a place to live as any."

"What, then, is making you so miserable?"

"Coming home is like traveling back to sad places. The Coulters are not as respectable as you think."

"I know. You called them wild. It had to have been a long time ago. I like your family. They're nice as nice can be."

Fern stared back out the window toward an abandoned barn. "It's easier for you as a man, that's all."

"You saying you sowed some wild oats?"

"Don't jump to conclusions." She sighed. "You're making me crazy."

He wanted to call her bluff, ask if she wanted him to turn the car around and head back to Nazareth. But in her mood, she might tell him to do just that. Instead, he let out an irritated sigh, like she had always done when she wanted her way.

"I said I'd go. Maybe it's this whole idea of me being a minister's wife. In Nazareth, they'd buy it. I don't know about here. I lose myself when I come home." She put away the mirror. "It's silly. I'm sorry."

"I choose who I marry. You think I'm going to put that through some filter, parade you around, get everyone's approval? Who I marry is my choice. You took me 'as is.' I don't care what happened back here in Oklahoma. It doesn't matter."

Fern leaned across the seat and kissed Jeb's cheek. Her jasmine scent mixed with the car exhaust.

Jeb stared at the road ahead, but kept stroking her hair. Fern was always surprising him. He still knew her better than anyone had ever known Fern Coulter. "It doesn't matter," he said again.

✣

Rachel Flauvert carried a tray of iced tea into her husband's study. "Mrs. Nubey, I made you some tea with mint." She placed the tray on a coffee table. "Here's a plate of cookies to tide you over until lunch."

"Don't leave us, Rachel," said Jonathan. He introduced her to Jeb and Fern. "Reverend Nubey hasn't officially given Miss Coulter his name yet, though."

"I don't mind," said Fern, taking a glass. "That's good tea, nice and sweet."

"None of that Yankee tea for us," said Rachel. Jeb liked her laugh and the way she used her arms when she talked. She was orchestrating everything, the party, where everyone sat, and seemed to be enjoying herself.

Jonathan said to Jeb, "Tell me how you came to be in the pulpit, Brother Nubey."

Jeb averted his eyes. Fern shifted in her chair.

"Is that a loaded question?" asked Jonathan. "It's all

right. Gracie filled me in on one thing; that you were cut from rough cloth, as he put it."

Jeb thought Fern looked as though she wanted to talk, so he let her.

"Jeb's not your conventional-type, run-of-the-mill preacher."

"Gracie has spoken highly of you, don't get me wrong," said Jonathan.

"Dr. Flauvert, I'm always going to tell you the truth. I was once a wanted man running from the Texarkana police," said Jeb.

Jonathan laughed. "There's a story you don't hear every day."

Rachel offered Fern more tea.

"If it had not been for the patience of Philemon Gracie and Fern Coulter, I'd still be running."

"Jeb's not giving himself due credit," said Fern.

Jonathan kept smiling, not once cooling to him, to either of them, so Jeb decided it was all right to relax and tell things as they were.

"I can attest to his education. He's read as many books as most lawyers," said Fern.

"Brother Nubey, you've found an ally in this fine lady here. If a woman of her virtue and a minister of Philemon's character speak so highly of you, it's good enough for me."

There was a faint cough, Fern's hand coming to her mouth.

"I'd like to say something," said Rachel.

"Go on then, dearest."

"I once knew of a man with a past and I heard the

story told that he went on to become the president of this country."

"Does a stained past disqualify you from the ministry, though?" asked Fern.

Jeb could not get comfortable in the chair.

"Not at all," Rachel mouthed. "Don't worry yourself."

"I mean, are we talking about a past or a reputation?" asked Jeb. "The difference is in what men know about us versus what God only knows."

Jonathan laughed.

"Everyone's got something, don't they?" asked Jeb.

"Goodness me, you men all do," said Rachel. "Ladies aren't allowed, though, are we, Fern?" Her hand was on top of Fern's now and she kept patting her.

Jeb got up and reached for the tea pitcher.

"Oh, let me," said Rachel.

Jeb stopped her. "My fiancée's glass is empty. She's always doing for me." He filled Fern's tea glass.

Fern looked up at him. She bit her bottom lip and looked down at Rachel's white rug. "You be careful, Jeb. We don't want to stain Mrs. Flauvert's rug."

ॐ

"Angel, Angel, come quick!" Abigail ran through the house.

Angel lazed on the screened-in back porch. She had taken to a hunting dog named Baxter, a sleek brown dog that inched his way into her lap, his large bottom half hanging down onto the porch. She was massaging his ears when she heard Abigail's shouts. "I'm back here," she hollered.

Abigail opened the door to the porch. "There you are! Look what came to the door, this instant!" She held out a telegram.

Angel pushed Baxter onto the floor. "What is it, Miz Abigail?" She was acting like someone had died.

"Girl, you know when you told me about your sister Claudia?"

Angel nodded.

"I started inquiring at that café in Norman, I telephoned there and I had them on the line and we were talking. They gave me the name of a man who might know the Drakes, and they kept saying 'might.' One thing led to another, Angel, and I got an address. I didn't want to get your hopes up, so I sent her a telegram telling her that you were here in Oklahoma." She held out the telegram. "Claudia replied. Look."

"You saying you found my sister?" Angel didn't know what to say.

Abigail threw her arms around Angel.

Ida May and Willie came bounding up the back steps. "What's all the hollering about?" asked Willie.

Angel read the telegram:

Heard you was in OK. stop Have to see you soon. stop Coming on a bus. stop Friday 8 a.m. stop Pick me up, will you? stop Claudia

"Angel, what is it?" asked Willie.

"It's a letter from Claudia!" Ida May jumped up and down and grabbed Angel.

Tears ran down her face. "I can't believe you did this

for us, Miz Abigail." She hugged Abigail Coulter. "I had given up."

"Let me see it," said Willie. He snatched the telegram from Angel. "It doesn't say whether or not she has kids. I hope she has a boy."

Angel plopped down on the settee. Abigail gave her a handkerchief and said, "I'll make cookies, how about? We need to celebrate." She went back into the house.

"What does Claudia look like, Angel?" asked Ida May.

"That's right, you were young when she left." Angel counted the years on one hand. "You weren't but two or so. Is that right?"

"Everybody said she looked like Momma," said Willie.

"Brown eyes, dark hair, long and hanging in curls around her shoulders. She was always pretty," said Angel. "Men were always fighting over her, according to Granny."

Willie sat down cross-legged on the porch floor. "Angel, does this mean we won't be going back to Nazareth?"

"We're going back next week, Willie," said Ida May. "Aren't we, Angel?"

"This changes a lot, doesn't it?" Willie took Baxter by the ears.

"Claudia probably has herself a house by now. Her husband lost his job, but maybe he's got a good one now. Aunt Kate told me he's a railroad man," said Angel.

"We can't leave Dud, can we, Angel?" asked Ida May. "What would he do? He can't take care of himself."

"Miss Coulter's going to take care of him, Ida May. Jeb is going to marry her, finally, and they'll have their own kids," said Angel.

Abigail opened the door. "I can't make cookies alone," she said after listening to Ida May raising her complaints. "Who can help?"

Willie beat Ida May to the kitchen.

"We can all help, Miz Abigail." Angel nudged Ida May into the house.

"Does Dud want us to go with Claudia?" asked Ida May.

"He has a life to live too, Ida May. We can't expect to live with him forever." She was happy to say that. There was nothing wrong with it.

"Does Claudia want us?" Ida May walked backward in front of Angel.

"Who knows how to use a cookie cutter?" asked Abigail.

Angel pointed to Ida May.

Abigail took Ida May's hand and led her into the kitchen. Angel stopped in the middle of the parlor holding the telegram. She read it over and over until her heart stopped pounding so fast.

✦

"You want Jeb to speak this Sunday morning, in downtown Oklahoma City?" asked Fern. "He's on sabbatical. Did you tell him that, Jeb?"

Rachel had to go. "I hear faculty arriving."

Jonathan smiled. "First Community is in need of a

speaker and I've taken their pulpit all summer while they've searched for a replacement minister. But our new students are arriving on campus this week. My faculty is arriving here this morning right this minute."

"Speak in a big church. You know Church in the Dell is a country church," said Jeb. There was a difference, he thought.

"They're accustomed to ministers passing through. This will give you a chance to get a feel for the place. They'll have a look at you, and you them. Fern, you'll get a taste for city life, although you strike me as the city type. Am I right?"

"I thought you wanted a rest, Jeb, that you needed time away from the pulpit?" Fern asked.

"I don't want to interrupt your sabbatical, Brother Nubey. If you'd rather not, I understand," said Jonathan.

Jeb said, "Fern and I ought to talk."

"This is where I make my getaway. I'll go and greet our guests, give you two some time alone." Jonathan left them in his study, closing the door behind him.

"What's gotten into you, Fern? Dr. Flauvert's offer is not set in stone. At least give me the chance to tell him I'm honored by his invitation. There's nothing wrong with that. I'd like to know what's gotten into you."

"What's gotten into you, is more like it. Jeb, you know me, know I'm not going to sit here like some big-eyed girl nodding and agreeing with everything that's said. There's a lot to discuss. You're exhausted and needing a rest and I was looking forward to time away from church. And while we're on the subject, here we are again making everything revolve around the church."

"For the minister, that's how life spins."

"Jeb, I understand your responsibilities. My father was a responsible man, a respectable doctor, but sometimes he forgot he was responsible for a family too."

"So this is about your father?"

She responded with an irritated sigh.

"Imagine, Fern, me in a city pulpit. No more small-town pettiness, smart folks with big ideas."

"Hear yourself, Jeb. You've already moved us into Oklahoma City."

"And what's wrong with that? I've slaved over Church in the Dell, and for little payback."

She didn't argue. "Nazareth is needy, I'll admit that."

"Fern, I've been speaking in the pulpit for quite some time. I can use a message from last week. We'll be in Oklahoma City. We'll get a couple of nice rooms, one for you and the girls and one for Willie and me. Monday, we'll see the sights, eat in a good restaurant. I'm thinking of you too."

"You've already decided then."

"We don't have to give them an answer this weekend, do we?"

"No, we don't." She got up from the chair and went to the window. Several couples were engaged in conversation out on the walk. "The Flauverts are good people."

"Fern, all I've ever known is hand-to-mouth."

"I finally got used to the idea of being a minister's

wife in Nazareth. I never imagined myself being anywhere else."

"We're giving them a look, is all."

A quiet moment passed between them.

"I guess we'd better join the Flauverts at their luncheon," she said, resignation seeping in. "I'm going to go
and freshen up. Rachel offered me her bedroom." She
picked up her handbag and snapped it closed. She kissed
Jeb and left him standing alone in Flauvert's study.

Jeb had not noticed until now how many bookcases
lined Flauvert's walls. It was a large study, and framed photographs hung decoratively around the room. Rachel stood
next to Jonathan in most of the photographs. She was a
plain woman, slender and tastefully dressed, her lips faintly
tinged.

Fern had never been plain or ordinary. She was complicated, more like, always asking questions. He liked that
about her, usually.

The door opened and Jonathan peered into the room.
"How did it go with the missus?"

"I'll accept your offer of speaking on Sunday."

"Fern's a smart woman."

"She's marrying me, isn't she?"

Jonathan opened the door wide. "I'd like to introduce
you to some of our faculty, one of whom is our son George.
He graduated college in May. Maybe before you head back
to Nazareth, I can meet your young charges."

"You'll like them too. They have their charms, Angel
especially."

"Nothing better for a church than a respectable minister and his family to lead the way. Come and try Sophie's chicken wings."

～

The afternoon wound down, the sun as gold as hay. The occasional car or horse and wagon rolling past the Coulters' front gate sent Angel to her feet. The telegram had not left her hands since Abigail handed it to her. The view from the screened-in back porch offered the best view of the road. Jeb and Fern had been due back from lunch for two hours.

Road dust lifted, hovering above a copse of trees beyond the horse stable. Angel leaned back against the settee and sighed until she heard the sound of a car motor rumbling down the shaded lane. Finally the Coulter Packard nosed into the clearing.

Miss Coulter wore a white hat and fumbled with it from the front passenger seat. Her face was tanning in the Oklahoma sun, but the women from Ardmore had a tendency to tan, at least the ones who played golf.

Fern talked to her more often, now that she and Jeb were engaged. She would like to have a mother like Fern, only not necessarily Fern. She could not explain her reasons precisely. Fern liked having her way and so did Angel. Fern could communicate exactly what she wanted with lightning speed, making it hard to calculate a reliable comeback. It was things like that that annoyed her.

But Ida May took to Fern, as had Willie, looking

more to Fern now for comfort. Willie's questions about Claudia indicated an alarm had gone off in both him and Ida May. She would have to study the matter.

She came to her feet and opened the back screen porch door wide, leaning out and faintly smiling at Jeb. Fern got out of the car carrying a dress store box. Angel held up the telegram and said, "It's from Claudia. She's here in Oklahoma."

"In town, your sister?" asked Jeb.

"Norman. She's coming Friday."

"Angel, I'm tickled to death! What good news, and here with us so close by. Does my mother know? How did Claudia find you here?" asked Fern.

"Miz Abigail made a telephone call and, after some time, she found her."

"She's a surprise a minute," said Fern. "Never said a word to me."

Jeb opened the door and Fern went inside. He took a breath, pursing his lips, but not saying anything at all.

"I can't believe it, can you, Jeb?" asked Angel.

"After all this time, no I can't." His brows came together, but he kept looking down, taking a breath as if he didn't know what to say.

Angel placed the telegram on the table next to the settee. "You think she'll want us, Jeb?"

"Of course she will. She's your sister, isn't she?"

"How do you feel about that, Jeb? Us maybe leaving to go and be with Claudia?" There was a pause and then Angel said, "That's what you've been waiting for, isn't it, Jeb?"

"You've been waiting for this day, Angel. It's not my business to say either way how I feel." He opened the door for her as he had for Fern. Instead of following Fern into the kitchen, he ascended the stairs. Halfway up, he stopped and said, "Be happy, Angel. That's all."

3

JEB SLEPT RESTLESSLY THURSDAY NIGHT. HE woke up at twelve, at one-sixteen, four o'clock, and again as Abigail's rooster crowed at five on Friday morning. His calves were tangled in the cotton linen sheets. The feather mattress had swallowed him up into its center and he sweated like a pig at slaughter. Plainly, morning came too soon.

Ida May ran down the hall singing a cereal ditty on the way to Abigail Coulter's washroom as she had every morning since they had arrived in Ardmore. Her high and tinny voice squeaked out the rhyme in step with her pounding feet.

It's good for growing babies, and grown-ups too to eat.
For all the family's breakfast, you can't beat Cream of Wheat.

The bedroom door opened. Angel stuck in her head and said, "Claudia's bus will be coming soon, thirty minutes. You'll be ready?"

Jeb kicked off the sheet. "I will. Where's my coffee, Biggest?"

"Downstairs. Who am I? The maid?" She laughed and closed the door.

Jeb showered, dressed, and, coming out into the hall, met Fern coming up the steps.

She kissed him and said, "I've never seen Angel so excited."

He walked past, towel-drying his hair.

"You forgot to shave," she said.

"I thought I'd go for coffee first."

"Did you sleep? You look like what the cat dragged in."

He stopped in front of a hall mirror and ran his fingers through his hair. "I don't sleep well away from home."

"Is that it?"

"What else would it be?" he asked.

"How do you feel about Claudia coming to town? You've not said a word since Angel told you."

"Angel needs her family. I'm happy for her," he told her. "It's as I said, that I don't sleep well away from home, that's all."

"You know this means that we won't be able to take the Welbys along with us into Oklahoma City tonight?"

That was a good thought.

"We can't go, just the two of us, babe, although I'm tempted."

Jeb kissed her forehead. "We have to go. I promised."

"I'll ask my sister Donna to join us. You've not met her. I'll see her this morning after you leave to pick up Claudia. I forgot about all that until Mother reminded me. She's going to make up my room today for Claudia after we leave."

"That means she's got all three Welbys and then Claudia too. You sure she doesn't mind?"

"Says she doesn't."

Jeb rested at the top of the staircase, staring down at the entry.

"Are you all right?" asked Fern. "What is it, Jeb?"

Angel's and Willie's voices drifted up from the kitchen.

"Maybe it is Claudia. Or Nazareth. Or both."

Myrna called them down to breakfast. The pork sausage smell drifted up the stairwell.

"I'll go and shave and then meet you downstairs," said Jeb. He lathered up and shaved and then put on a pair of brown trousers that would be good for travel for the day trip into Oklahoma City. Then he hurried downstairs. The Coulters sat around Abigail's kitchen table. Fern sat beside him and they ate in a hurry so that he could drive Angel downtown.

Ida May and Willie had already eaten. Willie kept peeking into the kitchen to see if Jeb was coming or not. He had a look about him that drew Jeb's attention. "You needing to say something, Willie Boy?"

"After you eat, maybe." He disappeared into the parlor.

Angel ran in breathless, holding a dark blue hat. "I'm

ready to go to the bus station, Jeb," she said. "You look awful."

Jeb picked up his napkin and fork and handed his plate to Myrna.

"We'll be waiting, Angel," said Fern. "Can't wait to meet the long-awaited Claudia." She kept her eyes planted on Angel, came out of her chair, and then held out her arms. "Give us a hug, girl."

Angel put her arms around Fern. Instead of letting go after a few seconds, Fern held on, drawing Angel close. Angel buried her face in Fern's shoulder.

Fern's face softened. She tightened her grip around Angel.

Angel's sniffling turned to sobbing. "It's—been—so—long!"

"Let it all out now, Angel. You'll want Claudia to see your smiling self," said Fern.

Abigail brought her hands to her face and kept saying, "Dear me, dear me."

Ida May ran and gave Angel a handkerchief.

"What's wrong with everyone?" asked Willie.

Jeb retrieved his hat from the hat stand and said, "Women's business, Willie Boy. Let's go outside."

Willie lagged behind Jeb, his gaze fixed behind him on the women all bawling in the kitchen. "Who gets the reason women cry all over one another?"

Jeb opened the door and led Willie out under the shade of an oak once planted by Fern's grandmother. "Speak to me, Willie. You look like you have something to say."

He stammered around for a minute before he finally said, "This may sound like I ain't as happy as Angel about Claudia coming. I am. But I've been wondering about us. I mean, does this mean that we're done with knowing you and Miss Coulter? Not that you ever asked for us. I know Angel finagled us under your roof."

"Willie, who says that Claudia is going to take you all in? Let's meet her first and let her have her say. As for Fern and me being done with you, as you put it, no, we'll never be done with you."

Willie cast his eyes across the pasture toward home.

"How do you want all of this to turn out?" asked Jeb.

"I wish I knew. Angel, she always knows what she wants and she'll be the first to tell you too. Why is it I never seem to know what I want?"

"Maybe you haven't been asked often enough."

Willie looked up at Jeb, as though he were having his first reflection on life. "Haven't we been a family, Jeb?" He crouched beneath the tree and wrote in the dirt with his finger.

"You're a smart boy, Willie. Give me your take on it."

"People who sleep under the same roof so's they can all take care of one another, get in one another's business and such."

"Do I get in your business?"

"All the time." He came to his feet. "If you didn't, wouldn't I go bad? I know I would."

"Families have to let go too. The question is, do you think it's time to move on, to join your sister?"

"I know I'm supposed to want to say yes, but something's keeping me from it." He laughed. "Fact is, I like things the way they are. Miss Coulter, she's a good lady and looks after us and I had this idea that after you-all married, she'd be my momma." He swallowed hard. "I sound like a fool."

Jeb wanted to promise Willie that he would never have to leave, that he would go and meet Claudia at the bus stop and then send her back home. The two of them stood staring at the ground. A crow flew overhead calling to the sun.

"I guess I'd better go and get your sister."

The door opened and Angel came through the doorway, wearing the blue hat.

Willie turned and marched out into the pasture. He walked with a halting gait, his shoulders squared.

⌒

Claudia's bus arrived five minutes late. Angel's eyes took in the stream of faces of the folks stepping off the bus, the people carrying suitcases and store bags packed with traveling items. There was one pretty auburn woman who assisted her two younger children down the steps and onto the street. Angel squinted in the hot sunshine and smiled at the lady. She walked around Angel and met her family under the depot's overhang.

Jeb gazed into the bus. After all those years, Angel said she feared that she had forgotten what Claudia looked like. A lone woman sat three seats from the front. She was looking down, her hat all that was visible.

"She didn't come," said Angel.

"Hold on, don't get yourself in a lather," said Jeb.

The woman rose, said something to the driver, and then made her way to the front of the bus. She had two children by the hand, neither as big as a minute. The driver's eyes softened as he followed the frail woman out of the bus. His head was cocked to one side, and when he saw Jeb and Angel waiting, he nodded as though he were handing off a fragile obligation.

"Claudia! Claudia!" Angel's hands came together almost in a prayer.

The woman had a small face, small like Ida May's, and eyes brown as pudding. She lowered her face and examined Angel. After she got the children onto the street, she shook her head and said, "I can't believe it. Angel?"

Angel trembled and her half smile gave way to, "Aren't you a sight!"

Claudia embraced her and Angel nearly knocked her over, which was not hard, since she weighed about as much as her two young'uns put together.

"I couldn't believe it when Mrs. Coulter told me she found you!"

"You're a sight too, girl. Daddy always said you'd be the beauty when you got grown, now look at you, all growed up."

Angel stepped back and took in her round-eyed brood. "You've got two babies. I heard that you were expecting again."

"I lost one, but no need to dampen the day with that kind of talk." She turned her eyes on Jeb.

Jeb introduced himself and took her by the hand. "I'll get your things if you'll point them out."

The driver alighted and led Jeb to the only remaining suitcase left near the bus on the street. Jeb thanked him. Angel heard him say to Jeb so Claudia wouldn't hear, "I give her my dinner. It was just some bread and cheese and an apple. She's nearly starved from hunger. I'm glad you-all are taking her in."

Jeb thanked him and turned and looked at the two sisters. Angel was enamored of Claudia, and as she talked, she reached and touched Claudia's hair. She had outgrown her older sister by a good three inches. She walked her under the depot overhang and then knelt next to the little boy, her nephew.

"This is John. John say something to your aunt Angel."

John buried his face in Claudia's skirt.

"He's beautiful, Claudia." Angel took the little girl's hand. "I don't know your name, Littlest." It was the name Jeb had given to Ida May.

"Thorne, give your aunt a smooch," said Claudia.

Angel came to her feet. "You named her after Momma?"

"I've missed her so badly, and when she was born, I saw Momma in her eyes, so I just naturally called her Thorne."

Thorne reached up for Angel and Angel took the little girl in her arms. She balanced her on her hip and said, "I'll never let go of you."

Thorne kissed her face.

Jeb took Claudia's suitcase from Angel. It hardly weighed anything at all. "This way to the car, ladies."

The two sisters talked all the way back to the Coulter estate. Angel asked about her husband, Bo, and his rail-road job.

"Bo went off to work last month like always. I'd fixed him cold chicken in his dinner bucket. He always liked that. That night, I sat out on the porch like I always did, me and 'ese two waiting for Daddy to come home. It was a hot night. I could hear the neighbors laughing over the picket fence out front, like everything was the same as always. We've had us a good house. But Bo never came home that night."

Jeb glanced obliquely at Angel.

"I went to the police, went around the train depot asking if anyone had seen Bo. Finally I saw one of his drinking buddies standing in the unemployment line. He told me him and Bo had lost their jobs two weeks before. I guess Bo never had the guts to tell me he'd lost his job."

"So he left you and the children," said Jeb. "Claudia, I'm sorry."

"Rent's come due. I was glad I had a little money put back, enough for a bus ticket. I know I should have spent it on the rent. But I've been so lonely for my family. I had to see you, Angel. Where's them other two?"

"Waiting at the Coulters' house. I've missed you too," said Angel. "I've been trying to find you for so long. You must not have gotten any of my letters."

"We moved around too much for that, I reckon. Aunt

Kate says you been living in Nazareth. Small world. That's where Bo and I first lived."

"I know. We came there looking for you. But your house was empty. You left this behind." Angel pulled out a small toy, a cloth rabbit.

Claudia laughed. "That was John's. Never knew what happened to it. You did find our old place. Aunt Kate told me in a letter Daddy sent you all off. I hated that. But Bo wouldn't hear of taking in family. He said we had enough to contend with. After that, we moved twice and I lost touch."

"I wondered why you didn't write to Aunt Kate, let her know where you were. I was worried sick, Claudia."

"Bo stopped all that. He was not one to let people into our lives. He brought home the money, wanted me to keep house and have babies. I figured I owed him that."

Angel came face forward in the front passenger seat, quiet.

"We're here," said Jeb.

"Would you look at this place? Whose house did you say this is?" asked Claudia.

"It's the home of my fiancée's family, the Coulters," said Jeb. "They're fixing up a room for you for the weekend." He drove them under the shade of an oak and parked. "How long did you say you were staying?"

"In her letter, Mrs. Coulter said you would be here until Tuesday. If Angel can front me some cash, I can leave Tuesday," said Claudia. "I'm not one to overstay my welcome."

Angel glanced at Jeb. "I'll get Claudia's luggage, Jeb,"

she said. She fetched the suitcase and then corralled Thorne, leading her up the brick walk to the back porch.

Claudia kept saying, "You're doing well for yourself." She followed Angel into the house.

Fern came out into the parlor. "Glad you're all back. I'm Fern. Angel, you can put her things in my room."

"I wouldn't want to take your room, ma'am," said Claudia.

"You'll love my room. It overlooks the pond. Jeb and I are leaving today for Oklahoma City."

"I live right outside there, Miss Coulter," said Claudia. "You heard of Norman?"

"I have." She turned to Jeb and said, "Jeb, Donna said she can come with us. She's glad to get away. A friend of hers works at the Skirvin Hotel and he's getting us two rooms for the weekend."

"Fancy place, the Skirvin," said Claudia. "I heard of that place."

"Jeb's got a dinner there tonight," said Fern. "We've got to get out of here. Jeb, you tried on those trousers Myrna fixed for you, didn't you?"

Jeb had forgotten. He pursed his lips.

"They're laid out on your bed. I've packed everything else."

"Angel, are you sure you'll be all right here, don't mind us leaving?" he asked.

"Claudia and I have a lot of catching up to do. Don't worry about us. Are you going upstairs?" she asked.

Jeb caught a look in her eye that said that they should go upstairs. "To try on my trousers, yes."

Angel followed him upstairs. Once they had made it to the upstairs landing, she said, "I don't have any money to give Claudia. How will she get home?"

"I'll see she gets a bus ticket home."

"Bo shouldn't have left her like that. But she shouldn't have come here counting on someone else to give her the money home. I don't know what she expects to do when she gets back to her place. Bo didn't pay their last month's rent and she found that out only yesterday."

"Maybe there's work for her in Oklahoma City. I'll ask around."

"I knew you'd help," she said, and hugged him. "I'm sorry as I can be about her, though. I didn't expect she'd be so bad off."

"I feel bad about leaving you all here with Mrs. Coulter."

"I'll see to everyone, Jeb."

"I know. You always do, Angel." She looked older than her years again. Her childhood slipped away once more when Claudia stepped off that bus.

⁓

Donna lugged her suitcases across the lawn, a set of blue baggage, one small case and one large. She was blond like Fern, but more deeply bronzed from a summer spent on the course at Dornick Hills. She walked with a wobble, wearing a pair of Grecian-looking heels that laced around her ankles. But her head tilted the same as Fern's, slightly back with her chin and nose up. It was a sure bet that they developed that posture as teens when all the Dornick Hills boys were chasing after the Coulter girls. She was pretty too, nearly as pretty as Fern.

"Let's split this joint!" she yelled. When she saw Jeb, her smile widened, showing off her teeth, and they were perfect little pearls.

Angel walked with Fern, following Donna and helping to carry one of Fern's bags. "Stop looking so sick with worry," she told Jeb.

"We'll come back Sunday instead of Monday," said Jeb.

"Not on my watch," said Donna. "I've got our rooms through Sunday night and Brian says they're the last two available rooms."

"It's up to Jeb," said Fern. She handed her luggage to him. "Donna, this is my fiancée, Jeb."

Donna extended her hand to him. He clasped it. He felt a fool to kiss a woman's hand. But she was standing there holding it out like everyone was a hand kisser.

Fern said, "I've heard the hotel has chilled air."

"It has everything. We're going to live like kings for three days straight. So when are you two tying the knot?" Donna asked.

"Soon. When Fern's ready," said Jeb.

"I thought I was waiting on you," said Fern.

"Why not marry here at the farm?" asked Donna.

Jeb turned and found Fern smiling. "Donna has a good idea. Want to marry here at your mother's place?" he asked.

"Why not?" She surprised the dickens out of him.

Angel's mouth fell open. "No, you mean it? When you

get back from Oklahoma City?" She was waving her hands around, excited.

"Isn't the dress you're wearing tonight new?" Donna helped load the luggage into the trunk.

Jeb said, "Fern, we can do it Tuesday, here in your mother's parlor."

"So what are we saying, that we're going to just up and do it?" There was a pause. "Donna, I'm getting married next week!" said Fern.

Donna squealed.

Fern threw her arms around Jeb. "This is so spur of the moment! We're nuts!"

"Not a moment too soon for me, Fern. I don't think I could wait a minute past Tuesday," said Jeb.

Abigail came out on the back porch. She opened the screen door, asking what in the world was going on.

"Can we do a wedding by Tuesday?" asked Fern.

"Jeb, she's joking, isn't she?" Abigail looked at Jeb.

"They're serious," said Angel.

Abigail met them out by the car. She kept saying that this was all a joke until she started crying.

෴

The Skirvin Hotel was a crowned jewel in Oklahoma City's downtown apex. The two towers boasted 525 rooms, a cabaret club, a drugstore, a handful of retail stores, a rooftop garden, and the prestigious Venetian Room. An air-chilling system cooled a coffee café.

A red-coated valet waiting under one of the hotel's

overhangs offered to park the Packard. Jeb handed him the key. Fern tipped the man.

"I'm starving," said Donna.

"May I suggest the Coffee Shop inside? You can enter from either the lobby or First Street. You'll like the stores at the Skirvin too," said the valet. "The ladies all hit the dress stores first here."

Jeb led the way through the glass doors into the marble-floored lobby.

Fern was admiring the Gothic lanterns suspended from the ceiling, and she knew they were Gothic, of course. "There's the Coffee Shop."

"Fern, since Brian has registered the rooms in my name, why don't you and Jeb go and find us a table. I'll check in," said Donna.

"Good. I'm up for some tea," said Fern.

Jeb and Fern took a seat near a window. Jeb looked out at the construction across the street. "No Depression going on in Oklahoma City."

"It's because of oil," said the waiter. "Plenty of work in the City, at least for us locals. Those migrants camped around the edges of town do give us grief."

Fern ordered vegetable soup and tea. "My sister will have the same thing," she said.

"I'll have the chicken special," said Jeb. "Coffee, black."

The waiter left to fill their beverage request.

"Maybe Claudia could work here at the Skirvin," said Jeb.

"There's also Packingtown. That's where they slaughter and package meat. I hear tell the jobs are plenteous there too," said Fern.

"Where's that?"

"Southwest of downtown. Exchange and Agnew," said the waiter, reappearing with their drinks. "Here, I got a cousin there that does all the hiring." He wrote it down and gave it to Jeb. "But the jobs go fast and you have to ask for him, he's the one who knows everything going on over there."

"Who wants keys?" Donna walked up, dangling two sets of room keys in front of her. She seated herself next to Fern and took a sip of tea. "If you two want to take one of the rooms, you're safe with me. I'm here for the sightseeing."

Jeb took one of the keys out of her hand. "I'll take one. Fern, you and your sister take the other."

"Where'd you snag him anyway?" Donna asked Fern.

"We met in Nazareth," said Jeb. "I think, though, I snagged Fern."

"You're not the first, just the first to hold on to her."

"Look, our food's arrived already," said Fern. She shot Donna a look.

"There's a good dress store. That valet wasn't lying. After we eat, I'm going to shop," said Donna.

"I think I'll rest a bit and then clean up for the party. Fern, you?" asked Jeb.

"Rest sounds good to me too."

"There's a band here tonight. If I'm wearing something new, I'd best skedaddle. You old folks can hit the hay, but I'm out of here." Donna picked up her key and headed out into the lobby.

"Donna is spirited," said Jeb.

"That's kind to say it like that. Walk you to your room?"

"This is a fancy place, Fern. I like seeing you in your natural surroundings. You fit in here much better than Nazareth. Whatever made you decide to leave?" He stood and offered her his arm.

"Oh, there's that drugstore. Let's stop in there and see what hair products we can pick up. It is nice to be back in the City."

Jeb walked her to the Skirvin Drugstore. Fern needed to rest, he could tell. The trip had made her anxious.

4

BRASS CURTAIN ARMLETS IN THE SHAPE OF
old ladies' elbows restrained the mohair drapes in the
Venetian Room. But it opened up the windows and gave
the Skirvin Hotel guests seated at the better tables a view
of the city by night. A bank of stormy-looking clouds
threatened the horizon, but the locals had all given up on
rain. The clouds draped the sky and erased any evidence of
sundown; but down the main drag the streetlights and the
neon signs of the better dining joints did the job of illuminating downtown Oklahoma City. Jeb thought it was a
good place for minds to drift from the sight of the tent
cities, where migrants camped around the town limits;
a body had to be driving in from Shawnee or thumbing it
into town to see that kind of thing anyway. It was the part

of town that was no different than Arkansas. But here at the Skirvin, worry drifted away with the band music.

A skinny woman nursing a martini opened a window. A Skirvin Hotel waiter juggled a tray of dishes, correcting a near spill, and that put everyone in a good mood. Lightning ricocheted over the rain-starved plains giving way to deep rumbles of thunder lifting from the throat of early nightfall. The Venetian lanterns dimmed, causing two young women to gasp like kids over cake. For that instant, the place was a slice of Venice.

Jeb rubbed the toe of one shoe against the back of his pants leg. "Seems like I've been here in a dream."

A master of ceremonies swayed on the platform, his posture stilted as he introduced a black jazz singer from Chicago. Her hair was blue in the dimmed light and her face emerged from the dark, led by two eyes shining out through the smoke.

Jeb got the feeling Fern was lightening up about starting over in Oklahoma City. On the way up in the elevator, she listened to his ideas for the Sunday sermon he planned to offer up at First Community.

She was dolled up for the night. Where some of the women went gallivanting around the dance floor, her head scarcely moved as she walked. Her dress was made of that soft, supple stuff, the kind of fabric that fell off the bed if you laid it on the edge, material floating and circular around her ankles, the folds undulating. She wore lavender and the dress seemed to swim among the other women under the lights; the beaded dresses flickered and reflected the overhead dance-floor lights like scales on tropical fish.

Fern could not have worn that dress in Nazareth. She walked, shoulders back, her slender neck rising out of the beads and the lavender cloth, skin as white as a freshly dusted beach.

Fern glanced around the Venetian Room looking through a tobacco haze floating above the couples. "Say, who are we looking for, Jeb?" she asked.

"Rachel Flauvert told me to look for a heavy man with silvering hair. Said he wears an orchid in his lapel."

"I forgot his name, Jeb. I can't remember anything today," said Fern. She kept touching the brooch fastened at the dip in her neckline that made a sort of X-marks-the-spot.

"Henry Oakley, wife Marion. I don't see Donna."

The elevator door behind them opened and Donna stepped out.

"I tried to wake you," said Fern. "I didn't know if you were coming or not."

Donna had picked up a new green dress, puffed sleeves. She stubbed out a cigarette in an ashtray at the door of the elevator. She spotted Jeb and Fern and joined them in the door of the Venetian Room. "If you-all want me to make myself scarce, I can find plenty to do in this place."

"Donna, you ought to join us," said Fern. "You don't know a stranger, and Jeb and I don't know any of these people."

Jeb agreed and said, "You know the Oakleys, don't you, Donna?"

"Do we know them, Fern? We didn't go to school

with them, but I remember Mother talking about the Oakleys, or maybe I did meet them, I don't know," said Donna. She let out a breath, her brown eyes sizing up the room. "Don't see too many dance partners," she said. Most of the guests were seated around the dining tables.

Jeb held out his hand. "Fern, I'm going to take your little sister for a spin."

"Fine, then. I'll ask around and see if anyone can point out the Oakleys," said Fern.

Donna accepted his arm, but asked, "Jeb, won't you get excommunicated for dancing?"

"Would it bother you if I did?

"Not in the least. Your funeral."

"A quick spin around the floor over there away from the lights won't hurt." He led her away from the dance floor's center. The singer chose a slow song, good for talking and asking Donna about her sister. Donna knew some steps. "Fern told me you were a good dancer."

"Not as good as Fern. She's good at everything. Dancing, golf, skiing."

"I've never been on skis. They don't have too much of that in Arkansas."

"She likes golf best. I heard about your golf game this week. Buddy told me." She even laughed like Fern, the laughter starting out low and throaty and then spilling out of her, her chest lifting and her head falling back.

"I admit defeat," he said.

"That's why she loves you, I guess you know. Some guys felt threatened by her back in Ardmore."

"I once thought you were called Faye. Did I imagine it?"

"Oh, that. I'm Donna Faye Coulter." Her dark eyes took in all the dancers moving in around them. "After college, I started going by my first name. I'm settling down. I want to find someone like Fern has, I mean, more seriously than before."

Jeb spun Donna and drew her back in front of him. "Did she date anyone seriously? Not that I care, but did she?"

"Who, Fern?" She coughed.

"It's all right to say. The past is the past and all that."

The dance ended. Donna clapped like the others, who had milled onto the floor. "Looks like Fern found your dinner party host."

Fern and a woman seated at a long banquet table talked. Fern was still standing. Jeb invited Donna to join him and they commenced to walk across the dance floor. He escorted her around several chairs and had one more table to get around when Fern turned and withdrew from the party. She left the Venetian Room and disappeared into the hallway.

"Big Sister must have needed the powder room," said Jeb.

Donna rested one hand on an empty chair at the head of the table. The other hand rested on her hip until her gaze seemed to land on a male guest seated at the banquet table's opposite end. "I'm going to go and join my sister in the powder room. You get us three chairs, will you, Jeb?"

She excused herself and left Jeb standing awkwardly alone, staring into the face of their host.

Eleven or so people were seated around the long table, faces pale in the candlelight, and eyes glassy. One woman across the table smiled and said, "You must be the fiancée of that beautiful woman who just dropped by? And I guess that was her sister just now?"

The man at the table's end glanced at Donna exiting the Venetian Room and then looked up at Jeb.

A woman wearing a gold-threaded outfit garnished right out front with a big bow smiled at Jeb. "Esther, don't you know her? That was Fern Coulter, Francis and Abigail's daughter. Can you believe it?"

The man next to her came to his feet and thrust out his hand. "Reverend Nubey, I'm Henry Oakley." He was a slightly younger man than Jeb had imagined, thick dark hair that glistened under the low-hanging lights. A bit of salt and pepper at the temple.

The woman in the bowed dress was his wife, he said, and then she introduced herself as a close friend of Rachel Flauvert. "I'm Marion. I hope we didn't scare off Miss Coulter."

"Did she mention where she was going?" asked Jeb.

The man seated at the table's end said, "I'm sure she'll be back." He glanced back toward the door and then pulled out an empty chair next to him. "Please have a seat next to me, Preacher."

"Walton, I won't let you hog Reverend Nubey all to yourself. Ignore him, Reverend," said Marion. She had reserved two chairs, one next to her for Fern, and then a chair across from her for Jeb. Her face reddened when she told Walton, "I'm pulling rank on you."

Walton conceded defeat.

Jeb shrugged apologetically for Walton's benefit and accepted Marion's invitation.

Marion slid a tray of hors d'oeuvres toward Jeb. "Get this away from me. I'll eat the whole plate of those things."

Jeb placed two of the concoctions on his plate, cucumbers pieced together with circles of bread and pasted with creamy spread. Marion took up all of the conversation after that, so Jeb settled back and listened, paying close enough attention to nod or answer with a "yes" or "no" whenever appropriate. His attention wandered down the table when the other eyes became fixed on two new arrivals to the table.

"Always the last to arrive, those two," Marion said to Jeb. She excused herself and got up to go and greet them.

Walton fingered a cigar without lighting it. He seemed as preoccupied as Jeb. His hair was frosted with a bit of gray; he had a thin nose, a slight crook in it, and an easy smile. He was having as much trouble as Jeb paying attention to the women's chatter. Walton turned once and looked back toward the door. Jeb followed his gaze.

"I hope your fiancée hasn't gotten lost," said Henry.

Walton leaned toward Henry and said, "Why don't I go and look for Fern and Donna. They can't have wandered too far away." He got up and left the table.

"I didn't know Walton knew the Coulter girls," said Marion, and then she worked her way back down to her chair and told Jeb, "They were young college girls when

Walton got out of law school. I thought they ran in different circles."

Before Jeb could protest, a waiter filled his wineglass.

Henry slid his hand over and moved the glass aside. "Most of these folks seated around here are Lutheran, Reverend. I hope you aren't offended."

"Not at all. So Fern knows you, Mrs. Oakley?"

"I'm Marion to everyone else. May as well call me that. I knew her daddy, so that probably makes me a speck in her constellation, but I watched her grow up, read about her golf matches in the paper. Everyone in law and medicine in Oklahoma all seemed to run in the same circles. Dornick Hills is the hive, if you catch my meaning. The Coulters knew everyone, but Fern didn't necessarily know everyone her father knew. You know girls, they have their own business to attend to. My mother and Fern's mother knew one another since college. But I'm older than Fern. Did you know Abigail was schooled in New York?"

"I think I knew that," said Jeb. He wondered why Fern and Donna did not return.

Donna appeared in the doorway, shot out a final stream of smoke, and saw Jeb. She smiled faintly, at least observably pleasant, and sauntered to the table. Jeb got up and offered her the chair on the other side of him.

She settled herself into the chair, leaned forward to look up and down both ends of the table and then asked, "Where's Fern?"

Jeb tossed down his napkin. "I thought she was with you."

"She was in the powder room, said she was coming

out here," she said. "I didn't know I needed to walk her back to the table."

Jeb excused himself to the Oakleys.

Donna apologized. "She can't have gone far." She asked Marion, "Is there a balcony in this hotel?"

"There's a rooftop garden," said Marion. "There was a brief rain, somebody said."

Donna said to Jeb, "You've noticed, haven't you, that Fern likes to stand outside after a rain?"

He didn't say. But he hadn't noticed. It had been too long since the last rain shower.

"It's been so hot and all, I wouldn't be surprised," said Donna.

He didn't know her well enough to tell if she was irritated with Fern. Jeb had taken a few steps when he heard Donna ask Marion, "Do you know where that Walton fellow went to?"

"Senator Baer's gone to look for your sister," said Marion.

"Senator?" asked Jeb.

"Dear one, I thought you knew," said Marion. "Senator Walton Baer."

꒰

Fern wasn't among the group of women who came out of the powder room laughing. Come to think of it, he hadn't seen her laugh the whole weekend. She was civil most of the day, but not her happy self, not the way she was in Nazareth—not even on the trip all the way from Nazareth to Ardmore. He felt like an insensitive fool to keep nudging her to go to this bash. Jeb found a building diagram down the hall from the elevator. He gave it a look. There was a right turn, and then a small lobby with a doorway leading guests out onto the roof. He had never seen such a sight, a little square of Eden on a hotel roof. Maybe it was like Fern to want to see such a thing, especially by night. He followed the hallway right and found the two glass doors. He pressed his face against the glass to see out. A couple necked near a potted tree. He pushed open the door.

The air was dank, steaming under the cloud barrier that turned the sky black, erasing the moon and stars, like Sanford's ink washing every point of light from heaven. A brown thrasher fluttered suddenly, bursting out of the foliage of an olive tree. Drops rained off the leaves, gold dripping under the lanterns. The stone pavement was shining and black, everything damp. A pondlike vapor hung over the terrace, but it couldn't have rained that much. A gardener had been out and watered it. Water hoses were wound up like snakes and put against the wall. The raised gardens were framed all around with wood, a tangle of mountain sumac and primrose petals dripping over the potent boxed soil.

Fern was where Donna said she might be. She stood near the rooftop balustrade, looking down on Oklahoma City. Her fingers lightly gripped the barrier. Jeb walked around the tree that blocked his view of her. Now she was in full sight. The rhinestone hairpins in the back of her hair flickered like a cat's eyes.

Walton leaned against the railing near her. She kept

looking away and he was talking to her in a low voice. "I was surprised to hear you were coming," he said.

Jeb slid his hands into his pockets and stepped sideways behind the tree.

"Who said I was coming?"

"Marion's daughter, Sybil, told Anna," said Walton. "She didn't know who you were, though. Did you know Sybil? It's been so long. At any rate, since college, Sybil's still my wife's best friend. They sit out on the patio all morning, gabbing and drinking coffee. I'm glad for Anna she still has Sybil."

Fern kept looking down at the street below. "I knew I shouldn't have come." She fumbled with something at her wrist. Walton reached and with both hands adjusted whatever bauble it was she fiddled with around her wrist. "Was I that bad, Fern?" he asked.

"We were all bad, Walton. That's the way things were back then."

The Oklahoma senator gripped the railing and his hand rested near the hand that bore Jeb's engagement ring. "Fern Coulter's marrying a preacher. I couldn't believe it when Marion introduced him. I guess you'll have to be good now. Abigail must be pleased, she never could keep a good leash on you."

"Hush, Walton."

The door opened behind Jeb. The necking couple took their party inside. The woman laughed, a loud, rolling flutter of laughter that echoed across the terrace. Fern turned and then froze. She moved away from the railing. "Jeb, is that you?"

Jeb came from behind the tree. "I was worried. I came looking for you."

"Evening, Reverend," said Walton.

She stared at him after he stepped out from behind the tree. "You should have said something. Told me you were here."

Jeb looked first at Fern and then Walton.

"Jeb, this is Senator Walton Baer," said Fern.

"We've met. Our host and hostess are probably wondering what happened to us." Jeb held out his hand. She sighed and then accepted his hand. Her fingers trembled slightly and then clasped his. Her husky grip was gone, but she followed him. Her palm was clammy. She kept her eyes to the pavement all the way across the terrace and then even as they walked down the hallway and into the Venetian Room.

She knelt and brushed away a soggy leaf from the hem of her gown. A trace of brown stained the hem. She sighed and then straightened upright.

Walton followed them. "No need to spoil a good party," he said. He slipped on his jacket. "I'm not hungry anyway. I hope we meet again, Reverend. See you, Fern." He turned and left.

"I'm getting a headache, Jeb. Can we leave?"

Donna spotted them. Her face brightened. She rested against her chair back to allow one of the waiters to fill her soup bowl. "They're bringing your food," she mouthed.

"Donna's already ordered for us. We ought to go in," said Jeb.

One by one, each dinner guest turned his or her face

from the table and looked at Fern, a set of curious eyes connecting back to Jeb, and then turning back to whisper.

"You going to tell me who Walton is?"

She lifted her face. "I knew him once."

"Where's his wife?"

"He didn't say." She took a breath. "He followed me, Jeb. I went outside to be alone. Don't make it something else."

"Do you want to be alone now?" He let go of her arm.

"This isn't right, what you're doing."

"What am I supposed to think, Fern? A man I don't know shows up and ends up out in some garden with my fiancée. You think I'm an idiot?"

"I know you're not, Jeb. But I told you I didn't want to come, didn't I?"

"So you knew this Walton would be here?"

"You're not listening, so what difference does it make?"

"Why'd he come alone?"

"I think he came to see me." She waved to acknowledge Donna. "We never brought things to a proper close. I think he wanted to make sure I was all right. Everyone's looking at us. Can we stop talking about it?" Marion waved at Jeb. Jeb cupped Fern's elbow with one hand, and clasped her wrist with the other. He steered her back toward the dinner party. Marion had commented about Walton finishing law school when Fern and Donna were in college. But she had never mentioned him before. "I hope we can return to the party and at least be civil."

Fern smiled at the hostess, but she didn't comment any further.

"I wish you would say something, Fern," said Jeb.

"I told you I didn't want to come."

⤶

Marion was talkative, telling Jeb that while he and Fern were out for their walk, Donna started a rumor about them. "She says you're getting married this week, is that right?"

"Tuesday, most likely in Abigail's church. A simple ceremony," said Jeb. But he said it without looking at Fern.

"I'm surprised Abigail isn't throwing you-all a big wedding. I'll bet she had no say in this," said Marion.

"She didn't at all," said Donna. "I think I was the instigator and Mother never lets that happen. I'll be surprised if she lets them up and get married without a big to-do."

Jeb tried to keep from looking at Walton's empty chair. His bowl was cleared by the wait staff.

"Let me see your ring, Fern." Marion extended her hand to Fern, who was seated next to her. The rock on Marion's hand could sink the table.

Fern held her hand up to Marion. Her tone was staid when she said, "It's very old. Jeb's mother left it to him."

"I've never seen diamonds in that sort of arrangement. It's a fine ring and the plainness of it is what I like best," Marion said to the entire party.

"I propose a toast," said one of the men.

"If it's all right with the preacher," said Henry Oakley.

Several of the men said, "Hear! Hear!"

Donna elbowed Fern until she lifted her water glass.

Jeb touched his glass to Fern's. There were shadows under her eyes. She was breathing heavier than usual, her chest rising and then sinking. As she lowered her glass, Marion began bending her ear again, wanting to know about her trousseau.

Henry touched Jeb's arm. "How about we get down to business, Reverend? Marion and I have been friends for years with Jon and Rachel Flauvert. They've traveled all over, you name it, Mexico, Peru, what have you. I think they've been to China or some such. We lost our last pastor to some big church outfit in New York. Jon Flauvert knows everyone, so when I was asked on behalf of First Community here in Oklahoma City to find a new minister, I knew he was the man to see about it."

Jeb listened to Henry talk about the founding of First Community and then told him, "Dr. Flauvert asked me to speak on Sunday. But it's happening kind of fast. I still have a lot of ties back in Nazareth."

"Understood. But we like what we've heard about you, so we hope you'll give us a look and we'll give you and your bride a look and see what happens."

"Tell us, Fern, what you think of coming here, of your husband taking the pulpit of a city church?" asked Marion.

Fern turned to look toward the restaurant entrance. Donna whispered something to her. She said, "I'm not sure."

"She hasn't had a minute to think about it, I'm sure," said Henry.

"I've made a life for myself in Nazareth. The people are good." The whole time Fern talked, she shifted her gaze from Marion and then back to Henry, avoiding Jeb's eyes. "Most, I'd say, are good."

Everyone laughed.

"The last thing I remembered saying about Nazareth was to Jeb before we left town. I wondered if we would live there the rest of our lives," she said.

"Is that what you want?" asked Marion.

"She said it didn't matter as long as she was with me," said Jeb.

Fern finally looked at him. "I don't think I said that." She was smiling for everyone, but there was that irritating tension between them.

Henry laughed and a couple of women leaned forward, elbows on the table.

The entree arrived and the soup bowls were removed. Donna had ordered a steak for Jeb. He thanked her for that. The waiter filled Jeb's glass again. The jazz singer was taking a break, so the band struck up a soft melody. The lights were dimmed so much that all members of the dinner party had a blue cast to their skin. The smoky haze made a halo around Fern's blond hair. She mostly listened to Marion gabbing, communicating by an occasional nod of the head. Donna kept looking at Fern and then Jeb. Her fingers nervously tapped the table.

Jeb closed his eyes when he chewed the first bite of steak. It was a perfect cut, fork tender. He had not dined on steak since the time before he and his brother, Charlie, went to work for a man named Leon Hampton in

Texarkana. Maybe it had been longer. He could taste the rareness of it, the tender pink juice flowing into his mouth. The fluid music lulled him into a relaxed state.

The woman sitting next to him wore a spangled shawl, the border threads dripping over her fingertips whenever she reached for her glass. Her husband invited her to get up and dance a slow one. Another couple got up from the table and then a young man walked all the way across the room and invited Donna to dance.

"Looks like we're the only old fogies left to hold down the fort," said Henry.

"Henry, why don't you ask Miss Coulter to dance?" asked Marion.

Fern glanced at Jeb. She didn't wait for his nod of approval, but got up and met Henry on the floor.

Marion turned around in her chair to watch them gliding around the floor. Then she faced Jeb and said, "That Fern is a pistol, sharp, sharp, I'm telling you. She'll be an interesting one to watch. Not your typical preacher's wife."

"Fern's a good woman," said Jeb.

"She's got eyes for you, I'll say that. The whole time we talked, she never took her eyes off you."

Jeb slid his glass across the table to the waiter, who filled it again.

"You like our little city, Reverend?"

He did not have to keep Marion occupied. As soon as she asked him something else, her eyes would fall on another of her friends and she would shout down the table, engaged in a new story.

Fern twirled under Henry's arm, an old dance step, but she had it right. It was not his first time to watch Fern dance. Henry snapped her out at arm's length and she laughed. Jeb finally looked back at Marion. "I like the city fine, Mrs. Oakley." He hadn't known until now that he did like Oklahoma City. "Folks don't seem quite as desperate here as back home in Nazareth. I don't know if you've heard, but there's a Depression on."

Marion laughed. "Waiter, how about a slice of key lime pie for the minister?"

Jeb saw that she was waiting for his approval. "Sure, I'd like that," he said.

The waiter served him and then Marion said, "There's desperate people here too, just like around the rest of the country. Migrants mostly. They've camped in tent cities around our city limits."

"We saw them."

"Folks around here don't like it. They call them free-loaders. I don't know how I feel about that. I guess you being a minister and all you have some things to say about that."

"I preach all the time. I'd rather hear what you have to say."

"You are a smart man, aren't you? Henry and I once knew hard times. We weren't raised with a silver spoon like the rest of this bunch. Both of us worked to put him through law school. Our first home was an upstairs room in a boardinghouse. We didn't have two nickels to rub to-gether. So I downright hurt for those families."

The dance ended. Fern and Donna met in the center

of the floor and then turned away from the Oakleys' table to go and freshen up. Henry sat down on the other side of Jeb and explained how the church committee voted in a new minister. His coffee cup was refilled. Jeb took a sip and then pushed it aside.

Henry asked, "Has anyone seen Senator Baer?"

"He's gone home to be with his wife," said Jeb.

One of Marion's friends seated herself on the other side of Jeb. She was out of breath from dancing. "Anna's not gotten out much since she fell ill."

"The senator's wife is sick?" asked Marion.

"She's not expected to live. You knew that, didn't you?"

⁓

Fern leaned against Jeb in the elevator.

Donna reached for her purse.

"Donna, don't light up another of those things. You smell like the Devil," said Fern.

He had not seen Fern so harsh with her sister before.

Donna's hand froze inside her purse. She withdrew it and then leaned against the back of the elevator. "For a minute, I thought Abigail had gotten in this elevator."

Jeb held Fern's hand. Her skin was cold. She stared up at the elevator dial over the door. A silver bracelet jingled out of her sleeve, exposing small gem droplets, emeralds and sapphires hanging from the bracelet.

She drew that hand up into her shawl.

"That's a nice piece of jewelry. Is that your mother's?" asked Jeb.

Donna leaned forward and lifted Fern's shawl. She

looked at Fern and said, "That's the bracelet Daddy bought you one year. Wasn't it a birthday gift when we were in college? I thought you'd lost it."

Fern touched the gems. "So did I." She and Donna exchanged glances.

Jeb said, "Did you find it at your mother's place?"

Fern let out a breath. She closed her eyes and the elevator doorbell sounded.

"Here's our floor," said Donna.

Jeb walked them both to their room. Fern unlocked the door. Before she could open it fully, Jeb placed his hand atop hers, on the doorknob.

"I'm tired," said Fern.

"I think you're right about something." Jeb opened the hotel room door all the way.

Fern looked at him.

"We should have stayed back in Ardmore."

"We all need rest," said Donna. She put her arm around Fern's back and they disappeared into the room.

It was just as well. The more talking he did, the more Fern retreated.

He remembered the first time he saw her. She wore linen. He caught trout in the stream behind Church in the Dell. The water rushed around his boots as he messed with a trotline and then looked up to see a being of light, her heels planted in the grass. It seemed it was morning and the sun was up and shining across her face. She was sure of herself.

Before she disappeared into the hotel room, her shoulders were stooped and she looked as though she had lost bits of herself along the highway between Arkansas and Oklahoma.

Jeb knocked on her door. Donna answered and he said, "I need Fern."

The room was quiet behind Donna. Finally Fern appeared.

"You forgot to say good night," said Jeb.

Fern stepped out into the hallway. The color on her cheeks had rivulets of white.

"I love you, Fern." He held her.

"I don't know why." She was crying.

He kissed her. When he drew back to look at her, he tasted salt and lipstick.

Donna closed the door behind her.

"I'll take you home right now, Fern, if that's what you want."

She wiped her eyes with the lapel of her robe. "Jeb, it's your turn to do what you want. I'm not telling you what to do."

"I'm not going to wreck us, Fern," said Jeb.

"You're not, you're not. Don't be this way. I'll get some rest. Tomorrow I'll be different. You study for Sunday. We'll do this, Jeb. I never thought I'd see you behind a city pulpit. But I should have, I should have known. I'm proud as can be. Shame on me for not saying so sooner." She kissed him again, her lips warm and swollen from crying. She slid her tongue between his lips and pressed herself against him.

"Come with me, to my place," he said. He held her face in his hands.

She pressed against him and his back went against the wall. She kissed him again. Then she let go of him, brought her hands to her face, and laughed. "You'll never finish that sermon with me around." She walked back to her door and knocked for her sister.

Donna opened the door. Her hair was tied up in rags. "May I help you?"

Fern took the door handle and said her good-nights. Behind the door, Donna muttered, "You look miserable." The door closed. The sound of the lock clicking into place told Jeb that the night was ended. He waited until he heard Fern and Donna laugh from inside the room.

He rode the elevator back up to the top floor and walked down the hallway and out into the rooftop garden. The clouds had cleared and the moon was nearly whole, like it had filled up with air and might break open. He stood on the spot warmed by Fern not an hour ago.

A waiter called from the glass doors, Indian-looking in the face. His open necktie hung loosely down his shirt. "I'm supposed to lock up. But I can come back if you need some more time. You going to be out here awhile, sir?"

"Five minutes, okay?" asked Jeb.

"Sure, glad to oblige. Want me to get you a drink, last call? You look like you need a whiskey."

Jeb turned it down, but thanked him. There was the scent of Fern's perfume hanging around. He smelled one of his cuffs. Her lipstick had smudged the sleeve.

Only an occasional car rattled past below. A flock of rock doves settled and nested along the roof. He tried to recall some of his sermon ideas, but Fern kept sifting into his thoughts. The door opened again and a woman's voice called. He turned, hoping that she had followed him and was still wearing that bathrobe and tasting of salt.

"Only me. I'm a maid here. The bartender asked me to come and lock up. Are you all right?" she asked.

"I needed some air is all." He gave the girl two bits for her time. He left the garden and took the elevator back to his floor. No light shone under Fern's door.

He did not know what he would say to her in the morning. But in a few days she would marry him. Weddings fix things, he had heard.

When he finally fell asleep, he slept restlessly, waking up a couple of times, but then falling into a deep hibernation, which shut his mind down and gave him blessed peace. He did not wake up again until the sun was shining through the window shades, reminding him that summer still lingered while the sameness of life evaporated.

5

OUTSIDE, PLANTING HIS FEET ON THE downtown sidewalk, Jeb watched the sun coming up. He could set his watch by the sun in August. He sniffed deeply, enjoying the café smells mingling with car exhaust. First one automobile and then another motored by, *click-and-click-and-clack.* The rubber tires rhythmically hammered the dusty brick streets.

A pencil salesman held out his cup. "Three for a penny," he told Jeb. He did not sound like an Okie, more like a Kansas boy, a bit of spit and polish to his manner. His suit was pinstriped, frayed at the jacket sleeves. His necktie was expertly tied and his shirt and trousers neatly pressed.

As Fern approached, Jeb dropped a penny into the

cup, but turned down the pencils. The man insisted Fern take the pencils, not wanting a handout. She accepted them and put another coin in his cup. Fern gave Jeb the newspaper she bought from a paperboy on the corner. "We'd best go inside. Donna's already ordered breakfast," she said. Donna held a table inside the Coffee Shop.

Two Indians in feathered derbies conversed in the lobby, stepping out of the way to tip their hats at Fern.

"The cook's out of biscuits, but they have hotcakes," said Donna.

Jeb sat between them, facing the windows street-side. The Coffee Shop's waiter gave him his order of pancakes and filled his coffee cup. A blue dish of grits was placed next to the breakfast plate.

"I haven't had a Sunday breakfast like this since I started teaching," said Donna. "Remember that restaurant, Fern, that Mother and Daddy took us to when we were small, that one up in Vermont? Didn't they make their own syrup? Taste this and see if it isn't as good."

Fern accepted the forkful of pancake from her sister and then said to Jeb, "Did you find the church out on your walk yesterday?"

"Three blocks from here. If you can't get there in those shoes, I can order a cab if you want." Jeb mixed his eggs with the grits.

Fern had changed out of her teaching shoes. She glanced down at her upturned heel. "I can walk. Donna, you going?"

"Sure. I need a little religion in my life," she said.

Fern picked up the saltshaker. She had replaced the

bracelet she wore Friday night with a snug gold rhinestone bracelet.

Jeb touched it and stroked her wrist.

"Do you like it?" she asked. "I bought it yesterday. Donna and I found a shop where an old woman makes every piece of jewelry by hand."

"Where? In the hotel?"

"No, two blocks west of here," she said.

"So you must have seen the church."

"I don't think we went that far, did we, Donna?"

"It's a whole block farther," said Donna.

"I look forward to seeing it today, Jeb. You know that, don't you?" asked Fern.

"I only meant that since you were so close, it seems you would have taken a walk around the place. You like gardens. The church is surrounded by trees and flowers."

She turned her hand up and clasped his hand. "You're right, I should have gone there already. I can't wait to see it." Her eyes lifted.

"Yesterday, seeing the church gardens, it came to me how little has been given to Church in the Dell."

"God prayed in a garden, didn't he?" asked Donna. "Is that what you-all are talking about?"

"If the people are happy, what's the difference?" asked Fern.

Jeb nodded, absentminded and staring out at the main drag, the Sunday drivers increasing in number. "The churches like First Community were few and far between where I grew up. Until now, I never gave much thought to steeples and gardens." He picked up his Bible and said, "I'd like to go early and see the inside of the sanctuary. Join me when you finish, ladies."

"It's still an hour until service time," said Fern.

"The two of you can come when you're ready." He rose and pretended not to notice how they stared after him.

～

The church doors were unlocked. Jeb strolled inside through a lobby, and entered another set of doors opening to a church aisle. A blue floral rug ran the length of the aisle pointing straight into the platform and the preaching lectern. As he walked down the aisle, voices quietly murmured from other rooms. He ascended the two steps to the top of the platform and then stood behind the lectern where he opened his Bible. The pages fell open, bookmarked. The electric light overhead illuminated the words more keenly than the single naked bulb hanging over the Church in the Dell lectern. There was a woody aroma in the room. He examined the ceiling. The beamed ceiling and the walls were laid with a golden oak, wood shining as though it had just been put in.

The rear door opened and a woman looked startled to see Jeb. "I hope I'm not disturbing you. I come in early to set up the Communion plates."

"Not at all. I'm Reverend Nubey," he said.

"We heard a new man was coming to take a turn in our pulpit. Glad to meet you," she said. "Have a look around. Our building is nearly a century old. It's been took good care of." She excused herself and disappeared into the lobby.

"If I may suggest, you can switch on that light over the lectern," said a voice. A young man, whose face had an eager boyish quality, walked quietly across the platform. He carried a tray of water, a pitcher and a single glass. "We thought you might need a drink as you preach, sir." He placed the tray on a stand behind Jeb. "Our last minister taught us to serve the pastor so that he could better serve others."

"I'm Reverend Nubey," said Jeb.

"Pleased, I'm Rowan. I help out wherever I'm needed." He filled the glass and handed it to Jeb and padded away through an exit door on the right side, where he disappeared into a room hidden behind the platform.

Jeb turned on the reading light. The pages were bright and legible. He sipped the water and then took off his jacket and laid it over a platform chair. The attention given to him made him relax and enjoy his surroundings.

Oak pews formed rows on either side of the sanctuary, big enough to seat five hundred or more congregants. Glass light fixtures hanging in suspended rows made the sanctuary glow. The only chandelier in the building hung over where he stood. There were stained-glass windows on both sides. He descended the stairs and walked between the end pews and the windows to study the artwork. Scenes depicted the Apostles and certain elements of the life of Christ leading up to His Passion.

Church in the Dell's small chapel existed only to serve the members who filled its pews, a sort of people holder, as it were. First Community's structure had taken on a traditional aesthetic.

"She was a cripple."

The voice startled Jeb. Henry Oakley had slipped up behind him.

"Sorry, Reverend. You seem to be enjoying some quiet time."

"Good morning, Henry. Who was a cripple?" asked Jeb.

"The artist who created all of these windows. She had polio as a girl."

Jeb and Henry walked the aisle. More people filtered into the sanctuary. Jeb listened as Henry described how the artist suffered to create the window glass. He commented about her tendency to use blue more than any other color and did that have anything to do with suffering. He didn't know and Jeb didn't venture a guess, Henry said, "It takes two days for the cleaning men to clean the windows." The glass rose from two feet above the floor to the ceiling. "The artist, she would hold up her arms until they ached, her neck hurting. So the janitors see the window cleaning as a mission."

"Henry, may I ask you the order of the service?"

"The choir will sing three congregational songs and then I will introduce you to the parishioners as our visiting minister. I don't know how you were installed at your last church, but until you tell us for certain you want to be considered for candidacy, we will instruct our members to consider you a visiting pastor from Arkansas."

"Have others preached here since your pastor left?"

"A revivalist and one missionary. And, of course, Jon Flauvert."

Jeb nodded as Henry spoke. He wanted to answer

right then and there that he would accept the post. Instead, he quietly listened and followed Henry out of the sanctuary.

The choir could be heard warming up in a room behind the platform. Henry continued showing Jeb the rest of the building. In the building's rear section was a large kitchen, next to a dining hall. "We have a soup kitchen for the migrants," he said. "For years, our ladies' committee fed the hobos that passed through, but after this Depression hit, the everyday folks started hitting the rails in search of work."

"I'm glad to know you're feeding them," said Jeb.

"The trains brought them right through town, right through Packingtown. Livestock is auctioned and butchered down around those parts."

"Glad there are places where people can go to get help. I'm trying to find work for a young woman there now."

"Oklahoma City was able to accommodate for a while. Problem is, one city like ours can't give a job to every person put out of work in this country. Some move on to California, some to Texas. Some stay and hope for help."

"Why is it that you've not been hit as hard as the rest of the country?"

"We've had dust storms and crop failures. But drive by our governor's mansion and see for yourself. Right out on the front lawn are oil derricks. We got more oil than we know what to do with. One of those oil men attends First Community."

"I see, I see. I suppose you understand how unusual it is to find a church doing well in hard times?" said Jeb.

"We've been hit, don't get me wrong. Some of our members have been put out of work. It's made us all live more practically now. But the oil fields have lessened the sting." He unlocked a few classroom doors as they walked down the hallway. "Here's the way I see things, we got this pocket of commerce here and don't know how long until it unravels. But as long as people in this country don't turn back to the horse and buggy, Oklahoma City's got a good shot at weathering out this Depression. I say the auto mobile io heic to stay. Some say I'll be proven wrong."

"Seems like even if all I have to keep it together is bale wire and bobby pins, I keep hanging on to my old Ford. Hard to remember what it was like without it."

"Can't say as I want to go back to sitting behind a mare myself. Let me show you our dining facility. We built it five years ago. When you close your message in prayer, you'll be escorted back to the dining hall. The deacons' wives have prepared a dinner for you. Hope you like fried chicken. We'll give the deacons a chance to meet with you then, if that's acceptable." The door opened to the choir room. Twenty or more choir members were slipping into robes. Henry led Jeb past them and into the dining hall. A dozen women were already popping open tablecloths and covering tables.

"I wasn't expecting dinner," said Jeb. He thanked him.

"Your fiancée and her sister are invited too. They'll have a chance to meet the women in our church." He led Jeb back into the hall.

The choir filed past them and up a set of steep stairs to the choir loft.

Henry led Jeb back to the lectern. "Are you ready, Reverend Nubey?" asked Henry.

"I am," said Jeb. He pulled on his coat and tightened his tie.

꙰

People filed into the sanctuary, taking up spaces as far as the front row. Jeb had never lectured in front of a crowd that size. The high rafters serviced the sound naturally. The music director led the choir in a crescendo that swelled until Jeb could feel the vibration in his ears.

Two other elders sat to the right of Henry on the platform while Jeb took his place left of Henry. He had not seen Fern or Donna since the music commenced, but it would be easy to lose a face in a sea of so many.

"Do you ever get the jitters, Reverend?" Henry asked. "I've always wondered if preachers got wet feet every Sunday. You don't have to answer."

"I always thought a big church might scare me. Maybe it does. I'll answer you after the sermon." If he admitted to being nervous, it would only make things worse.

Henry laughed and Jeb tugged at his collar.

"I could use some of that water," said Jeb.

Henry poured him a glass from the pitcher left by young Rowan.

"Must be at least seven hundred in attendance here this morning. Our old pastor, Reverend Miller, used to say it was harder to preach to a sparse auditorium."

Jeb's throat felt parched in spite of the drink of water. The third song ended and the choir was seated. Henry introduced Jeb in as simple a manner as he had said he would. Jeb decided to search as he spoke, until he found Fern's face. The sight of her in the earlier days at Church in the Dell, when he preached so wet-behind-the-ears, always calmed him. This morning he needed to see her smiling up at him in a room full of strange eyes staring back. Most of the men were dressed in dark suits, the ladies in hats and dresses of blue and yellow, pink and white. He offered a prayer, but as the congregants bowed their heads, he peered through his lashes searching for Fern. Had she worn a hat? He could not remember. There was a whole herd of women's hats bowing out in those pews. Was her dress green or pink? Why hadn't he noticed? He remembered her shoes, her long toes pressed into black-and-white alligator leather, but nothing else, nothing helpful.

He made his opening comments. The next sip of water seemed to help. He commenced the message. During the sermon, he methodically looked left to right, making eye contact, and then assessing what he felt he was reading as the congregation's approval. He was met with so much disapproval in his first year at Church in the Dell that he learned to appreciate the sight of smiling, relaxed faces.

An usher opened one of the oak doors and helped a woman through the door in the rear of the sanctuary. Behind her a smartly dressed man followed. The usher seated the couple in a pew, second to the last row on the right side. The man assisted the woman, who looked to be his wife, handing her a pocketbook after she settled into her seat. He then sat forward, his hands gripping the pew in front of him as he looked up and down the aisle. It was Senator Walton Baer and he was looking for someone.

A woman in the front row shifted uncomfortably, most likely in response to a pause held out a moment too long by Jeb. He looked back down at the text and closed his eyes like ministers do to allow a point to seep in. He continued his next point and his mind took on two tasks, the first being to deliver the message he came to deliver, and secondly, to find Fern.

By the final point, the sermon overtook his thoughts. The steady pace of the message found a good rhythm. An occasional nod of a church member's head spurred him to continue to feed the hungry faithful who had gone too long without a shepherd. Jeb felt a unity of soul. They needed him.

He said, "And in conclusion," and the several women from the food committee slipped out of their chairs. A musician returned to the piano stool and played a chorus, a soft backdrop cadence to underpin his final comments.

Before he asked members to bow for prayer, Fern's soft blond crown appeared from behind a woman's large hat. She was too far away for him to read her face. She'd always been the one he looked to for encouragement. But in a church of this size, her face was nearly indistinguishable. He turned back to the right, where he found Senator Baer looking at Fern. Then he sat back next to his wife.

After Jeb's concluding prayer, Henry Oakley escorted him off the platform. Jeb was flanked by an entire committee of men, who followed him down the hall and into the dining hall.

Marion was holding the rear door open when Jeb and Henry arrived. "I'll go and find your fiancée and her sister. You're seated at the head table, Reverend Nubey, next to Henry and me and our deacon board and their wives. I hope you find everything to your satisfaction."

He was hoping to find Fern and Donna following the deacons into the hall, but they most likely had gotten lost in the throng of retreating church members.

"I couldn't be more pleased, Mrs Oakley. Things couldn't be more perfect."

Jeb was led to the head table and seated in the center chair. His plate was picked up by one of the ladies wearing a blue apron. She told him that she would fill his plate and asked him about some of his favorite selections. He told her what sounded good to him. Another woman filled his iced-tea glass and placed a saucer of bread in front of him.

The other deacons and their wives filled their plates at a serving table and then joined Jeb. He assumed the chair next to him would be reserved for Fern. But first the chair to one side of him was taken and then the other, so he thought that perhaps Fern would be seated across from him. Then another woman wrestling a baby took that chair.

The gathering was not as small as he thought it would be. The hall filled with about a hundred or more members.

Henry described first this one and then that one as either a leader in the town or a person who was in the habit of making a large donation to First Community.

"Each of these families has a vested interest in First Community. They are best described as men and women who care about this church."

The hall doors were closed. Henry stood and offered a prayer of blessing on the church as well as on Jeb.

The deacons and wives all commenced eating.

"I'll bet Marion and Fern have gotten tied up," said Henry.

Finally the doors opened and Marion escorted Fern and Donna into the hall. She led them to the serving tables, where they made their selections. Fern looked all around and finally saw Jeb. She and Donna spoke for a moment and then the two of them took their plates to a table in the back of the room.

Marion returned to the head table and sat next to Henry. She looked all around the table, saw how the seats had filled up, and said, "Dear, we can't have this! Where's Miss Coulter's seat?" She wasn't hiding how she scowled at Henry.

"My wife knows I can't handle these things alone," said Henry to Jeb. He got up and waited as Marion began to shift the members around the table.

"I'll go and fetch Fern and Donna," said Jeb. Before making it to the back, he was stopped first by one church member and then another, each one praising his morning sermon. He walked up to the rear table and found them both eating but saying nothing at all. He was still feeling the vinegar of his morning message and the accolades when Donna said, "Well, have you come down to pay your subjects a visit?"

"They have a seat for the two of you up front. I can help you carry something, Fern." He held out hands.

"I saw no seats for us, did you, Donna?"

"It was a mistake. Marion is correcting all of that, if you'll just come with me."

"We're fine, Jeb. Really. You go ahead and join your party," said Fern. "Donna and I are just kidding around."

"But they've gone to all the trouble of giving up their seats just so you can join me."

"I'm honored, Jeb. But I've already settled into my dinner."

She was beginning to get under his skin. "You know, if you hadn't taken so long, this wouldn't have happened in the first place. Where were you anyway, talking to someone? Never mind, it doesn't matter."

She sipped her tea.

Donna kept staring down at her plate.

"I saw Senator Baer and his wife, if that matters. If you care to know that I saw him," said Jeb.

"I saw him too."

"What was he doing here anyway?" asked Jeb.

"His wife has gone to this church for years. He comes with her. She's really sick."

"I know, I know." Jeb shoved his hands into his pockets, got right in her face, and muttered, "Are you telling me a man that you once had some sort of fling with attends this church?"

"You're loud."

"I'm done," said Donna. She picked up her plate. "I'm going back to the hotel to rest. See you there, Fern."

"Don't leave," said Jeb. "I'm sorry. But today's been good until now. I thought you'd want to be a part of it, Fern. Or at the least, tell me what a good job I did this morning. So if you don't mind, I'd appreciate it if the two of you would kindly pick up your plates and join me for a nice meal."

Several people at the next table turned and whispered.

Fern's fork froze in midair. She slowly pulled her napkin out of her lap and draped it over her forearm. She pushed her chair away from the table and picked up her plate.

"I've really had enough to eat. But thank you for the offer, Jeb. I mean that." Donna gave Fern a peck on the cheek, picked up her handbag, and left.

"That was embarrassing," said Fern.

Jeb led the way back to the head table. Marion greeted them and kept saying to Fern, "How awful, how can we make it up to you?" until Fern got up and gave Marion a squeeze around the shoulders. She assured her that she was fine.

Marion asked, "Henry, where did Senator Baer and his wife, Anna, go?" She said to Jeb and Fern, "We seated them next to the Blooms, since Sybil is Anna's best friend."

"I spoke with them," said Fern. "Anna could hardly get out of bed this morning."

"Sybil must not know or she would have told me," said Marion.

"All I know is what Walton told me," said Fern. "He seemed troubled over it. Donna and I thought he looked kind of weathered around the eyes."

"This has aged him. Anna fought it for a good six months, but of late, she seems to be losing ground," said Marion.

One of the deacons' wives said, "Reverend Nubey, your message was right on the nose this morning."

Several of the other deacons and their wives joined in raving over Jeb.

Jeb said, "I must say I've never known such a feeling as preaching to such a large congregation."

"You'll have to try it more often, Reverend," said Marion.

Several of the guests laughed.

"Maybe I will and soon," said Jeb. His tea glass was filled again.

"You must be used to hearing people bragging on your fiancée," Marion said to Fern.

Fern pushed out her chair to go and refill her tea glass. She returned with a plate of cake for herself.

Marion must have forgotten what she had asked Fern. In the babble of the other women and the deacons, everyone lost track of who asked what and who did not respond, all except Jeb.

6

Monday delivered a nearly bone-white sky over the Coulter farm. A wall of thinly white clouds covered a sky that brought no relief or rain upon the land.

Angel sat on Abigail's front porch steps cradling Thorne in her arms. The three-year-old was prone to clinging. She squealed so loud from breakfast on that Angel worried that Ms. Abigail would grow weary of Claudia and her children. So she took her outside and sang to her. The little girl stared straight ahead, the pointer finger on her right hand twirling Angel's hair into a spiral. Angel sang a song her mother, Thorne, had sung out on their front porch.

Inside all morning, Claudia's oldest boy, John, ran all

over Abigail's house like a scalded pup. He ran from the parlor to the back of the house, into the kitchen, arms out as he made motor noises. He finally collapsed on Abigail's parlor sofa sound asleep. Angel turned around occasionally to keep an eye on him through the screen door.

Claudia leaned against a fence post out near the northern cow pasture. A small herd of Coulter cattle grazed on the yellowing grass. A ring of smoke floated over her head. She enjoyed a cigarette she rolled that morning on the dining-room table, scraping into a paper the residue of loose tobacco from a tin Bo left behind. After she stubbed it out on the fence post, she walked back toward Angel on the front porch. Her cotton dress swayed front to back, sheer in the sunlight, a pale pink, practically white fabric. The silhouette of her legs showed through the cotton fabric, lean as a newly birthed fawn.

Thorne let out a sigh. Her head slumped against Angel and she was out. Angel stood up, holding the little girl underneath her back, her small face pressed into her body. "She's nodded off," she told Claudia.

Claudia was relieved. "I can't remember the last time I had a minute to think or take a smoke. Ever since Bo took off, I've had both of them two hanging on me every minute of the day. I think they was scared when their daddy didn't come home."

"I'll take her upstairs and lay her on my bed."

"You've had her all morning. Here, I'll take her." Claudia held out her arms and draped Thorne over one shoulder, holding the cigarette in her teeth. She carried her indoors.

Willie ran out of the house, followed by a breathless boy cousin. "Miz Abigail, she says you got a phone call, Angel."

"Who would call me?" she said to herself. Ms. Abigail was the only person she knew who had a telephone. None of her kin had ever paid to have one put in. She got up from the porch stoop and went inside. She walked past a mirror hung above a table in the living room. Thorne left a round wet place on her shoulder seam.

Ms. Abigail's maid, Myrna, stood with one arm extended holding out the telephone receiver. She wiped down the kitchen table with the other.

"Who is it?" asked Angel.

"Beats me. I never ask those things, hon," she said. "Mrs. Coulter asked me to give you the phone. She took to her bed for a nap." She picked up a load of laundry and carried it out the back door to the clothesline.

Angel held the telephone receiver to her ear. "This is Angel."

The voice was male and languid, although somewhat muted, like he was standing out in a wind. "Hi, sweet cakes. Long time no hear from. Bet you never expected to hear from me."

"Who is this?" she asked.

"This is fun. We could make it a game."

"I'm going to hang up."

"It's Nash. Remember? The Studebaker?"

She tried to remember what she had said to Nash that would cause him to call. Then she remembered how he asked for the telephone number of the place she was staying. Guys like him asked for phone numbers all the time back in Nazareth, men who pass through town looking for a small-town girl to hang on their arm on a Saturday night. She never paid them any mind and never expected Nash would call. "I don't think I can talk to you."

"Why not? It's my nickel. Say, you owe me one anyway."

"You ought to know," said Angel.

"I gave you my number. You could have at least paid me the courtesy of a call."

"What do you want?"

"I don't like to travel alone and I thought you'd like to see the world. Country life is too quiet for my tastes."

There was a pause.

"My sister Claudia Drake is here. She lives in Norman." She meant that she would be busy visiting with her sister. But none of the words came out as she had intended.

"Better idea. I could pick you up there."

Angel's pulse quickened. Her breath was coming faster. "I can't talk to you." She slid the phone back onto the hook.

Ida May came up from the cellar, having fetched a jar of grape jelly. "Your voice sounds funny," she said to Angel. "Who was that anyway?"

"Here, let me open the jelly jar for you," said Angel.

"It's not for me. Miz Myrna had me fetch it for supper tonight."

John woke up. His voice went off like a siren. Angel walked into the living room and collected him from the sofa. The side of his face was red and damp from spit, his right cheek dimpled from the woolen sofa threads.

Claudia stood staring out the front living-room window at the cattle eating breakfast from the yellow grass. She seemed unaware of John's cries.

❧

The arduous drive back to Ardmore caused Fern to retreat into a book. Donna made a bed on the backseat. Her breath became rhythmic as sleep overtook her.

"I hope that all of the kids we left on your mother's doorstep haven't been too much for her," said Jeb.

"I couldn't tell if she cared or not," said Fern. "She's hard to read."

Jeb pulled into a filling station to fuel up. The evening porch light was left on, giving the lot a jaundiced cast. Inside the station, the attendant read the morning paper. He pulled down his feet from the desktop when he saw Jeb waving from his car. He came out and offered to fill the tank.

Jeb slipped back into the car. Fern marked her book with a crocheted marker and slid it under the seat. She laid her head against the seat and fixed her eyes ahead.

The attendant washed the window in front of her and smiled in at Fern. She managed a faint smile and then closed her eyes.

"You haven't asked me about my meeting with Henry after the dinner yesterday. Do you want to know anything at all?" asked Jeb.

"I do, Jeb. This is all so fast, that's all." Her voice sounded stretched thin.

"The committee has asked me to agree to become a serious candidate."

"And did you tell them you would?"

"I said I'd pray."

"That was a good answer."

"The dickens you say! I want this church, I want it for us!"

She opened her eyes. The attendant tapped on Jeb's window. Jeb rolled down the window and paid him.

"Then tell them you'll take it."

"You know I can't. Not until you and I have worked out all our matters." He started the engine.

Fern pushed up from her relaxed posture and looked at him. "I saw the way those people catered to you yesterday, Jeb. They were all but saluting when you walked in the door. Church in the Dell has been a hard church to pastor, I know that. I've wanted you to give up, at times, but you didn't. You stuck it out and over time, you've done some good. But this city church has you reeling from all of the attention they've shown you and I'm not ignorant of that either." She slipped her feet out of her good shoes. She had a pair of white cotton socks in her pocketbook. She dug them out and pulled them onto her feet over the stockings. "You need time to clear your head, Jeb."

"My mind is clear. This is the place for us, Fern. We've found the Welbys' kin and a place to start over."

"Claudia Drake is a mess. You aren't suggesting that she is prepared to take in Angel and the kids, are you? She can't feed what children she does have."

"You heard the guy at the Skirvin. I found her some

work. Even Henry said I had made a good connection for her, had one of his church members get some material to give Claudia. The girl lives right outside Oklahoma City, for heaven's sakes. If we're there, we can check on them, help them out. We can have it all, a new congregation, better pay, and give the Welbys back their family."

"Life is not that easily fixed, Jeb."

"Until now, it wasn't."

"You've made up your mind, so what else is there to talk about?"

"There's more to tell. The pay is really good, Fern. You can stay at home if you want."

"I teach because I want."

"I know. The Coulter girls choose to work. You're like your daddy. But you won't have to, that's all I'm saying."

Donna sighed and stretched out her arms.

Fern peered around the seat. "You finally awake?"

"I think you need to listen to Jeb, if you ask me," she said. "I never knew what you saw in that scrubby little town, Fern. You never did fit the bill for a small-town preacher's wife."

"I liked you better asleep."

"Now we're getting somewhere," said Jeb.

"Not that I ever saw you as a preacher's wife either," said Donna.

They drove past several little towns. Around noon, a red-and-blue light flashed ahead, an advertisement for hot-plate specials from inside a diner window. Jeb offered to buy Donna's lunch, obliged to an ally.

✌

Myrna called the Welby children and Claudia and her brood in for a noontime meal. Abigail took her meal in her room. That troubled Angel a tad. She hoped that with Claudia's family showing up, that they weren't wearing out their welcome. "Is Miz Abigail feeling poorly?" she asked Myrna.

"Oh, she is fine, girl, don't trouble over it. Sometimes since Mr. Coulter passed, she likes to take her meal in her bedroom. She and Mr. Coulter used to take tea out on the patio outside her room. Wouldn't surprise me if she sits out there to think about those times."

The table was set up family-style with bowls of vegetables set in the table's middle section. Myrna made beans with ham and fried potatoes. She added two leaves to the table after Claudia showed up. Ida May carried a large bottle of ketchup to the table. She had been running errands all morning for Myrna in the same manner she had for either Angel or Fern back in Nazareth. Myrna took to Ida May as affectionately as all of the other women at Church in the Dell.

Willie and Darrell, Fern's young nephew, came inside panting, their faces gleaming with sweat. They ran hoops all morning down the hill from the pasture. Myrna made them remove their berets.

Claudia sat holding Thorne as the girl wanted nothing to do with the baby chair Abigail kept for her grandchildren. John sat near Angel. She tied a rag around his neck and asked him if he liked potatoes.

"Corn bread is right out of the oven and I see Ida May has put butter on the table already." She cut the round of corn bread into triangles and served it on a platter. "You all can bless your food and eat," said Myrna. She had already fixed a plate for herself. She excused herself from the family and carried her plate into her quarters, right outside the kitchen.

Angel asked grace. She made Willie draw back his hand. "Hand the corn bread platter first to Claudia, Willie. Serve company first."

Claudia accepted the serving plate. She served herself and handed the platter to Ida May. Angel got up and served her sister with beans and potatoes, since her lap was full of Thorne. Claudia smelled the food, her eyes closed. "I haven't seen potatoes in years. Nor ham in the beans, nor piccalilli relish, nor onion slice." She blew on a piece of potato, dipped it in ketchup, and held it in front of Thorne's mouth. "You've done good by your brother and sister, Angel. I couldn't have done no better. Fact is, I probably wouldn't have done near as good."

"It's because of Jeb and Miss Fern."

"And the good people at Church in the Dell," said Willie. He waited for the bread platter to return from around the table. He forked corn bread onto his plate. "Everybody gives up a little of what they have and it ends up enough."

Darrell watched Willie shovel potatoes into his mouth. His laughter dribbled out of him, a nervous squeal.

"Truth is, Bo had a good job. We had enough, more

than some, maybe not as much as others. But what he didn't drink up, he gambled away."

Angel gave another cooled potato cube to John.

"In spite of that, I never thought he'd be the type to up and leave," said Claudia. "Granny told me once that she saw meanness in Bo's eyes. It took some time to see things as she saw them, but she was right."

Angel buttered her bread and broke off a corner for John. "What are you going to do, Claudia, get a job?"

"How am I going to do that? I can't leave these two behind."

"Bo ought to be horsewhipped," said Willie.

Angel asked Ida May to fetch the iced-tea pitcher. She said to Claudia, "Have you ever heard from Daddy?"

"Not since he sent you off with Lana."

"You knew about that, then?"

"I got his letter, the last one I ever got."

Angel and Willie exchanged glances. Angel said, "So he told you that Lana was bringing us to your place."

Claudia stopped crumbling corn bread over her beans.

"If you knew we were on the way, why'd you leave?" Willie asked.

"I shouldn't have said nothing," said Claudia.

"So you and Bo up and left after you knew we were coming to live with you?" Angel asked.

"That's a fine howdy-do, Claudia." Willie put both wrists on the table, his gaze resting accusingly on Claudia.

"You don't understand how things was with us. Bo wasn't good with John and then we had little Thorne on the way. I knew he wouldn't be good to either of you."

"We could have starved, Claudia," said Angel. "Ida May was sickly. You knew all of that and you left us behind. Even Daddy did better by us. At least he wrote to tell you we were coming."

"That was a bad time," said Willie. "After Lana took off with a salesman, we hitched a ride with a crazy woman. She stole everything we had and left us out in the rain." He described that night well, not leaving anything to the imagination.

"I was scared," said Ida May.

"So was I," said Angel. "I thought we'd all been left for dead."

A tear trickled down Claudia's cheek. She set Thorne on the floor, brought the napkin to her face, and sobbed.

Angel, Willie, and Ida May stared at one another and then at their oldest sister.

"I made the wrong choice," said Claudia. "I should have picked you. I was afraid that I couldn't make it without Bo."

"You were right about that," said Willie.

"Willie, don't make it worse than it is." Angel wiped the sheen from John's mouth.

"When you got the letter from Daddy, is that when you decided to leave?" asked Ida May. She set the tea pitcher on the table.

"It wasn't exactly like that, no. Bo had gotten a telegram with a job offer to work for the railroad near Oklahoma City. I told him about Daddy's letter and that you would be on the way soon. I asked if he would let me stay behind and wait for you-all and then send for us. He told me that if I didn't leave then and there with him, that I'd be on my own. He knew he had me." She refilled her tea glass. "He gave me almost no time to pack up our belongings. We left the next morning before sunup."

"You could tell," said Angel. She paused for a second or more before saying, "I don't blame you, Claudia, for what you did. It's hard to know what to do when you got no one to call." She gave Willie a look.

"I even tried to write you a letter, Angel. But he tore it up, burned it in the cookstove," said Claudia. She wiped her eyes again.

"Angel's right. I won't hold it against you," said Willie. "So you married a louse. You made a mistake."

"It wasn't always like that between me and Bo," said Claudia. She blew her nose into the napkin. "We made a few memories, the two of us. But it never accounted to much, not like the times I had with you-all."

Ida May scooted her chair away from the table. She walked up beside Claudia and threw her arms around her.

Claudia kissed Ida May's cheek. She hesitated as if she needed time to form her next sentence. "There's something I need to ask you, Angel."

Angel rested her face in her hands and nodded at Claudia.

"I'd like to ask you to come and stay with me until I get back on my feet. If you watch these two, then I can find a good job."

"Claudia, you couldn't feed all of us," said Angel.

"Not Willie and Ida May, I couldn't. But with you helping out, I could see to our needs."

Ida May withdrew from Claudia.

"Don't get in a huff, Little Sister. I'd send for you and your brother soon as I could," said Claudia.

"Angel's got school to finish," said Willie. "Miss Fern's got her studying to become a teacher."

"They's no time for that, Willie. We got to think about Thorne and little John now."

Angel stiffened. "Willie's right. I want to become a teacher."

"Welbys help out their own, Angel. You need to learn that now, get your feet on the ground."

Angel helped John to the floor and gave him an extra bite of potato to suck on. She asked Ida May to help her clear the table.

"I'm asking you to think about it, Angel. I'm tired of our family being strung out all over the country. It's time we put back together what Momma and Daddy let fall to pieces."

Angel gathered the plates into a stack and carried them into the kitchen. She called Myrna out of her room and told her, "I'll help you with the dishes."

Myrna said, "You're a guest of Miss Coulter. You don't have to bother."

"Not really a guest, Myrna, when you think about it. Jeb and Fern will be married soon. We're almost family, aren't we?"

"You're right, girl. I should have thought of that already."

ॐ

Jeb drove down the road and up the Coulter drive. The car undulated over the hills and dips in the drive. Fern slid her feet back into her shoes.

Ida May came running down the hill. Her red face gleamed and her dress tail was hiked up in back as she ran. Jeb slowed and opened his window to ask her, "Need a lift, Littlest?"

"Claudia is taking Angel away, but we can't go. I don't want Angel to leave, Dub."

Donna opened the back car door and invited Ida May inside. She was ripe; the potent sweat of a girl was no different than a boy's. She told Fern about going to church with Miz Abigail and about the new calf in the barn.

"Who told you Claudia was taking Angel? Taking her where?" asked Jeb.

"I heard them say so over dinner. It made Willie mad. He wouldn't play with me."

Fern let out a breath.

Jeb pulled underneath the oak behind the house. He got out and opened the trunk for the women, setting their suitcases out for them. Fern picked up the largest case. "I guess you got your second wish," she said.

Abigail came out onto the back porch. She smoothed her hair with her fingers and then smiled at her girls. "Ida May, I wondered where you were off to. You spotted them before me. That girl's got eyes, eyes, I tell you."

Donna pulled out a pack of smokes.

"Fern, you and Jeb need to hear this, I got something I want to say," said Abigail.

Fern's brow tensed. She and Donna exchanged gazes.

"I've been worrying over this wedding. Since you-all told all our friends about it in Oklahoma City, the phone's not stopped ringing." Abigail's tone was less than enthusiastic. "Not to mention all the relations who haven't been invited." She kept clasping her hands in front of her, bending her fingers until the veins on her hands stood out.

"What's the deal, Mrs. Coulter?" asked Jeb.

"If you marry tomorrow, then half the state will be offended. No one can come on that short of a notice and everyone wants to come. You know how it is, Fern. Most of those people are well-moneyed, and what with your situation, it's in poor taste to up and marry and not give anyone a chance at a wedding gift. You have two uncles who would want to be here, and that doesn't include golf club families and the Oklahoma City families."

"I apologize, Abigail. I didn't know it mattered," said Jeb.

Fern let out a sigh.

"Fern, you know I don't try to impose society on you, but marrying a minister means you'll need a good start. If you at least give me until December, I could pull this thing off, I know I could."

"Fine, Mother. We can call it off," said Fern.

"Not just like that, not like that, Fern?" Donna huffed. "Aren't you going to stand up to her, give her a good round or two?"

"Donna, this isn't your business," said Abigail.

"Daddy would have told her to stand up to you," said Donna.

Fern carried her suitcase around Abigail and into the house.

"You're going to talk to her, right?" Donna asked Jeb. She shot out a stream of smoke.

Jeb picked up his suitcase and took it to Fern's Packard. "If there's no wedding tomorrow, there's no need to unpack."

"This is not right. I don't understand either one of you," said Donna. She glared at Abigail.

"What just happened?" asked Abigail. "I didn't mean for it all to blow to pieces. She didn't mean cancel the wedding, not really, did she?"

Jeb walked past Abigail and touched her shoulder. "It's not your doing, Abigail."

"I don't think she meant it like that," said Donna. "Don't jump to conclusions. Go and talk to her."

Jeb found Fern sitting on the edge of her bed. Her back was to him. "I'm going to turn down the pastorate at First Community," he said.

She cried, so he gave her a handkerchief.

Jeb recounted the moments from the time he had met her, when he was a charlatan on the run from the law using three abandoned kids as a front, until the time that Gracie helped him carve out a life of legitimacy. "I've been trying to save the world for too long, Fern. It's time I focused on us."

"I don't want you to throw it away. I saw you Sunday. You were brilliant." She hadn't told him that until now.

"You make me brilliant. I know I'm not. I can tell you don't want to move back here. You've made a life in Nazareth. We have." He looked toward the closed door and then back at Fern. "I'm going to help Claudia get that job in Oklahoma City. She can take Angel with her now to help out. As soon as they're on their feet, I'll send Willie and Ida May to join them. Angel is almost grown. She has wanted nothing but to live with her family. I've wanted nothing but to live with you. We're going to spend the time between now and December doing a better job of getting to know one another. Then we'll give Abigail that big church wedding she's been wanting." He got down on one knee. "I'd like to ask you again. Will you?"

⤳

Angel had heard the commotion, Ida May caterwauling about Jeb and Fern driving up. Donna said they went upstairs. She walked up to the door to hear Fern accepting Jeb's decisions without argument. That wasn't like her. Jeb seemed to be promising to send the Welbys away with Claudia. She had not imagined Fern would agree. As a matter of fact, she expected to sit down as soon as they returned tonight and laugh with Fern about Claudia's stupid proposal. But all she could hear Fern doing was laughing. She wanted her to stop. Fern had always been a strong woman. She was the reason Angel decided to teach. This was not happening. Fern was not allowing her to slip away without a fight. *Say something, Fern! Make things right, like you always do.*

7

ANGEL LOADED HER SISTER'S BELONGINGS
into the Coulter car. Jeb was passing her coming and
going from the house to the car. She was quiet and keeping to the task of getting her things and Claudia's belongings loaded for the bus trip. Her hair was combed back
plain, the auburn so nearly red in the bright sun she looked
like another person entirely. She put on an older dark green
dress and flat-heeled shoes for traveling. Her face was tight
and her mouth drawn up small. She did not apply any of
the cosmetics she had taken to wearing since June.

Jeb understood Claudia's happiness over the job offer
to mean relief for Angel. She had wanted nothing but to be
reunited with Claudia since Jeb first met her. Angel was
going to be a free agent once and for all. Jeb figured that

because she always fought him for his control over her, she'd be glad to be shed of him. She had to appreciate what he was doing not only for Claudia but for her, Willie, and Ida May. Most of the kids put out on the streets had it far worse. She knew that.

She padded across the grass, holding two books, and still would not look at him.

Ida May hugged the porch pillar. She erupted into convulsive sobs. It seemed she had stopped believing her sister was not going to leave her for good. Everyone, including Abigail and Fern, told her that Angel had to follow Claudia early on to help her get back on her feet. After Claudia could pay rent and keep up the grocery tab, then Ida May and Willie would join them in Norman. It had been said to death. Still, Ida May tailed Angel out of the house, lamenting like a kid thrown out on the street.

Fern carried a few more of Angel's things out, following her close behind. Jeb and Fern agreed they would drop Angel and her sister and kids off at the bus stop and then return for Willie and Ida May. Fern said good-bye to Donna Faye, but not Abigail. Abigail always cried, she said, not in a way to make her feel good, but to feel guilty. She would hold off on telling her mother good-bye until she was climbing into the Packard. That would be the end of it.

Fern kept asking Angel about Claudia's small bag of belongings.

"It's all—all she has," said Angel. She sounded out of breath, sidetracked of course by the packing and trying to always keep an eye out for Claudia's two. Thorne and John were delirious. Aunt Angel was their new savior.

Fern folded up a few bills and told Angel, "Be sure Claudia buys food as soon as you land in Norman."

Jeb took all the folding money he brought for the trip, save what they needed to get home, and gave it to Claudia after breakfast.

Claudia came onto the porch holding Thorne on her left hip. She gripped John by the forearm. He was fidgeting and tugging at his mother, pulling one way and then another until she finally let go of him. Freedom at last! He bolted for the open yard going after the ball left behind by Darrell. He kicked at it, but his short legs drove it only a foot or two.

"I guess we'd better head out," Angel said to Claudia. "Bus'll be leaving in an hour."

Abigail looked out through the screen door. Her shoulders lifted, a sigh rushing out. She kept saying, "I hadn't counted on Fern leaving so soon," muttering how Tuesday should have meant that they would stay Tuesday night. The heat was all else she could talk about. She pushed the door open with her toe. "Here's a bite to eat, both of you. Angel, Claudia, take this food along and give those kids a good meal on that bus ride." The bag was oversized, a big woven hemp bag that Myrna used for her shopping. Myrna put in some peanuts, Abigail said, a half loaf of bread, already sliced, a small jar of jelly, two apples. Abigail listed every item out loud, explaining how the fried chicken was wrapped tightly in cheesecloth, plus a handful of coins thrown in for milk if they could buy it along the way.

"I don't know what to say," said Angel. She kissed Abigail's cheek and accepted the oversized lunch. She lugged it to the trunk and tucked it next to her suitcase. Fern walked beside her as they crossed the yard, Fern doing most of the talking.

Angel whistled, came down on one knee, held out her arms, and took charge of John. Claudia looked mystified by her control over the boy. John took to her like she was his momma. Angel smiled, her eyes drinking him in, though heavy-lidded. The boy clambered up her like she was the best tree on the street. He wrapped his legs around her, slightly leaning back and head bowed, talking quietly about the ball he claimed for his own.

Claudia said, "Reverend, I never thought I'd see them all again and looking so good. You've done good by them and now by me. I'll pay you back."

Her offer made Jeb ill at ease. Angel looked at him long enough that he could finally, by a nod of his head, direct her away from Claudia and her brood. Angel met him beside the front porch and freed John to streak back across the yard.

"Don't let things go too long," said Jeb. He placed his hands on either side of her face. "What I mean is, Claudia may not notice things as fast as you. Fern is going to give you her telephone number. If you need help, you call." Jeb kept holding her face so that she had to look at him and not cast her eyes away.

"This seems like a dream, doesn't it?" she asked.

He didn't know how to answer.

"Jeb, I know I've carried on about finding my sister. It's not what I expected," said Angel. "Do you ever get what you expect?"

Jeb turned his back to the others so no one else would hear. All she had to say was that she did not want to go. "You've never been one to hold back. Tell me what you want, Angel."

Angel looked at Fern and then at her sister. She never was a girl to let go of tears so easily, and this moment would be no different. She finally said, "For everyone to find their own life." Her eyes drifted to the ground. "You have to find it with someone, though. You with Fern. Me, Willie, and Ida May with Claudia." When she looked up again, she was pleading. "Tell me I'm right. It's important."

He pulled out another bill from the dwindling roll and gave it to her.

"You need that to get home," she said.

"I'll make it home."

Angel wrapped her arms around Jeb and buried her face against him. She shook for a minute, and then a tear soaked into his shirt. Jeb kept patting the small of her back. Finally she let go of him. He gave her a handkerchief from his pocket to clean her eyes. She looked grown-up after that.

⌇

The August heat sent everyone into the bus depot's shaded areas, the awnings with their blue paint and signs advertising haircuts and liniment, the sprawling sweet gum leaves flapping like a girl's hands turned up and responding to laughter. Jeb and the women waited at the depot long enough for the line down the walk to expand from the waiting benches to the ticket terminal and then they moved gratefully into the shade. Fern struck up a talk about Angel's schooling. Jeb had not bothered to ask Angel about her studies. She was in charge of all of that back in Nazareth, so he figured Claudia and Angel had worked out the particulars.

"Claudia won't know her hours until we get to Norman," Angel told her.

"But you'll continue in school no matter." Fern kept glancing over at Claudia, who had inched into a spot on a shaded depot bench.

"Of course, what else?" asked Jeb.

"If you're looking after John and Thorne while Claudia works, how will that work?" Fern would not let up.

"Put it off until later?" Angel said it like a question.

"Jeb, you need to say something," said Fern.

Angel swallowed. She kicked a dust puff up from the ground with the toe of her shoe.

Jeb shook his head and said, "I didn't agree to that."

Angel shifted onto her right foot. Her hip jutted out and she sighed as though she were being grilled. She shaded her eyes with one hand. "How did you think this was going to work, Jeb? I can't run after Claudia's two and go to school. I'll have to wait."

"Wait how long?" asked Fern. "You'll fall behind. Jeb, remember how hard she worked to get caught up with her classmates back in Nazareth?"

Claudia got up from her perch. She broke off a corner of the bread loaf and gave it to John, who was jumping up and down wanting to feed the pigeons. John promptly disintegrated the bread between his palms and tossed crumbs into the air like he was tossing up sand.

"That was supposed to be for lunch," Jeb said to Fern.

Fern extended her fingers and touched Jeb's arm.

Claudia joined the circle and said, "If you don't mind my two cents, Reverend, I read ever' bit of the letter you give me on that meatpacking job. There's a five-to-midnight shift. I'll go for that and then Angel can still mind her studies."

Jeb walked away from the women toward the street to steer Thorne back toward her brother. He hefted her onto the bench, picked up John, hurled him up laughing like a lunatic and then plopped him next to his sister. The boy scraped precious bread from between his fingertips to the waiting flock.

The skin around Fern's temple relaxed and she talked to Claudia and Angel as if they would all be back together again soon. She had Angel dig out a slip of paper from her drawstring purse. She scrawled down her telephone number and tucked it back into Angel's bag. The bus to Norman pulled up. Jeb helped Angel carry her suitcase to the bus. Claudia stepped up into the bus, eyes straight ahead, herding John and Thorne up the steps and into a front-row seat. John stood up and looked out the window, his eyes big as headlights until he spotted his aunt. Angel motioned for him to settle into his seat and mouthed, "I'm coming," so the boy would stop troubling over her.

Fern hugged Angel. Angel was not as affected as she had been at the house saying good-bye to Jeb. She had not said much to Fern in the last few hours. There was a final kiss she planted on Fern's cheek, the same as her good-bye to Abigail. Time was spinning away from them and she let it go without a single complaint. She waved at Jeb from the bus steps. The door closed between them.

Fern said, "Jeb, where are you going?"

He kept walking behind the bus to see if Angel might turn and wave wildly for the bus to stop, yelling in that way of hers that she had changed her mind. Other passengers waved from the window as they departed. But the bus swallowed Angel whole. She was not in his sights any longer. He was out of breath in the heat. The sun was eating his brain. The bus turned right. There was a flash of girl in the window, pale and full of quiet craving.

"She's gone," said Fern. "I wasn't ready."

⌒

There was a stop five minutes before noon. The sudden jolt on the bus brakes brought Angel out of a thin sleep. Her neck hurt from dozing in a sitting position. Claudia turned completely around in her seat and smiled when Angel's lids came open. The passenger seated across the aisle from Angel smelled like cigars rolled in bourbon, a cloying smell for a woman dressed so well. Thorne was stretched out across Angel's lap, limp as a dishrag, her right arm hanging out into the air, her left arm straight up, fingers closed in a relaxed fist. Angel was hungry. Claudia had taken charge of the food. John stuffed his face the whole trip from Ardmore.

The bus stopped in Pauls Valley. Ten or maybe even a dozen passengers got up and filed out of the bus. The driver held to the grab bar and facing them said, "We'll be here in Pauls Valley a half hour, folks, so if you want to get out, stretch your legs, or get a bite to eat, feel free."

Angel rubbed Thorne's forehead and kept saying her name until her eyes came slowly open. "Let's step outside and have us some lunch, Thorne," she said.

Claudia and John fled out of the bus and took a seat under a sprawling black walnut tree. Angel carried Thorne and laid her on the grass next to Claudia. The hem of the girl's dress had come loose. Angel said she would fix it when they got to Claudia's place.

"If I still have a place," said Claudia.

"Jeb gave you money, Claudia. Landlords don't turn down cash on the barrelhead." Angel pulled open the sack. Myrna's fried chicken had come loose from the cheesecloth. Angel drew out a leg for Thorne and one for herself. One end of the bread loaf looked like mice had been at it, of course. She tore off two nice pieces and handed one to Thorne, who was finally sitting up.

Two women stopped on the corner to gab, townsfolk out for a walk. They each sipped on a cold Coke. Claudia smiled at them. They raked her over with their eyes and took a few steps back to find shade under a drugstore awning. One of them lit a cigarette.

Angel finished her chicken and bread. She pulled out a napkin and cleaned Thorne's greasy fingers and mouth.

Her skirt rode up around her diaper. A rash ring showed around the legs of the diaper. "She's wet and needs a change, Claudia."

"I'm almost out of clean diapers. We'd best make do with what she's got on."

"She's eaten up with rash, Claudia."

"It'll clear up."

Thorne scratched at her diaper.

"I thought you did the wash yesterday. You ought to have plenty of diapers," said Angel.

"My hands were too full with these two to do it all. Why you think I need you, Angel?"

The two women under the drugstore awning left and one threw down what remained of her smoldering cigarette. Claudia got up, and when they were out of eyesight, she retrieved the butt and took a drag on it.

"I thought you had plenty of smokes." Angel put away the dinner sack and cleaned up the bones.

"All I had was what Bo left behind. Still got a card of papers. I could buy a tin here in this drugstore."

"We need the money for food and rent, though."

"Just a tin is all." She went inside.

Angel turned her attention back on Thorne. A few of the passengers were eavesdropping, having nothing better to do for the next fifteen minutes. John crawled into Angel's lap and laid his head against her shoulder. "My belly's full, Aunt Angel."

"I know, John. I'm glad." She dug through Claudia's bag and found the last clean diaper. She laid Thorne back in the grass.

Out of boredom, the passengers went back to their lunches.

꒰

Willie and Ida May accepted the pillows given to them by Abigail for the trip home. They each claimed a corner in the rear car seat.

Fern kissed Abigail and Donna Faye good-bye.

Jeb thanked Abigail and Myrna for their hospitality and started the engine. Abigail cried liberally as Fern had prophesied. Myrna dallied on the porch picking sprigs from some of Abigail's plants, not actually watching them pull away, but doing other things as if time had taught her to keep busy when Abigail's offspring pulled out of the family drive. Jeb turned right onto the road and glanced for the last time at Abigail. Myrna had her arm around her mistress, coaxing her inside.

"I don't know why Mother wants to annoy me like that," said Fern. "She always gets so overwrought."

"Shame on Abigail. She ought to give a cheer as we pull away," said Jeb.

"I'd like that," said Fern.

Jeb wondered how far Angel's bus had traveled, if Claudia would ration their meals correctly, or if the ride was bumpy or dusty. Angel had taken to Fern's fostering of womanly needs more than his and had grown spoiled. She would do well to run after Claudia's children, but then she had not known much else since being put out by her family to look after Willie and Ida May. Of course the women at Church in the Dell and Fern saw to things like helping

Angel keep a few dresses done up for church and Saturday night goings-on. Claudia did not strike him as the type of woman who would think about those things. "Angel looks out for herself well enough, doesn't she?" he asked Fern.

"Better than most, I'd say."

A single drop of rain hit the windshield. Jeb leaned forward and glanced up. There was a cloud cover, a few acres of gray-and-white cumulus stretching over Carter County. But the smattering of storms that came through Oklahoma on this trip only teased them with a brief sprinkling of rain and a barren show of lightning; nothing that promised the end of the drought. "When did your mother say that last dust storm hit?"

"Last March, wasn't it?"

"Miz Abigail says it was like the end of the world," said Willie. "I wish I coulda seen it. Nothing big ever happens in Nazareth."

Ida May opened her mouth and sighed out a yawn and then a big burp. Willie doubled over laughing. Ida May covered her face and laughed too. Fern told her to rest her eyes and take a nap on Abigail's feather pillow. Ida May smiled at Fern, and after she closed her eyes, she said, "Angel said that you was going to make a good momma. She was right."

Fern looked pained by the comment. She pulled her hair up to one side into a comb so that she could rest her head comfortably. "Angel didn't say much to me today. How about you?"

"Not a lot. So much on her mind, I guess. Finally after all this time, she gets her wish. I think Claudia needed her worse than she needed Claudia, though. I don't know. I don't know."

"Did you ask Angel if she wanted to go to Norman?"

"Sure she wanted to go," said Jeb. "What else has she wanted all this time?"

"You know that for a fact?"

"I wouldn't have let her go otherwise. What makes you say that?"

"Angel never actually said she wanted to go. But then again, she was always one to let you know if she wanted something."

"Of course! She's not one to be pressured," said Jeb.

"I agree with that."

There was a quiet that fell between them.

"Claudia has a lot on her plate, though. I wonder if it's too much for Angel." The winding road straightened for a good ten or twenty miles. Jeb lost track of time as he put more and more road behind them. Fern stopped commenting, but as to how much time had passed since her last comment, he couldn't say. "I never actually asked Angel if she wanted to go. Should I have done that?"

"It never hurts to ask."

A road sign sticking out near the highway advertised fuel and window cleaning. The glass was already dirty from the road dust. Jeb pulled into the filling-station lot. He turned off the engine and sat staring straight ahead. "I may have made a mistake," he said.

Fern stared out her window too. Her fingertips slowly massaged her lips. She did not help him one way or another.

༚

"Aunt Angel, we're here!" John voiced it so loudly from the center aisle, the passengers seated around him laughed.

Thorne climbed back into Angel's lap expecting again to be carried off the bus. Several people shoved past them. Finally a Spanish-looking man seated in the back of the bus stopped and let them out into the aisle. Angel picked up the bag she carried on, along with her purse, and hefted Thorne onto her hip. Claudia and John waited out on the walk. "Welcome to the big city of Norman," said Claudia.

A clap of dry thunder made Thorne holler.

"I wish to goodness the sky'd stop threatening us. Just let us have it!" Claudia spread her arms, but then said, "I wasn't yelling at God. Just the sky."

Angel stared at her impassively.

"What with you being brought up by a preacher and all, I didn't want to offend your upbringing," said Claudia.

"Claudia, don't start."

"I'm not funning."

"Shut up! Do we hitch a ride or walk to your place?" Angel asked.

"One or the other. We walk a piece, then rest a piece. It's a good half-hour walk."

"Daddy took the truck," said John. "I hate him."

Claudia smacked John's mouth. He cried.

Angel set down her suitcase, stepped up, and took his hand. She had watched Claudia backhand John more than once at Abigail's, but was starting to have her fill. She picked up her luggage again and struck up a bit of chatter to busy his mind and to calm him.

Claudia wanted to maintain control over the boy. "Don't coddle him. Boys are hard to raise. You got to give it back to them or they grow up wild like Bo. His momma says she's to blame for him taking off on us."

John was already mad as wet bees and shook his head vigorously. "Granny said it was you to blame!"

Angel stepped between them and then trailed behind Claudia, holding tightly to John's hand for the first mile. The roads running around the shops and houses in Norman were bricked, but as they left the pretty row houses and a place called The Diner, the bricks gave way to the hard-pounded dirt roads. The occasional motorist left them in a cloud of smothering dust.

Finally a hay truck pulled to the side. The farmer's arm came out the window and motioned them aboard. Angel was grateful Claudia traveled so light, but her own bag felt like iron weights. The muscles in her right shoulder ached. She threw the bag onto the bed and helped John scramble onto a hay bale. The farmer drove them two miles. Claudia crawled up to the cab and pounded on the top. The driver slowed to a stop at a crossroads near a country house. "This is our getting-off spot," she said.

Angel followed her down a country lane. There was a pretty house encircled with a white picket fence. On the fence hung a small hand-painted sign that said, HOUSE FOR RENT. Claudia picked up the sign and carried it under one arm. She opened the gate and allowed John and Thorne to run inside. Thorne immediately took up with a gray cat, which wound around her stubby legs.

"Claudia, you never told me you had such a house," said Angel.

"Oh, this ain't mine. This is the landlady's house. Ours is out back." She walked around the house and then down a stone walk. She pointed to a shack, a slapdash nailed-together job of scrap wood and tin. The picket fence separated the two houses like the good from the bad. She laid the sign on the porch facedown. "Looks like Mrs. Abercrombie is up to her old tricks." She mounted the concrete steps and yanked on the lock and chain bolted to the front door. "She pulls these shenanigans to bully me about her money."

"How much do you owe?" asked Angel.

"Fifteen, plus two dollars for milk."

"That's almost everything Jeb gave you."

"Take her half and see if she'll buy it," said Claudia. She handed a roll of bills to Angel.

"Why on earth would you think she'd take it from me?"

"You got a nice face. Bo always got around her with a smile. Me, I'm not too good at maneuvering women like Abercrombie."

Angel headed across the yard. Before she could reach Mrs. Abercrombie's backyard, the woman came out of her house and stopped Angel at the gate. "Who be you?" she asked.

"I'm Angel Welby, Claudia's sister. I came to help out my sister." She handed the woman the money.

She flipped open the roll. "That's only half. Not good enough."

"Claudia's getting a good job at Packingtown. She'll have the other half soon." Angel was too tired to smile. The heat was making it hard to breathe.

"I got other boarders that'll pay twice what the Drakes have been paying me and they say they'll pay up front. None of this half now, half later business."

"She's lying," Claudia said from the porch.

Mrs. Abercrombie kept her words for Angel only, as if Claudia were not looking at her across the yard. "I got bills to pay too."

Angel pulled another couple of bills out of her purse, the money Fern had given them for extra food. Mrs. Abercrombie accepted it. She handed Angel a key to the bolt lock. "Bring me back the hardware. I might need it again, knowing that Drake woman."

"We'll see you're paid on time from now on," said Angel.

"You got a believable face, girl. Whether or not it's true, we'll see, I reckon." She kept studying Angel. "I got some corn to bring in tomorrow. Not a lot, mind you, what with the drought and all. You help me shuck and can it, and I'll pay you for it."

"I can do that. I used to help a woman back in Nazareth with the canning. May I have the shucks when they're finished, ma'am?"

"Suit yourself."

"I'd like to make a doll each for Thorne and John."

The woman took a step closer to Angel and asked, "Ain't you got no other family, girl?"

"Not with me, no, ma'am. My sister and brother live back in Nazareth, Arkansas."

"Nazareth?"

An apple pie cooled in the kitchen window.

Angel hesitated.

"You an orphan?"

"Not that, no, ma'am."

"I remember now. Your sister told me you kids was put out by your folks. Shame you ain't got nowhere left to belong."

"I belong here with my sister, ma'am."

Claudia yelled across the backyard at John.

"That sister of yours ain't right. She's got the brains of a rabbit. I hope you know that."

Angel thanked her for taking the partial rent payment. "You got a little food we can buy? I got another dollar I can give you."

The woman said, "I got stew and apple pie. I can ladle you out some stew in a jar for yourself and those kids and a slice of pie you can share. I wouldn't do it for that sister of yours." She went inside and came out with the stew and pie.

Angel gave her the dollar and she turned it down. She didn't know what to say to the woman. The stew smelled like something from back in Nazareth that a woman named Josie Hipps would bring by from time to time. She put that thought out of her head. She was done with Nazareth and back with family.

8

JEB LET FERN KEEP TO HERSELF THE WHOLE way home. Since Willie and Ida May dozed off and on in the rear car seat, she had to keep a lid on private matters about the past anyway. She did a good job of keeping the chatter on an even keel, how nice to see Donna again and her brothers and how big the Coulter nephews and nieces had grown. Not once did she bring up Walton Baer, and a good thing, because whatever she decided to spill out about him would be at her own discretion, no prompting whatsoever on his part.

The matter of the Oklahoma City pulpit swam around his head, but he held off beating that dead horse, keeping his promise. He finally figured out the things about her that had been a mystery to him. Patience had to play its course. Once he assured her the matter was settled, they would not marry until December and after that they would settle down in Nazareth like they planned all along, the tension lifted. Her cheeks turned red as berries again, and even her hands talked as she spoke, her long slender index fingers lifting and tapping the air like a person sending a telegraph.

"Jeb, I see the sign ahead for DeQueen. Let's stop and stretch our legs, why don't we, at that downtown café? You remember the one, don't you?" she asked.

"You want to wake up Willie and Ida May?"

Fern turned and wiggled Willie's big toe. It stuck out of his sock.

The town sign for DeQueen welcomed them back across the Arkansas border. Fern slipped on her shoes and tucked the strands of hair around her ears up into a blue hat.

On the side of the road, a faded black car full of children sat broken down. Four children peered out the windows as they drove past. A woman, wearing a dress that may have once been green, leaned against the hood, her face in her hands. The wind was hot, hot like blue blazes. The woman's skirt flapped around her calves. Jeb pulled aside. When he got out, the woman waved him on, saying in a raspy voice, "My husband hitched a ride to go for gas. We run out two hours ago."

"Anything I can do to help, ma'am?" asked Jeb.

She said no. Jeb said he was sorry and that was when she ran her hand down her thigh, her eyes drinking him up. Jeb wanted to yell at her. What else was she hiding from her old man? Fern stuck her head out the open window and offered a loaf of Abigail's bread. "May we offer your children a bite to eat?" she asked.

The woman said, "I'll take that if you don't mind." She averted her eyes.

Jeb handed the bread through the open car window to the oldest girl seated up front so he wouldn't have to look the woman in the face again. The kids inside dove for the bread like gulls fishing out of the ocean. He got back in the car and drove until Fern spotted a roadside café outside DeQueen. The café stood out on a stark lot; a load-bearing square, built of masonry blocks, painted white.

Jeb got out and put on his hat to block the sun.

Fern led them inside to a table near a window. "It's as hot out there as Oklahoma," she said.

Willie ordered a Coke and a ham sandwich. Ida May wanted the same thing.

Fern dithered back and forth between the house stew and the Blue Plate Special. The woman serving the counter customers—two besides their clan—had a dog face, hair softly glistening on her upper lip, and big sausage arms that rested against her hips. She kept sighing, a sort of whistling sound that hissed from her nostrils like a baby bird. Fern snickered before her hand could cover her mouth, so unlike her since she got onto Jeb and Willie in the past for laughing at strangers. Ida May glanced curiously from her stool, leaning to see around Willie. Finally she laughed for no reason other than the sight of Fern burying her face in the menu.

The waitress asked Jeb, "She going to order or not?"

Fern said apologetically, "I'll take the stew and crackers. Iced tea."

Jeb ordered a hamburger and coffee. He gathered up the menus and handed them to the waitress. She huffed and disappeared back into the kitchen.

Fern blushed to the point of her ears turning red. "I don't know what's gotten into me," she said. She unbuttoned her top button and fanned her neck.

"I'm glad you're happy," said Jeb. "Glad to the bone, Fern."

She tried to compensate for her behavior. She came off the stool when the waitress came out with the tray of soda pops and took each drink off the tray for her and passed them around. Then she excused herself to the only bathroom in the café, maybe the whole highway.

Willie did not laugh at any of Fern's shenanigans. Jeb slid Willie's Coke down the counter and set it in front of him. Willie kept staring down at his boots, his toes tapping the counter.

"What's on your mind?" asked Jeb.

Willie shrugged.

Jeb blew on his coffee and then set it back in the saucer. Angel said little to Fern on the trip to the bus depot. Willie was giving Fern the silent treatment too. Jeb said, "I shouldn't have let Angel go."

"I know why you did it. So does Angel," said Willie.

Jeb turned the stool toward Willie.

"It was for Miss Coulter."

"Fern had nothing to do with it, Willie."

Willie hefted the large iced-down drink to his lips and took a long draft.

"Fern doesn't deserve the blame. Angel chose to leave."

"She told Claudia she wasn't going. Then she said you and Miss Coulter was into some sort of feud. That was when you decided Angel had to go. After they go up and get things squared away in Norman, then me and Ida May have to foller."

Jeb set him straight. "You have it all mixed up, Willie Boy."

"Angel was outside your door. She heard the whole thing."

"That's not how it came down at all."

Fern came out of the restroom. Her skin was damp, her sleeves and skirt clinging to her limbs. "It's hot as an oven in there," she said.

The waitress pushed out from the back kitchen doors. She carried all four plates on her arms. Ida May clapped. Each order was exactly as it should be.

"One, two, three, four, and no more," said Ida May.

෴

Angel ran after Thorne across the lawn, holding her shoes out front. "You can't run barefoot, Thorne! There's nettles in the grass."

Thorne ran directly across the pasturelike grass straight into a nettle pile. She howled and jumped on one foot, holding the other foot in the air. Angel scooped her into her arms and carried her to the fence between

Claudia's place and Mrs. Abercrombie's. She plopped Thorne onto a flat-topped fence post. Thorne bared her teeth while Angel pulled out every tiny nettle from her pink foot. She slid ankle stockings onto her feet and then strapped on the shoes.

"They're hot!" said Thorne.

Angel clasped the buckles on the shoes and then plopped her on the ground. Her wrist slid against the fence post. She picked up a splinter and it stung all the way to the vein. John yelled from the front porch for Angel to come and get him. He was afraid always that Mrs. Abercrombie's milk cow would jump the fence and trample him to death. His daddy had made him afraid, according to Claudia, to make him obedient. Angel turned her back to John.

Claudia stored away the extra milk they bought on the bus ride and the leftover chicken and the bread and then took to her bed, ailing from a sick headache. Angel wanted John to go and climb in bed with his mother. He followed Angel around like a stray. She sat flat on her bottom in the grass and began to work at the splinter. John's wailing subsided and the screen door slammed hard behind him.

Mrs. Abercrombie carted out the leftovers from her and her son's dinner and raked it into a bucket. She yelled for her son, Edwin, to empty the slop bucket.

The splinter went deep, but left a good dark bit hanging out. Angel dug at the tip until a clear liquid came out of her skin alongside the splinter. The Abercrombies' back door squeaked open. Angel slumped onto her belly. The grass around the fence post was tall tickle grass, yellowing from the drought. She parted it to look through at the Abercrombies' son. She thought she saw him before, but decided she didn't know him. He was grown and not a youth, but not old. Angel snaked backward onto her knees and then turned around to sit back against the fence post. She licked her arm and cleaned up the faint pink trickle from the splinter wound.

Edwin carried the bucket out to the distant hog pen and then back.

Angel closed her eyes. Miz Abigail had taken them all to church Sunday morning. She liked the choir best. Miz Abigail sang one of the songs louder than the others, and then all afternoon, Angel could not shake it, as hard as she tried. She pursed her lips and whistled what part she recollected.

Footsteps on the tickle grass drew near, crackling beneath two large Abercrombie boots.

Angel whistled again.

"You bringing omens, girl," said Edwin Abercrombie.

Angel leaned away from the fence post to get a look at him. He wore a pair of black riding boots, steel-toed. "I don't know nothing about no omens," she said.

"A whistling woman and a crowing hen always come to no good end." He laughed, showing off a missing upper tooth in the back of his mouth.

Nothing about him was funny. She returned to her perch slumped against the fence post. The sun was finally going down behind Mrs. Abercrombie's house.

"You Claudia Drake's sister?"

Angel tried to think of anything to say that might slightly offend him enough to make him leave. Without Jeb around, she was out of practice. Instead, she sighed. The hot wind kicked up again, blowing dust across the yard. She shielded her eyes with her arms.

"Maybe you can talk some sense into her," he said. "I been telling her that man of hers ain't coming back."

Angel roused from her slumped posture and said, "It's her business."

"I been trying to get her to go out for drinks on Saturday night, for laughs is all. You ought to tell her to go. I'll bet you're smarter than Claudia. You're prettier, that's for sure. I'll bet she hates that."

Claudia came out onto the porch. "Angel, is Ed bothering you?"

Angel got up and ambled across the yard, meeting Claudia on the porch. She turned and stared down Edwin, feeling the power of her sister close by.

Edwin dropped the slop bucket and crossed his arms. He never took his eyes off them.

"You stay away from Edwin Abercrombie," said Claudia. It was whispered so only Angel heard. "He's mine. I've waited long enough for Bo."

ॐ

Nazareth was quiet and black as coffee. Only the backroom light from Will Honeysack's grocery interrupted the monotony of darkness down the row of shops and the jailhouse. As they turned into town, the bank window reflected the headlights. Jeb geared down to keep from hitting a stray cat, which had taken up with Faith Bottoms at the Clip and Curl. A paperboy knelt on the walk in front of Honeysack's, bundling newspapers for the morning sales, six hours away. Ida May roused from Willie's lap, where she had curled up to doze, to say, "I've got a headache," and then fell back to sleep.

Fern's head lay pressed against the glass. She slept a good hour, both her hands curled in her lap. The engagement ring caught a bit of moon, scattering a dusting of light particles inside the car. Jeb passed the library, where he once kissed Fern and gave her the ring out front. He remembered her standing in the snow.

She blew out a breath, as though she were entering the deepest sleep. The moon had a circle of white. Fern did not so much as flutter a lash. No amount of money would make him wake her yet, not with the ring of the moon casting a light on them both.

Tomorrow she would go to the Stanton School and do up her classroom for the fall. The principal would respect her and say how he wished he could pay her more. She would blush and say it was enough. The teacher across the hall would split a box of chalk with her and she would act as though it were all she needed. She would wear a pair of practical flats like the other teachers and no one would think of her as one of Francis Coulter's crazy girls.

Bringing her home was a wedding gift. He finally figured out the distance between Ardmore and Nazareth. Plenty of miles to rebuild a life. She was more like him now. Nothing wrong with that, a touch of wildness about her. She wasn't so prim. Why did he think she was? Had he wanted her to be so different from him? Not in the least. Nothing wrong with that.

"Jeb, are we home?" Fern asked in a whisper.

Jeb stroked her engagement hand and said, "Best you get ready. I'll drop you off at your door."

She leaned across the seat and touched Jeb's face. "You look tired," she said. "I should have driven part of the way. I must have gone out like a drunkard."

He drove them out of downtown and past Long's Pond.

Fern took a gander at the moon. "You're quiet."

The car turned down the snaking drive to her house. He helped her take her suitcases inside, the store sacks full of bric-a-brac and whatnot, all things she and Donna raked up in Oklahoma City. "That's a big haul," he said.

"I buy too much when I'm with Donna." She wrapped her arms around him, clasping her hands at the back of his neck. Jeb kissed her. She let go of him and said, "You're not yourself." He kissed her again, longer, and pulled her close to him. That felt right. "I must be tired," he said.

She flipped on the lamp near the window and then looked into his eyes. She invited him to drop by the school after his morning rounds. He said he wanted to. She bought it and he told her good night.

⁂

Behind Stanton School, a few leaves had turned on one of the thick maples. The locals said autumn would not come because of the drought, but that the leaves would most likely brown up and drop off. Autumn needed to come soon. The drought had taken nearly all of the life out of the land. The air would cool. Nothing could stop the cooling down of the land, summer's passing on, not even a drought. He yearned for winter, to chop wood and fill the potbellied stove. The kindling box stood dry. The drought had done some good. Not all was lost.

He could not see Fern through the classroom window.

The truck was cold and slow to start after sitting idle for all of his days away in Oklahoma. Jeb lifted the hood and tinkered with the engine. Fern would sweep out her room. He checked the radiator for water. The teachers would swap stories out in the hall. Jeb cleaned out the floor of the cab. He should have done that before coming to see her. He could not think of why he hurried off to the school before doing his errands. Will Honeysack left a note on his door. He had to go and check on a sick woman in the hollow, Tilly Churchill. Fern was a day behind the other teachers. She needed more time to count books up in the attic, boxes coated with black dust, books moved down in September only to be packed back up when it was time to plant the spring crops.

He pulled out his pocket watch and checked the time. Willie was home with Ida May now. He had to keep a closer watch with Angel gone. Fern had not glanced out her window yet because she had so much to do; everyone in Stanton School counted on her for so many things. They were allowed to need her and depend on her. He gunned the truck and left for the hollow.

He passed Ivey Long, who would not give up his horse and buggy. Ivey whistled long and high and snapped his whip in the air. It annoyed Jeb. Ivey was behind on things. Not even his grown kids could talk sense into him, get him to accept change. He'd bet Ivey had not been out of town in three decades, but that was true of most people of Nazareth.

Tilly Churchill was wrapped up in a blanket, sweating out a fever in a front-porch rocker. Jeb said, "You'd do better to toss off that blanket." He took it off her, even though she complained. "I'm going inside, Miz Churchill, to get you a ladle of water." Before she protested, he slipped inside. He found the water pail full and the ladle on the hook in the kitchen. The tin ladle was cold and he filled it to the brim and took her a drink. He made her sip.

She said, "You're awfully bossy today, Reverend. You and that schoolteacher in a feud?"

He gave her another drink, said a prayer over her, and then headed for his truck. "There's no one in a feud, Miz Churchill. Fern and I are getting married in December. We're happy as anybody has a right to be."

"You forgot to tell your face then."

He headed into town for a newspaper. He could go for a cup of Beulah's coffee at the diner, a quiet spot where a man could think.

꒳

Claudia had been gone since sunup. Edwin Abercrombie met her out on the porch after promising her a ride into Packingtown. She kept asking him if he knew the man's name from the slaughterhouse that Jeb gave her. Angel wanted her to leave the cash behind. They could go later and buy food and milk. But Claudia wanted to take advantage of the free ride. She would come home with food and whatever else they needed. Maybe a toy for the baby, she said. She was giddy. Edwin took off his hat in the house and chatted up polite niceties with Angel. He told her a clean joke, not funny, and had buffed his shoes. He had Claudia laughing all the way out to his newly polished car. She wore red pumps and black stockings seamed straight up the back.

Angel opened the doors in Claudia's small kitchen. The cabinets were tall and narrow, the doors primitive and rough-hewn, rope pulls for opening and shutting. Claudia had a smattering of dishes, two bowls in one of Momma's patterns. Large numbers were painted inside the cabinets. Angel kept opening the doors and then shutting them until it came to her that she once had seen such narrow boxes out in her papaw's shed. The Abercrombies had nailed old ammunition boxes to the kitchen walls, boxes saved from the war. The numbers, her papaw told her, were supply numbers used for infantry inventory. Maybe Edwin put them up. Or else Bo took them after Granny died. It would be like him to take whatever he wanted without asking.

Claudia had not a speck of food to be found, not a spoonful of cornmeal or even a single yam. Angel cut up the remaining loaf of Abigail's bread and pulled yesterday's bottle of milk from the icebox. She fed Thorne and John most of it and then sliced up an apple from the Coulters' withering orchard. It tasted both sweet and sour. Tart, Myrna said, for cooking pies. John sighed, rolling his eyes in ecstasy when he bit into his portion.

"There's more coming, John. Momma's bringing more food," said Angel. She helped John onto the floor and then Thorne. The floor looked like it could use a good sweeping. She found the broom out back, sewn into a corner by a web. She took that and a mop and cleaned the kitchen. She folded the blanket and put up the pillows and shoved the mattress against the wall where she slept with Thorne.

By the time she cleaned the inside windows, it was nigh close to noon. Tapping heels clipped across the front porch.

"Momma!" yelled Thorne.

Angel met Claudia at the door. "Is that a smile?" asked Angel. "Are you telling me you got the job?"

"Oh, Angel, I got it!" She set down a sack and threw her arms around Angel's neck.

John ran to look into the sack. He pulled out a small train. He set it on the floor and looked through the bag. "Food, Momma?"

"We'll have all the food we need, baby. Momma's got a new job," said Claudia.

"But you bought food with the money, right, Claudia?" asked Angel.

"Edwin had to get to work. I had stopped at this little store outside Packingtown, thinking we had all the time in the world. I bought John that train."

"I'll go and buy more food from Mrs. Abercrombie. Where's the money?" Angel held out her hand.

"I had to buy work clothes. They make you wear this uniform at the slaughterhouse, blues they call them, and these white aprons, as if that would do any good in a slaughterhouse."

John shook Claudia's uniform out onto the floor.

Claudia sighed. "Angel, don't give me that look. Edwin said that he would bring us a sack of food tonight after he got off work, plenty to get by, he said, until I make it to the first paycheck. Stop looking at me like that. I should have borrowed a smoke off him while I was at it. I hope I don't lose my mind."

"So you must be starting work tonight? Is Edwin taking you?"

"There's a truck that comes by every morning one mile from here. They do it for the Packingtown workers. They don't dock us much for the ride." She let down her hair. "I start tomorrow."

Angel slumped down in the chair. "You were supposed to take the night shift."

"What do you mean?"

"School, Claudia. I start school, remember?"

"Angel, you're going to have to forget about that until we can get on our feet. Now I did the best I could with what I had. If your reverend friend hadn't have give me that name, I would have been standing out in the heat all day like most of the fools I saw turned away today. I took what they give me."

Angel got up and went outside. She sat on the front stoop. Mrs. Abercrombie and her son argued inside their house, the kitchen windows open. She yelled at Edwin for promising grub to the moochers. She called Claudia a tramp. On the back porch, the cat was lapping milk from a dish.

Angel had left her drawstring bag on the porch, left it out all night and did not notice it until now. She dug through it until she pulled out the piece of paper she fished out for Fern at the bus stop. Fern had written down her telephone number and even Will Honeysack's number in case she could not reach her. She folded the paper in two. On the back of the paper was more writing. She turned it over. In fine-printed letters was the name *NASH* and a telephone number. That's what he meant when he said he slipped her his number. She flipped over the paper and looked at Fern's name and then back again at Nash's.

Claudia yelled at John from inside for crying. Angel buried her head in her arms. The sun bore down hot from the sky that held nothing, nothing except blue emptiness. Rain was gone for good, like everything and everyone else. The telephone rang across the yard from inside the Abercrombies' place. Angel could see Mrs. Abercrombie cross the house inside and answer her telephone next to the windowsill, where she cooled pies. The window was without a screen and seldom latched. Mrs. Abercrombie ought to take care of her things. There was a Depression on. People tended to take without asking.

9

JEB CRUSHED ORBS OF PECANS UNDER A dishrag, hammering the nuts open, blow by blow, tossing them into a basket for Ida May to shell. Freda Honeysack called her to the back of the store after dawn and showed her the sacks of pecans, forty pounds delivered the night before. She gave Ida May a sackful for a penny, but then refused the penny.

Jeb invited Ida May to ride into town for his newspaper run. She said she needed to buy pencils. School started in nine days, nine days for Ida May to moan about walking to school without her sister or how Angel fixed her braids up and ribboned them.

Jeb counted the cracked pecans and said, "That ought to be enough, Ida May."

"The dough is too dry." She put her head down on the kitchen table and cried.

"Add a spoonful of water, Ida May, for crying out loud!"

Ida May lifted her head and then laid it down sideways on the table. She contorted her mouth until her chin flattened and turned white. One tear dropped onto the tablecloth, another down her nose. She raised her head, sniffed, and said, "Who was the letter from?"

"I didn't pick up mail today. Freda didn't say I had any," said Jeb.

She used her sleeves to dry her eyes. "Mrs. Honeysack gave me the mail today. I told you, I know I did."

"Ida May, you never gave me the mail. Where is it?"

She fished through her smock, turned sideways, and cupped her hand to her mouth. She ran outside. The truck door squeaked open and then clicked, not quite shut all the way. She ran inside, waving the envelope. "I forgot. Don't look at me that way." She gave Jeb the letter. "I can't remember nothing now with Angel gone."

Jeb turned over the letter. "Philemon Gracie." It was his second from Gracie within the last month. He took the letter to his study table and used a letter opener to slice it open. He slid his reading glasses down his nose and read to himself. "He says he plans a trip to Nazareth," said Jeb.

Ida May perked up. She liked Philemon's children, although his daughters were too old for her. But his son was of a good age for throwing rocks down in the creek.

Philemon's brother found him a good doctor, one who

helped his stomach to heal. Jeb read the next paragraph in silence and then read it again:

> By now, you have guessed that I am bored with sitting around mending. I assumed you would turn down the Oklahoma City pulpit unless you could be confident of a good successor for Church in the Dell. That is why I'm writing to tell you that I am fit and able to return to shepherd the Nazareth flock again. In case you've not heard, the pulpit committee at First Community Church was ecstatic to have found a candidate so quickly. Congratulations, Jeb! I couldn't be prouder than if you were my own son.

He took off his reading spectacles.

"What else did he say?" asked Ida May. She picked up the nut picker and culled pecans from the cracked shells.

Jeb tucked the letter back into the envelope. He looked at his watch. If Will Honeysack knew about any of this, he would not have been able to keep it under his hat. Jeb had seen him twice since returning from Oklahoma.

Ida May cupped her hand to her mouth again. "Miss Fern came by yesterday," she said.

"You forgot to tell me that too, I guess."

Ida May spread her fingers out on either side of her face. "All's I know is that she was wearing her mean face when she left. I been seeing that a lot lately on her. What did you do?"

Jeb put on his hat and tucked the letter into his jacket.

"Don't bake that pie until I get back. I don't want you and Willie making any fires with me gone."

"Are you going to the school?" asked Ida May.

"I'll be right back, Littlest."

"You could ask Miss Fern if she'd like to come and finish putting together this pie. That's where you're going, isn't it?"

～

Angel met Mrs. Abercrombie as the early sun was turning the back porch yellow. She took her up on the offer to shuck and cut up corn even if she couldn't stand the sight of her son. She sat in the shade of the screened-in porch. Edwin had gone to work. Claudia too. Angel showed John and Thorne how to make a doll by winding thread around two shucks. Thorne called her baby "Bean."

Mrs. Abercrombie yelled from inside, "I got to go into town for a bit. There's a tent revival." Some women were picking her up, she said. She looked out the window at Angel. "You got fast hands, girl. Maybe I'll have you shelling beans next summer."

"Your corns sure come in puny, ma'am," said Angel.

"I know, but some ain't got any corn at all. I'm thankful to God for what he give me."

John asked Angel for a bite to eat.

"That girl's kids are always hungry," said Mrs. Abercrombie. "When I stopped helping her is when she finally got herself a job, though."

"She couldn't work until she had someone to watch her kids, all due respect," said Angel.

"Shouldn't have got herself in such a tight spot. Don't make no sense. Girls like her get the cart before the horse, then expect others to get them out of their problems."

Angel sliced the cob at the stalk and then set the corn straight up on a cutting board, where she cut straight down. The kernels fell onto the board like small yellow teeth.

"You're not like your sister, are you? You don't ever ask for no one to feel sorry for you."

Angel cut another row. "I hear you got a cow needs milking. I can milk her for you twice a day."

"You done that before?"

"It's not hard."

"Twice a day, I'll pay you a quart of milk," said Mrs. Abercrombie.

"Twice a day is worth two quarts of milk," said Angel.

"Two quarts, then. But I don't want to hear you moaning after the first cold snap that it's too cold to milk."

"Two quarts a day, ma'am. Deal."

"I got some corn bread left from last night and some cow's milk already cooled in the jug. May as well make use of it. Stir some up in a glass and feed those two kids, but don't tell your sister. She never gets to the end of need. Can't give her an inch."

"You're a good woman, Mrs. Abercrombie," said Angel. "I'll wash down your corn for canning if that's what you want."

"I can see why Claudia went after you." Mrs. Abercrombie picked up her handbag and left.

Angel slipped off the porch and, from the corner,

watched her disappear in a dust cloud. She returned to find John and Thorne standing wait for her. John overheard Mrs. Abercrombie's offer of corn bread and milk.

"Let's not mess up her kitchen. The two of you wait on the porch and I'll go inside and bring out the food." She raked the corn into a large brown bowl. The bowl was no more than half full, not enough to can. The woman had bats in the head if she thought she had a mess big enough for canning. Angel took the bowl inside, washed it good, and set it on the counter. She found the milk jug inside the icebox. The corn bread was covered in a plate on the stove. Angel pulled two glasses out of the cupboard and poured them half full of milk. She crumbled the corn bread into the milk and stirred through.

John climbed onto one of the chairs on the back porch. Angel lifted Thorne and seated her next to John. "Here's your spoon and your corn bread milk. Stay put, both of you. I'm going back inside to fix a glass for me."

The telephone rang. Angel let it ring a good long time. What with the party lines and all, the call could be for one of any of the families that lived out along the road-ways of rural Norman.

She sat at Mrs. Abercrombie's table and ate alone for the first time in days. The house was cleaned up neat as a pin, but a strong odor blew in and hung in the air like Edwin had gone and butchered a hog. Framed photos were nailed across the wall near the kitchen table, one each of what looked to be grandchildren and one of Mrs. Aber-crombie and a man that had to be her husband. Claudia never mentioned what became of Mr. Abercrombie,

Edwin's daddy. Angel figured he died, since Mrs. Abercrombie did not act like a deserted woman. Whatever happened to him, he left her in a good way and what with Edwin's job they did quite well for themselves. A Victrola, recent model, sat on a table right outside the kitchen next to a stand-up radio. The rug on the floor was most likely made by Mrs. Abercrombie, a braided oval the colors of Christmas candy. She made a lot of her things by hand: a moppish yarn dog, twenty or more doilies hanging over every piece of furniture, two dolls most likely kept for grandkids, and a shawl folded up and kept on the arm of a chair.

She watched Thorne and John through the back screen door. Thorne slid off the chair, both hands in the air, balancing her drink and spoon. She crouched down and commenced to play with Bean and the gray cat. She gave the cat a new name each time it appeared. For the moment, it was Dew.

Angel kept looking at the telephone. The corn needed to be placed in the icebox, so she did that. Then she washed up her glass and spoon and left them on a towel to dry. She stuck her hand into her smock pocket and pulled out the piece of paper bearing Fern's telephone number on one side and Nash's number on the other. She picked up the receiver. Two women gabbed back and forth. One of them heard the break in the line and asked who was there. Angel placed the receiver back on the hook.

She went back outside and cleaned up the corn silk and the remaining husks. She shoved them into a dry bushel basket. Then she gathered up the naked cobs, packing them into the slop bucket. Thorne yawned. She would soon go down for a nap. "Let's go back to the house," said Angel.

John protested. He liked Mrs. Abercrombie's house. Angel coaxed him off the porch. She led them across the yard, opened Claudia's door, and blocked the cat from coming inside. Thorne padded to the mattress on the floor and curled up, holding the cornhusk doll next to her. John clambered onto the mattress next to his sister and closed his eyes. Angel retreated to the porch and waited for the kids to doze off. She read the telephone numbers again. Fern had nice handwriting: her *f* a flourish of confidence, the *e* a forward movement into the *r*. The *n* lapsed into a graceful mark that flew completely off the page. Fern taught Angel her penmanship. She hated her for that and the way she smelled the spine of a moldy book before shelving it. She hated how Miss Coulter harped on proving arithmetic, dividing into multiplying, chalk tapping the slate like a woodpecker until the numbers locked together in Angel's head, equations popping out, the annoying snap of the ruler, the straight edge rigidly guiding the pencil, the lines so straight, all of life woven perfectly as she planned. She hated her for finding happiness in Nazareth. No one could love Nazareth except her. Miss Coulter always had her way.

The sun finally went behind some empty clouds. Four buzzards circled a pasture distantly. There was the wafting of smells from the hog pen mingling with sweet hay and nodding clusters of Saint-Andrew's-cross. Angel cut across the front lawn, meandering around the white picket fence.

The telephone had not rung, not since lunch. Since she was the last to leave, the door to the screen porch blew open, unlatched. The cat ran onto the porch. The door closed, tapped open, slammed shut again, bounced, and fell ajar. The open kitchen window sucked air from the outside in, the curtain billowing in and out, lapping onto the sill. The cat jumped onto the sill, made a circle, and then crouched to nap.

Her hands were sweaty. Fern's number was smudged, but still legible. She flipped over the paper. Nash's handwriting was spare and hurriedly scribbled. He was in a hurry when she met him and even the day he called her at Abigail's. He never said where he was staying. She could call and get some mobster on the line for all she knew. She could not prove Nash ran with a pack of dogs. But she knew his kind. She knew better, had been taught better.

She made it to Mrs. Abercrombie's screened in porch.

Edwin's car sputtered from the front of the Abercrombies' house, choked, and then died. A buzzard glided straight down from the sky and landed on a pasture post. The screen door slammed shut behind Angel as she went back into Claudia's house. She curled up in her sister's bed. Claudia had not one book in the house to read or paper to write on. Until now, she had not noticed the bedroom ceiling was mottled by round gray patches, flakes of gray ashes dotting the whitewashed tins, as though Bo stubbed out his cigarettes on the ceiling. Or maybe Claudia did it after Bo left her. She could not explain it, so she closed her eyes.

꒰

Jeb lagged out in the hallway at Stanton School. One of the teachers glanced into the hall, waving at Jeb, and then disappeared back into the classroom. Fern's husky voice echoed from inside her empty room. She chatted it up with Frank Harrison, one of the students' out-of-work dads who did odd jobs around the school, such as sweeping the halls and bringing books out of the attic. Jeb tipped back in the chair against the wall. Fern's door came open and she thanked Mr. Harrison for his help. She looked surprised to see Jeb and surprised him. He came down hard on the four chair legs. "Fern!"

"You know Mr. Harrison, Reverend Nubey," she said.

Jeb extended his hand to the janitor. "I've come by to take Miss Coulter away from her duties for a breath of air and soup at the diner."

"You should have told me. I've promised to join two of the teachers," said Fern.

Jeb blinked, his hand resting atop the breast of the jacket that held Gracie's letter. Mr. Harrison excused himself.

She held up her sack and said, "We're eating out on the back steps. You can join us." Her tone was flat.

Fern sat next to the other two women on the steps. The shade reached across the steps but not down to the bottom step, where Jeb took his seat. He turned a bit to engage the women in talk, but they talked mostly to one another. Fern finished up a ham biscuit.

Jeb could not wait any longer, so he got up and said,

"Something's come up, Fern. Maybe later today, sometime, we could talk?"

The two teachers glanced at Fern. One said, "I'm done." She got up and the other teacher followed her back into the building.

"I didn't mean to break up the party," said Jeb. He climbed the steps and sat down next to her.

Fern rolled up her lunch sack. "I was expecting you yesterday."

Jeb wanted to rebound from his momentary lapse in courage, to tell her that he got tied up in church matters, sick people to see. "I know" was all he could think to say.

"Are we in trouble, Jeb?"

"Not in my book," he said.

"Tell me what's going to happen, if the tide's going out on us."

He imagined how things would be if he handed her the letter, how matters would turn around. She would congratulate him as she should have done in Oklahoma City. They would kiss and start packing. He had trouble forming the words. "Fern, I got a letter from Gracie." He pulled it out of his jacket and handed it to her.

She snapped open the letter and read it. She looked at him for a long while without saying anything at all. Then she said, "He's coming back. Gracie's coming back. Never did I expect it."

They both stared into the woods. Green pecans clung tightly on the limbs, ready at any moment to burst open.

She looked at him and he felt a chill, as though it

were the first time she saw him. "You're going to Oklahoma City, Jeb. I see it in your eyes."

He didn't like the flatness of her tone, the way she left her name out, the funny way she looked away and coughed.

"Stop talking like that, like this is about me. I'm not me, Fern, anyway, not the way I am when we are us. I'm not going without you." He made it clear so that she would not misunderstand.

She wrapped her arms around herself like winter had moved in.

"I belong in that pulpit, Fern. Can't you see it all unfolding? It's the hand of God. I've never known it to be so obvious. Not ever have I seen it so clearly like this. When God drops His hammer, it's done." He clapped his hands in the air. A breath seeped out of him. It felt good to let the words spill forth, lay out the obvious. He waited for her to say anything that would soften the tension between them, watched the way the bow on her dress lifted as she swallowed hard.

"He's cruel, then." She lifted from the steps and fled into the school.

An early autumn wind blew and several nuts dropped from the trees.

The shade receded. The sun shone down brightly where she had been sitting.

❧

Angel dreamed that someone came up on the porch. The unwieldy drum of shoes rattled the windows in their casings. The house shook and then fell still. The cool air blowing in from the open door sent dust swirling across the floor. Angel came awake, thinking the door had been sucked closed. She opened her eyes. Edwin Abercrombie was standing in Claudia's bedroom watching her sleep. She jerked up, spraddle-legged on the mattress.

"Did I startle you?" he asked. He smiled down at her.

"Claudia's not here."

Edwin stopped smiling. "Does she have to be? I mean, we can talk, just the two of us, can't we?"

She slid off the bed. Edwin was between her and the door. "You smell like whiskey," she said.

"I'm not drunk. Just a little mellow, wanted some company. Don't you get lonely for company staying over here all day?" He stretched out his hand and leaned against the door frame.

"You should leave."

"Can't you be civil, girl? I heard you was a Christian girl, brought up by a reverend. Did I hear wrong?"

Thorne sighed in her sleep from the mattress right outside the bedroom door.

"What about 'love thy neighbor' and all that?" he asked.

"Mrs. Abercrombie wouldn't want you over here like this," she said.

"Momma's gone off to a quilting bee."

Angel backed up, her thighs hitting Claudia's bedpost. "Look, Edwin, I don't like you and I don't want you here."

Claudia called from the front of the house. "Anyone home?"

Edwin turned around and said, "There she is! Claudia, your little sister and I were just having a talk. You asked me to meet you here, five on the dot."

Angel walked quickly around Edwin and met Claudia in the front room.

Claudia dragged in, holding a small bag.

John came awake and jostled Thorne. He showed his momma his cornhusk doll and ran straight into her, holding the doll in the air and flying it all the way into his mother's arms.

"I'm glad to see you," said Angel. "I was starting to worry."

"What's to worry about?" asked Edwin. "I was keeping your little sister company until you got home, Claudia."

Claudia thanked him, her voice wrung out from the day.

John wanted to know the contents of Claudia's bag.

"It ain't much, but look what Momma got us, babies." She pulled out a bag of peas, some bacon wrapped in butcher paper, and coffee. She said to Angel, "I told the boss man I had to keep my babies fed and he give me a small advance, enough to get us through to Friday." She hauled out three bright red apples and two potatoes and showed them to John.

Angel took the peas to the kerosene stove, rinsed them, and put them on to boil. She turned on the back burner to heat water for coffee. She could not stand to look at Edwin for another minute.

Claudia eased out of her work shoes. Slaughterhouse blood had dripped onto the toes. She held up her bare feet, grimacing. Her toes were red from standing on her feet all day. She glanced at Thorne, who was up from the floor, hand in her mouth, staring at her momma. "Momma worked her hind end off today, little girl." She told Angel, "They got me wrapping meat." She drew out a beef shank wrapped in paper. "Ain't but a half pound. It's all they'd give me."

"Good enough for stew," said Angel. She hurriedly shook coffee out into the top of the coffeepot.

Edwin was still standing in the bedroom doorway.

"What was it you wanted anyway?" Angel asked him. "Claudia's tired and we've got work to do. No time for company."

"Angel, be polite," said Claudia? "I asked him over." She asked Edwin to have a seat, stay for coffee. She set John on the floor and got up. "I look a mess."

"Want to go out for drinks, Claudia?" he said. "Nothing else, I swear."

Claudia laughed. "Angel, would you look! Edwin's blushing. You shy, boy?"

Edwin laughed too.

"I could go for a drink," said Claudia. "I think I deserve one."

Angel shot her a look.

"Not long, though. Angel's been at it all day with these two." Claudia didn't look at Angel when she said it.

Edwin crouched next to Claudia. He picked up one of her shoes and turned it over. He ran his finger through the small hole in the sole. "I know a place can fix these," he said.

Angel tossed the bacon into the icebox. She sighed, turning on her heels, and glared at both of them.

"He says he can have my shoes fixed, Angel. Ain't it nice of him?" Claudia asked.

"I'm not watching these two so you can be with him!"

"Don't talk like that to your sister. She's took you in and working in a place no woman ought to have to work to feed that big mouth of yours," said Edwin.

Claudia held her ears. "Y'all stop! You're going at each other like two cats!"

Angel dropped the potatoes into the sink and threw the knife down. "I'm not staying another minute with him in the house!" She left the house and headed for the pasture. Claudia yelled after her, "Where you think you're going?"

"Got a cow to milk." She cut across the pasture. A briar cut into her calf. She yanked it out of her skin and kept running. The two-story barn was in the field, a stone's throw west of the Abercrombies' shallow pond.

The cow ate in one of the stalls. Angel checked the udder and found it bloated. She seated herself and parked a clean pail under the cow. A clean rag hung over the stall. She used that to wipe the teat. She closed her eyes, remembering how Jeb's neighbor Ivey Long had milked. She rested her forehead against the cow's side, lifted her knuckles into soft skin, and then, using her finger and thumb, pulled down on the udder. Nothing came out. She tried again and several more times. Finally she pressed her face against the cow and sighed. She propped her foot against the pail so the cow would not kick it away. Ivey had sung to his cows. She hummed and stroked the cow's belly and then pulled on the udder again. Milk streamed into the pail. She rotated the fingers until her whole hand gripped the udder, pull, swish, pull, swish. The pail filled finally. She milked until only a bit of white liquid dribbled from the teat.

She hefted the pail and milk sloshed onto the barn floor. Angel carried the milk all the way back to Mrs. Abercrombie's house, with not much care for what spilled or what stayed in the pail. She carried the milk pail onto the back porch. The cat leaped out of the window onto the slatted floor. She put the animal out and latched the back door. The milk would keep for a bit while she made a telephone call.

Mrs. Abercrombie came into the kitchen holding a box of food she'd brought home from town. "Would you look! You've already got that cow milked. Aren't you a caution." She opened her pocketbook and drew out two bits. She pressed the coins into Angel's hand. "You keep that now and don't let that sister of yours take it."

"I won't, ma'am," said Angel. She thanked her. Edwin had not shown his face yet, so she ran into the pasture. She watched the house until the sun went down. Edwin and Claudia came out onto the porch, laughing and hollering for Angel to come back. Angel kept hidden behind some scrub. Edwin got in his car and left. A sulphurous moon came out.

Mrs. Abercrombie came out onto her porch to rock. Angel ran up to the picket fence and yelled for Claudia. Claudia came to the door red-faced. Mrs. Abercrombie called politely to Angel and wished her a good evening. Angel wished her well and then asked Claudia, "Did you need me? Were you calling for me?"

Claudia slammed her door shut.

"Brains of a rabbit," said Mrs. Abercrombie.

10

*I*T's HIGH TIME YOU TOOK UP WHERE YOUR
sister left off. Crying buckets won't do you any good,
Ida May. She's done too much for you. I've got to see to
church matters and you can't lollygag behind, you can't.
You help your brother this morning. I'll be back after I see
Mrs. Honeysack." Jeb was to arrive at her house, according
to Freda Honeysack, for breakfast bright and early. The
ladies' Tuesday quilting bee cooked up breakfast for the
preacher. Jeb stirred a pot of mush on the stove for the little ones who had to stay behind.

Willie came in to him and said, "I want to show you
the streambed first." His upper lip was wet. The boy had
already been down to the creek. His hands rested on his
hips and his shoulders jutted forward. He was panting and

smelled like the creek, a whiff of algae and tadpole. He kept shaking his head and saying, "I never seen it like this."

Jeb told Ida May to keep her hands from the burner and not to poke her finger in the butter.

The first day of September was no better than August. The hard blue sky, the hot dry air was for the tolerant. Overnight a wind had come up and sifted silt onto tree leaves and the hood of the truck. Jeb followed Willie down the dirt path. The creek bank smelled rotten, like low tide to the tenth. The stream was languishing. It yielded only a trickle of water. Willie ran up and down the bank, straining to see the hope of green flickers in the shallows, a fin breaking the water's surface. No such luck. Jeb took the upstream path. The water had shriveled to puddles in some places, not a good drink for a hunting dog. He knelt near the spot where the waterline had receded. Willie whistled. He found a handful of fingerlings, three huddled in a pool.

Jeb toed a fish bone. The large stones mothering the streambed were mud-caked. The banks cracked in rivulets. Sheets of dehydrated algae turned pale in the shade.

"Never, ever. Have you ever?" asked Willie.

"She'll be back in the spring," said Jeb. "Sky can't hold back the rain for good." He was sorry for the boy having lost his fishing hole.

Willie slogged up the path home, sag-shouldered.

Ida May stood in the doorway in a flour-sack slip. She closed her fist up tight, holding a button, she said. A dress was draped over her arm. "Willie, sew on the button for me," she said. She tried to give it to him. "Jeb won't, he won't."

Willie ignored her and collected his fish hooks off the kitchen table. "You got to do for yourself now, Ida May." He put the hooks into a cigar box.

"You fishing or not?" she asked.

"Can't, can I? Creek's dried up."

"Good, see now, you sew it on."

Jeb took the dress from Ida May. "Let's ask Miss Josie to give you a button-mending lesson. She won't mind." He thought that having one less female underfoot would take off some of the load. He was wrong.

Ida May closed her eyes and slumped down in a kitchen chair. He wanted to thrash her. "You needing this for school Monday?" he asked.

"The other dresses is too small," she said.

Willie backed out of the room. "Don't look at me like I'm the one to do it."

"Freda Honeysack will help out. I'm going to her place this morning." He took the button and the dress and promised to bring home a plate of food. "Eat your mush for now," he told them. "Ida May, help your brother do up the dishes after." He grabbed his brown jacket, for looks.

Ida May lagged behind him, stopping on the porch.

Jeb drove away. He would not give her the satisfaction of a look back.

Women covered Freda's porch. They were all dolled up in Sunday things, silk flowers pinned on dresses and hats. Josie stopped him on the steps and asked after Ida May. Jeb showed her the dress and the button. She took it and told him, "I'd best stop by and see to her and Willie. I heard they'd be joining Angel soon in Oklahoma." Her lips trembled. "It's good they'll be back with family," she said. Her eyes were wet. She stroked her lashes with one finger. "I know you do what's best for the Welbys. Never a thought for yourself." She covered her mouth and said twice, "Excuse me."

"Ida May's a mess over her sister," said Jeb. "She'd take kindly to a visit." He commandeered a route around the women.

Freda burst out of the kitchen, her face happy. She set out a plate of eggs. The table was spread with a tablecloth on which sat a bowl of oranges. Will got a good deal on those oranges, she said. "We didn't plan nothing big," she kept saying. "But enough."

Freda was the best of the deacons' wives. Not once had she raised sand, not the whole time he'd known her, not like some of the other wives. She was a rock. Will told her all the time they'd still be married in heaven. Freda worked as hard as a man, could sit at Will's side and put down a rug at the store or nail up a new shelf. Will could not do without her.

"You didn't have to do all this," said Jeb. "Why the big to-do?"

She talked about this, that, and the other. It had been too long since Church in the Dell had done something for their preacher. The offerings were down, she said, but that wasn't news. Jeb followed her back into the kitchen. She closed the door behind him. "We heard you might leave," she said. "Not everyone has heard. Don't think they all know out there. But Will heard."

Jeb thought first of Fern. She would never tell a deacon, but in a weak moment, a teacher or two. "Who said?"

"A little bird from up north."

That changed things. "Philemon Gracie," said Jeb.

"He sent Will a letter and apologized for hooking you up with that Oklahoma bunch. He's proud for you, Jeb. Do you really want to live in Oklahoma? I can see Fern doing that, her family being up there. Is she happy? I guess she would be. We should have taken better care of you."

She had no business knowing ahead of the others, especially not Fern. But the look she gave him, the simpering glances, were hard to take. "I'm not taking the Oklahoma church," said Jeb. It was the first time he said it aloud. The decision was made this morning. He was up all night. Fern had not been to see him since the last afternoon two days ago when she walked into the school and left him on the back steps. She'd not ever go back to Oklahoma. He'd not go without her. He started the letter to Gracie to let him know. It was on his desk. He only needed to sign and post it.

"Does Fern know?" asked Freda.

"I'm telling her today."

"You can tell her now: Josie invited her. You look surprised. Reverend, is everything all right?"

Jeb pushed open the kitchen door. The parlor was filling up. Fern stood in the doorway, holding her hat in her hands. Josie was bending her ear about the wedding. Bernice told her how she liked her in brown, how well her shoes matched, and that hat, how it flattered her blond hair. Fern pretended to listen, glancing once at Jeb.

Bernice kept waving her hands to get the women into their chairs. "Come in, Reverend, join us." She put Jeb at the head of the table, Fern next to him.

Fern was quiet, giving the churchwomen the talking rights. He started to tell her how glad he was to see her. But if she gave him a look, the women could all read one another. Fern was smothered with wedding talk.

"You feeling all right, Miss Coulter?" asked Freda. "I'll bet you need rest after such a long drive."

Fern talked about the hours she and the other teachers spent getting the classrooms ready for Monday. "I'm tired from all that," she said.

Jeb gave thanks.

Freda rushed out from the kitchen and served sausages. The women cooed. Josie passed the eggs down to Jeb and asked Fern about her visit with her mother.

"Good, good. I saw my sister and my brothers. We lost Angel to Claudia, though. Everyone's heard the news, I guess," said Fern. "Not too many secrets in Nazareth."

He could hand it to her, she could keep up a good front.

"I can't bear it," said Josie. "What will I do without Ida May?"

Freda said to Jeb, "I heard you almost up and got hitched."

"If Donna Faye had had her way, yes, we would have. But Fern's mother, Abigail, wants a big church wedding," said Jeb.

"Tell us the date, then, I can't stand it!" said Josie.

"December, on the tenth," said Fern.

"Child, you waited long enough, I'll give you that!" said Freda.

Fern fielded the questions about the dress, the Ardmore church. She had dressed plain for the churchwomen, it was obvious. She was brown, head to foot, a wren.

"But we wanted you to marry here," said Bernice. "You belong to us, not Oklahoma, no offense to your kin. Reverend, say something."

Jeb drank the coffee. He watched Fern for any sign that she might bolt at any minute. She smiled as often as she was asked another question. He told himself that he was imagining things out of school, such as the subtle absence of conviction in her voice when she announced the wedding date. No matter. That was a devil in his head. He cast it down. When she told Josie, "Donna will stand with me. Jeb hasn't said who will stand with him," she sounded like a woman delivering bad news about a crop not coming in well. But he knew her better. She was obviously distressed over Angel joining Claudia. The questions from the women were coming at her rapid-fire and she had never been like other women, coy and preening, desperate to win their approval. He knew that. She was not sitting there politely eating her eggs while quietly hating him. He wanted to tell her to stop averting her eyes. The others, who did not know her as well as he, might misinterpret the lackluster manner in which she described their upcoming nuptials. Her hands stayed in her lap, but not so that she wouldn't accidentally touch him while reaching for her coffee. Her hands in her lap, her eyes not reaching his. It was time to pull out the show card. "I have something to say," he said.

Freda looked up all the way from the other end of the table. "Ladies, our minister would like to say a few words."

Fern laid down her fork and fixed her eyes on Jeb, no lack of polite acknowledgement there.

"While we were in Oklahoma, a church invited me into their pulpit. They've lost their minister," he said.

Bernice and Josie bartered glances.

"I'm proud to say that they offered me their pulpit, but I am making plans to kindly turn it down," said Jeb.

"What a relief! Fern, are you glad?" asked Freda. She played up her part too quickly.

Fern's mouth opened slightly.

Jeb told Fern, "I couldn't wait to tell you. I hope you don't mind."

"You were right, Freda, right as rain," said Bernice. "Home cooking can turn a man's heart back home."

A faint gasp issued from the end of the table. Bernice was kindly nudged by Josie. A silent code fell upon the circle of women. Jeb fixed his eyes on Freda.

Freda held her hands up and said, "Reverend, I swear, I only told Bernice."

The churchwomen glanced at one another, one or two biting their lips.

"Bernice told the rest of us," said Josie.

Everyone except Fern was laughing.

Claudia finally picked up her first pay, enough to stave off Mrs. Abercrombie, buy a sack of meal and a pound of beans. Having found herself in Mrs. Abercrombie's good graces, Angel borrowed some lard and a chunk of salt pork fat. She pinched an egg from the henhouse after her morning milking. Before evening, the kitchen smelled like fritters crisping. The pork fat she cut up and put in the beans for flavoring.

"Friday night, finally!" said Claudia.

Angel lifted the lid on the skillet and flipped the fritters.

Claudia thought they smelled like Granny's back in Snow Hill.

"I learned these from a woman in Nazareth. She poured syrup on top. We got any syrup, Claudia?"

Claudia rifled through the cabinet. She pulled out a bottle. "Will molasses do? Here's a dab."

"Anything sweet," said Angel. She remembered how Willie poured syrup over his beans and corn bread, anything to satisfy his sweet tooth. She hoped he tried hard in his arithmetic. He could not, could not quit his studies. She stayed after him enough. Jeb had best not let Willie know that she was not enrolled in school in Norman. He would use any excuse. What was the use, she thought. She wouldn't tell Jeb. "You get mail here?" she asked. She had not seen a letter carrier.

"All the mail goes to the Abercrombies. You can write to that preacher, but I'd give him her address. If you get a letter, she ought to give it to you. Me, I never got a piece of mail once, not since I moved in here. But Bo wouldn't let me post mail, so I figure if anyone had ever sent me any, he would have took it."

Angel scooped out the fritters and drained them on a towel. "What made you stay with Bo, Claudia? Were you sorry you left Nazareth?"

Claudia shooed Thorne away. "Not now, baby. Momma's too tired to rock you. I don't know. I wish now I would have stayed behind. But Bo wouldn't mind taking a swing at me. He wanted me under his thumb. He knew I couldn't make it without him."

"You're making it, Claudia."

"All 'cause of you." She pulled a cigarette out of her work shirt pocket. She tapped it on the chair arm and then lit it. "Ain't you ever cared about a boy, Angel?"

Angel turned off the cookstove. "Beans are done. We can eat."

Claudia told John to get in his seat and keep still. The boy had the wiggles. He was keen on supper.

"Jeb and I fought over boys I liked. There was this one, I took off with him to Hot Springs," said Angel.

"I can't see you doing that."

Angel liked how Claudia saw her as one so taken by goodness. "He said he loved me. Jeb put a stop to it, though, came after me."

"Sounds like Reverend loved you better."

Angel ladled beans onto the plates. She put the fritters on another plate and set them in the table's center. "I told myself he loved me better than Daddy or Momma."

"Maybe he does."

"I'm not his own. He's going to start a family of his

own with Miss Coulter. When it all boils down to it, he's glad to be shed of me."

"I doubt that."

"Miss Coulter too." Angel poured molasses over John's fritters and showed him how to sop.

A shotgun fired outside.

Thorne shrieked.

"Hush that! Uncle Edwin's shooting bottles off the pasture fence, is all," said Claudia

Angel stared blankly. She poured John his milk.

Claudia savored a bite of fritter, her eyes closed. "Edwin told the kids to call him that. Uncle Edwin." She dropped a piece of fresh onion onto her beans, but was staring at Angel. "You need to get used to having Edwin around, Angel. He's good to me. Not like Bo. And you need to know too that he wants to take me out tonight. There's this dance in town." Claudia stopped her fork in midair. "You don't have a thing in the world to do. Stop looking at me like I'm a bad person."

"It's not my care. You do for yourself what you want. But you're still married to Bo."

"Only because I'm saving up for a divorce. Where is my husband, Angel? Do you see him anywhere around here? John, you see hide or hair of your daddy? He's gone, Angel. Do I know where? I don't."

Edwin fired another round toward the back nine.

"What makes you think Edwin is an ounce better?" asked Angel.

"He's good to me."

"You said that. But why have a man around at all? Why not wait, give yourself time?"

"I'm lonely," said Claudia. "I can't stand it by myself."

"You've got me. Soon Willie and Ida May will come. After that, you can go find a better job. Who says we have to stay here?"

"One of these days, you'll meet someone, Angel. He'll turn that pretty head of yours. You'll see, you'll see."

Claudia traded men like dishes from an oatmeal box. Bo walked out and Edwin walked in. She never said "yea" or "nay" or "kiss my foot." She was picked, not the other way around. A man with a good set of wheels could give her his name. Good enough. Good enough. She was up for auction again.

"How late you staying out?" asked Angel.

"You sound like Momma."

"Not Momma. I sound like Jeb."

❧

"The coat is a good color on you," said Fern. They stood out back under Freda's oaks, away from the churchwomen. She finally relaxed, in a better humor than at the school Wednesday.

"It's the time of year for brown," he said. "Yours is good too." She always talked better of clothes than he, what with her experience and all in buying better things.

Jeb offered her his arm. She ought to see Freda's rock garden, he thought. What with the drought and all, it was the only thing, Freda said, that could live. The trees were already losing leaves. They started shedding in August, what with the lack of water. It was a shady walk, still. Two churchwomen came up from the path, locking arms and giggling. "You two are lucky," said one. She was Bernice's neighbor, a Dalton. Effie, was it? No, she was Elizabeth, and as they passed on the path, she said, "Love is a fleeting thing these days."

A brass spout cloaked in ivy hung over a graduation of rocks. Jeb twisted the spigot, the water dashing onto the rocks, splattering. They moved their feet. "It's meant to be a waterfall," he said.

Fern turned the handle a quarter turn back. The water slowed, cascading over the top black rock, against the next, and the next, collecting in a circular well in Freda's stone pool. "You've wet your sleeve," she said, brushing the spots, her cotton handkerchief depositing damp lint on the brown. "I've had Willie in my thoughts," she said. Her voice was composed, as if she read from a list of assignments for her students, taking a breath as each big-eyed kid waited and held on her every word. "He might not try as hard at school, not like he did when Angel kept an eye out for him. Then he'll have other things on his mind, what's the use of starting school and then up and leaving for Norman, things like that. Boys like him are hard to keep interested in school. You've never said, you know, when he and Ida May might join Claudia and Angel." She shoved the handkerchief in her pocketbook. "It's one of the things on my mind."

Jeb had not thought of it, but he agreed with her. But he held on to that single word in the middle of her sentence, "one," as in, there will be a two, three, and possibly a four. "I'll stay after him." As to the when of the matter, when would Willie and Ida May leave for Norman, there was the matter of getting Angel's first letter and that could take weeks. Claudia left one address behind, that of a neighbor who took in her mail. It was hard to know when Willie and Ida May would go. "There's no hurry, you know. I wasn't hurrying Angel. It was the situation and all, you know." She might like the other rock garden, he thought, and the well was most likely low. He flipped off the spigot. Down farther, he kept leading her, walking past Will's shed, a tractor clutch leaning against a trunk, and a stack of empty clay pots. She stayed alongside him until at last, among a mix of cacti and rocks, they found the garden and stood at its circular wall. Freda's wicker chair sat to the side. He held out the chair and Fern sat down.

"I think I liked the other one better," she said. It was the water, most likely. Women were taken in by water, lakes, the sea.

"We can go back," he said.

"Stay," she said. "May as well." She liked the little rock wall, she said, made of stone and broken glass. The sun moved overhead reflecting off the broken glass, or was it refracting? She knew the difference, had always kept those details straight for him so that he could reserve energy for the bigger matters. She touched the glass, the blue pieces in particular. They were cobalt, she said. The Mexican glass was nice too, and did Freda help Will make the wall, she must have, for Will would not see a use for broken pieces. A man like him didn't have that kind of eye. "You ought to go to Oklahoma City," she said. "Think of Angel, how she'd like having us close by."

Fern said "us." He was not mistaken. But the heat was baking his mind. Jeb pulled off her hat. Her scalp was damp. He smoothed the blond strands sticking up and kissed her head. He knelt beside the wicker chair and touched the cobalt blue and the Mexican glass. Her fingers touched his. "Was that 'us' you said?" he asked. She kissed Jeb. Her skin was damp from the heat. Her lips had the faint taste of cosmetics. He never had known what to call that taste, candle or paint. He dreamed that taste. She came out of the chair and he got up. They kissed again. "We're us," she said. "That's what you said."

He liked the perfection of her at that moment. He had not posted the letter yet to Gracie. Also perfect. She closed her eyes, and her mouth lifted, met his. Bernice's neighbor spoiled the quiet and tittered behind the tree planted by Will's grandfather. He got the idea all at once to ask her if she was sure about Oklahoma City. But there was no need to ask. He knew her better than anyone.

II

M RS. ABERCROMBIE SET THE PAIL OUT, A
note attached asking Angel to leave the milk on
the porch. A man picked her up. Angel saw the whole
thing. He parked to the side of the road and she met him.
Mrs. Abercrombie didn't even casually mention his name.
She stole away, still the widow in the black dress, her husband's brooch pinned to her breast, her face brighter, color
on her cheeks as if pinched, but more likely it was rouge.
She stopped running with the old biddies from the holi-
ness tent meetings. Wrapped in the note was two bits and
please don't give it to your sister.

The cow had given good for the last three weeks, her
belly engorged as the sun was crowning. A slew of crows
burst out of the harvested cornfield, black feathers scatter-

ing into the autumn wind. Angel could lie in the barn's loft now and nap on the hay, not blistering. The day was slow to come, October so full and the hay bristling, the moon and sun sharing the sky. Angel liked walking through the veil between daylight and dark, the milk pail swinging. She whistled loud as a man. She thought, curse Edwin Abercrombie. He, a sorry excuse of a man, not even a man, but a maggot. She spit hard. He had left for work already. Spit twice.

She got the cat off the porch and set the milk inside, dropping the pail down into Mrs. Abercrombie's sink. There was the smell of lye. The woman made her soap and cleaned the hard surfaces so much that Claudia said that everything in Mrs. Abercrombie's house was wearing away.

Schoolkids laughed outside. Four walked past from down the lane, two big and two small, carrying books in belts slung over their shoulders. Every morning, they walked past the picket fence. Angel set the latch to keep the cat out, ran out and down Mrs. Abercrombie's steps, yelling to make the oldest girl look her way. Angel offered her name. "I'm Angel."

The girl's hair was in a halo of curls too old for her face. She walked, putting on lipstick. She asked Angel, "What you need?"

"I just moved in with family," said Angel. She pointed to Mrs. Abercrombie's house. No use pointing out the shack out back. "Where do you go to school?"

"Mount Holly, up a piece," said the girl. "What's your age?"

"Seventeen. I'm nearly done. You got a teacher you like?" asked Angel.

The girl cajoled, "Ain't nobody likes teachers."

Angel asked her name.

"Loretta."

John called out for Angel from out back of Mrs. Abercrombie's house.

"We got to go," said the girl.

A truck rumbled toward them. Claudia came dragging Thorne, buttoning up her work shirt. "Where you been? I can't get dressed and watch 'ese two at once. Here's my ride already. Thanks for nothing." She yanked the cigarette from her mouth. "You got to stop worrying about Abercrombie's milk cow. What's she doing anyway, paying you on the side or something? I don't want to know. Although, if you have extra, I could use it for the dinner wagon. They got these tamales for a dime apiece. You got money or don't you?"

Angel stretched out her arms to Thorne, who jumped and grabbed hold of Angel's neck.

"John's standing out on the porch in his drawer tail. Best get back to him before he catches his death."

"We need milk, some beans. You need me to write it down?" asked Angel.

The truck slowed and stopped. One of the men whistled at Claudia as she climbed up into the truckbed. Angel handed her the two bits. "Milk and beans. Don't forget."

Thorne laid her head on Angel's shoulder. "Let's go back to bed, Aunt Angel."

The truck pulled away. The schoolchildren ran out of

the road and climbed over a pasture fence. The entire
bunch of them turned down the road marked as Mt. Holly.
That oldest was not going to appreciate what was taught
that day, she thought.

Claudia squeezed in between two men holding to the
rails. A laborer was making her laugh already. Angel took
Thorne's hand. "Tell Momma good-bye," she said. Claudia
forgot to look back.

ॐ

In the first week of October, Gracie arrived on the parsonage doorstep, his three offspring in tow. The oldest girl,
Emily, was eighteen, never prettier. Her hair was trimmed
short, all the rage back in Cincinnati. Ida May kept holding Emily's hand, touching her fingertips. She was taken
with the older girl. The first order of business, Jeb decided,
was to return Ida May to Angel. Willie took Philip out
back. Ida May asked Emily to do up her braids. Emily and
Agatha took Ida May out to a chair seated under the trees.

"Gracie, it's you. Hard to believe it," said Jeb. He was
hard-pressed to find a place for him to sit. Crates were
stacked in the parlor, for the churchmen would come by
later to load his belongings into his truck.

"How about the front porch?" asked Gracie. "I've
missed it."

Jeb let him lead the way. Gracie lost half of his weight
getting well. His stomach was flatter and his face looked
lean, pink, his eyes clear and lucid. He left Nazareth
straight from the hospital after a two-week stint that nearly
killed him. Gracie rocked briskly and carried on about the

Cincinnati doctors, how they goaded and prodded. "I believe I got well to spite them," he said. His brother Geoffrey had done well for himself and looked out for all of them. "The girls were happy to see their cousins. They'll write one another, I imagine, keep in touch. It's good we went back, Jeb."

"Your letter surprised me," said Jeb.

"I hope you didn't feel pushed away from the litter, so to speak. My old college friend Jon Flauvert and I had been corresponding. When he heard I was feeling my oats again, he wanted to put my name in the hat for that city church. I thought about it a good five minutes. But I'm an old warhorse. Best to stable me out in the country where I'll do less harm. That's when I thought of you. Not many men would rebound like you did, from jail to the pulpit. But how would it be, I thought, if you finally got a new start where you weren't always trying to prove yourself?" He stopped his rocker. "I wasn't manipulating you, though."

"Of course not." Jeb grinned.

"Fern's got to be happy," said Gracie.

Jeb nodded.

"She was always too smart for Nazareth. Only woman I ever knew who read Pascal for recreation. Girl like her will keep you on your toes."

Jeb had not yet seen her this morning. She packed and crated for the last three weeks, selling off her furniture to the churchwomen. This morning she was saying good-bye to her students. "She had her reservations. I can't lie," said Jeb.

"I remember when she came to this town. She

showed up at church in bright blue, wearing one of those hats she wears. Drove the women crazy with worry. She was too pretty. But smart, as I said. Wasn't long until she was making friends. Had one of the women make her up a few plain dresses. The women took to her after that."

"I must say, when she goes home, she dresses for Fern, no one else." All glitter and high heels, he thought, but she deserved a few secrets.

"She was a surprise, how a woman with her culture would tolerate the petty jealousies of a small town. It says a lot about her character."

Jeb remembered her standing out on the rooftop garden over Oklahoma City, the lavender beads on that dress. That sorry Walton could not take his eyes off her.

"I didn't cause trouble between the two of you, did I?" asked Gracie.

"Not a bit. Geoffrey and Dolly helping you move?"

"Not this go-round. He hired a man with a truck. Should arrive sometime tonight."

"Will and Freda have arranged to have your things moved in after they get us all moved out. I'm going to miss him." Freda kept cooking for Jeb and the kids until he made her stop. "They're good people. Stuck by me when no one else would."

"I've missed him myself. Now have I counted wrong, or are you shy a child? Where's your oldest charge, Angel?"

"Oklahoma. She finally found her sister."

"I'll bet she's grateful."

"I'm going to go and check in on her. Ida May's

pining for her. I sent her a letter telling her that we're on our way. She has no idea, none at all."

"I can see God putting this all together," said Gracie.

"That's what I told Fern." Jeb was pleased Gracie agreed with him.

Fern pulled into the dirt circle behind Gracie's car. She lit up at the sight of Gracie. "I don't have room in my car for one more thing. We'll have to tie Willie and Ida May to the hood. You are a sight for sore eyes, Reverend Gracie," she gushed.

Gracie pushed up out of the rocker. Fern met him on the porch. She hugged his neck twice and kept saying, "You look better than all of us." Her eyes were moist.

"I know it was hard saying good-bye," Jeb said to her. "She means a lot to the students."

"Don't I know it. I imagined the town lynching me upon my arrival. Not only are they losing a minister, but a star schoolteacher."

"Lynch you? Never," said Fern. "The whole town is excited to have you back in the pulpit. I'll have to warn you a couple of widows have set their caps."

Gracie looked good. Jeb couldn't take his eyes off him. He had taken him in like a stray and taught him how to love. Then along came a first-rate pulpit post and Gracie passed it off to him. "I'll never be able to repay you for all you've done."

"Too early for swan songs, Jeb. You and your fine lady have to take me into town for one of those chocolate malteds. Fidel's, right? Ever since you got me my first one, I've thought about nothing else since."

"We'd best take two cars then. We'll have to take the kids," said Fern. She escorted Gracie out to his car.

Jeb whistled for Willie. The kids assembled out front and Fern lined them all out as she always did. She would make a fine minister's wife.

৲ৎ

Mrs. Abercrombie said she wanted all of the handkerchiefs washed, dried out on the grass, and ironed. Angel was to scrub six in one tub and she would wash another half dozen in the other. The lye made them clean, the grass took out stains.

Angel swiped each one with the bar soap, scrubbed the fabric against the washboard, and then plunged them into the tub of water. One stained as red as the lipstick she wore that morning was stubborn as blood to get out. When she examined it, Mrs. Abercrombie cut her eyes away. Angel swiped it a second time and scrubbed it doubly hard against the washboard. "Any mail come for me?" she asked.

"You asked me that yesterday," said Mrs. Abercrombie, a little edgier than she said it the day before.

Jeb had been so busy, she thought, what with getting married soon. Fern would be changing the furniture around. They had not had a second to think about a letter. Still, Jeb knew her address, knew that Claudia would spend every penny on food or cigarettes, leaving nothing behind to post a letter.

"Can't you phone your family?"

Mrs. Abercrombie knew Claudia had no phone. Angel plunged another handkerchief into the lye water. Jeb had not written, though, and that was saying that he was glad to be shed of her. It was Fern that was at the end of it all, but she mostly blamed Jeb. He would have to be blind not to notice that Claudia could not hold her own. He was going to stop it, she thought, that morning before the bus came. He had the look she waited for, troubled. He took her aside. That was when her heart leaped clear into her throat. That was when she expected him to tell her that he wouldn't let her leave. He gave her money instead. Claudia could not hold her own. What was in his mind? She would never be able to take in Willie and Ida May. Now she was trapped in Norman, not going to school, watching Claudia throw herself at Edwin Abercrombie.

"You can use my telephone, girl. One call, not more than a minute. You've earned enough for a telephone call."

Angel stared at her, her hands soaking in the lye water.

"You got a telephone number or don't you?"

"I do, ma'am," said Angel. "I'll go and fetch it." She told John and Thorne to play nice on Mrs. Abercrombie's back porch. The number was in her pocketbook, Fern's number on one side, Nash's on the other. Things were not well, she would tell Miss Coulter. Jeb needed to come for her. But what was Fern expecting, for her to be adult about Claudia? To make herself useful. Even Fern agreed, though, that she ought to be in school. That was what she would say first, spill that one out and see what Fern said. Only Fern would be at school and not home.

Mrs. Abercrombie wrung out a handkerchief, spread it out on the grass.

"I got the number," said Angel.

"You know how to place a call, girl?" she asked.

"I do, ma'am. I'll only take a minute. Save those hand-kerchiefs out and I'll finish them as you want, ma'am." Angel took the number inside. Jeb mentioned Will Honeysack. Will and Freda worked every day at the store. Fern had not written down that number, but she almost knew it. Angel picked up the receiver and said to the operator, "I need to speak to Will Honeysack in Nazareth, Arkansas, at Honeysack's General Store. His number begins two, four, three, and can you get me the rest?"

The operator said she would give it a try. She returned, having found the number, and made the connection for Angel. The phone rang once, twice, a third and a fourth. Finally a young man answered, "Honeysack's General!"

Angel asked him his name. He was Alfred, a boy who graduated last year from Stanton School. "I need Will or Freda," said Angel.

"Won't get them today," said Alfred. "They've gone off to help their new preacher move in."

Angel could not swallow. "Why did they get a new preacher?" she asked.

"The old one quit, I reckon," he said.

Angel figured he was confused. "Do you know where he is? I mean, the other preacher? This is important." He was irritating, not knowledgeable at all like Will's old employee, Val.

"Can't say as I know. Today's my first day."

Mrs. Abercrombie yelled outside that the minute was about up.

Angel slammed down the receiver. "I didn't get an answer," Angel said through the door. "All right if I try another number?"

She muttered loudly enough that Angel felt she could take it as a yes. She picked up the receiver and read the number to the operator off the back of the card. A click and then the first ring. There were seven rings and Mrs. Abercrombie was yelling again. Angel was about to return the receiver to the hook when she heard a voice. She leaned into the mouthpiece and said, "Is someone there?"

"Bill Foster. Who is this?"

"I'm Angel. Nash asked me to call. Is this the right number?"

There was some muttering in the background. Finally a familiar voice came through the earpiece. "Angel Welby from Arkansas?"

Angel breathed in deeply. "Oklahoma, I'm in Oklahoma now."

"You sound good, girlie. How's that sister treating you in . . . Norman, is it?"

Her bottom lip trembled. "Not so bad."

"Hey, you all right?"

A sob slipped out.

"I'm one hour from Norman. You need a ride out?"

"I don't know, that is—"

Mrs. Abercrombie was coming up onto the porch.

"I have to go."

"Give me your number. Let me check on you, you don't sound so good," said Nash.

"Mrs. Abercrombie, what is your number?" Angel said it plainly, facing her as she came through the door.

"Franklin, one, oh, two, nine, nine. Is that your family?" Angel forced a smile. She nodded.

"I heard," said Nash. "I'll call you back tomorrow." Angel placed the receiver back on the hook.

"How nice you got in touch. Now you won't be so troubled," said Mrs. Abercrombie.

⁂

"I don't think I can let you go, Jeb," said Will. "I can't get it all straight in my head that this is the right thing. But I trust you." Freda waited in the car, not able, she said, to say good-bye.

The truck was pulling in with the Gracies' belongings.

Fern was inside saying good-bye to Gracie and the girls.

"Gracie did all this, you know," said Jeb. "Not because he wanted Church in the Dell for himself."

Will knew the same as he did. "He was thinking of you."

Fern came out of the parsonage. She kept patting Philemon and telling him how good he looked. "I guess we're ready. Josie gave me some cookies for Willie and Ida May for the road."

"Fern, how about a kiss for an old man?" asked Will.

"Don't you make me cry," said Fern. She kissed his cheek and waved out at Freda.

"You can't get married without us, you know that," said Will.

"Of course, you'll come, you'll come," said Jeb.

"Philemon says he'll officiate at the wedding, Jeb. I asked him and he said he'd not miss it."

Jeb put his arms around Will. Fern kept putting her handkerchief to her face. Jeb could not muster the word "good-bye."

"See you in December then?" Jeb said.

Will would not let go.

12

A SET OF WHEELS FOR US," HE SAID. HE WAS
holding up a set of car keys. Henry gave it to him. It
was an old car that had belonged to Henry's father; the car
had sat out in his garage since his father died. "They must
have seen your old truck." Fern laughed.

Jeb ushered Fern from her car, his hand at her back,
taking measured steps on the faintly green grass to give her
the full breadth of the place. She carried a box of kitchen
gadgets, she said, from Abigail's, and had dropped in at the
grocer's to boot. The least she could do was cook him a decent meal. She kept her other things at Abigail's house,
where she planned to stay until the wedding. His gear he
stowed in the bedroom: a desk for studying, his suits, one
brown, one black, the one Myrna fixed up from Fern's

daddy's closet; the sofa. But the rest of the house was stark and echoing Fern's absence. "Are you happy at your mother's place?" he asked.

"For now. I shouldn't mind the drive to church on Sundays. Give me time to think along the way," she said. "You've a good-size yard. Lots of trees, like the old place. But different."

"Better though, I think." Except for the fact it had no creek out back. Willie mourned over it. But he made his bed in a storage room away from Ida May. "I thought you'd like to know the last minister's wife had gardens." He imagined Fern would garden. "Lots of places for flowers. Twice the room. And a few ladies from the church brought a small bed each for Willie and Ida May. Gives them a place to sleep for now." The neighborhood was blocks from the church too, a sleepy street of bungalows, yellow, white, blue, and green.

She barely glanced at the gardens. "Have you decided yet when they should join Angel and Claudia? Has either of them said?"

"Ida May, of course, wants Angel to come home, that is, to live here. She was too young to remember Claudia. We'll pay a visit come Friday to Norman. I said that in my letter to Angel, I'm pretty certain. She ought to be expecting us. After a couple of visits with their sister, I expect Willie and Ida May will want to stay. Family is family. Since you have time on your hands, I thought we all should go this first go-round."

"Mother wouldn't have it any other way than that I would be teaching in Ardmore. You know how fast she gets in my business. It's not a permanent job, but the school's not far from the house. One of their teachers has gone home to have a baby." She pulled her sweater closed to guard against the brisk air. "I told them I'd do it."

Fern had talked, hadn't she, of finally having some time to do as she pleased. Of course she never had to work, no more than Donna. "Take off Friday then to be with me. You know I'm not as good around Angel as you are. And Claudia is a real piece of work. I lose patience."

"You'll do fine. I've promised already, Jeb. They're expecting me. Can't leave a new mother in limbo," she said. There was that air that he knew so well, that way she had of making known her will and wishes. It was all set then. Fern had a teaching position in Ardmore. She always did as she pleased.

"Good enough, good enough," he said.

"You're annoyed," she said.

"Not in the least."

"Disappointed."

"You surprise me, is all."

"I can't sit around the house all day. You know I can only take my mother in small doses. It's best I stay busy," she said. She did not sound put out or irritated. He would try and give back in return. Today was Monday. "When do you start?" he asked.

"Not until Thursday."

Ida May yelled from the front landing. "Miss Coulter, come see my room. Angel is going to love it."

"Be right there," said Fern. She carried the kitchen bric-a-brac through the front door. It was all she brought this go-round, nothing else of her own. She was pleasant about the distance between them, but she had always been levelheaded. It was good they had time to plan the wedding, talk out things that they had not had the time to work out in Nazareth. Jeb knew it was idiotic to trouble over small things like Fern taking a teaching job in Ardmore. She wasn't a married woman yet. What was a teacher to do but teach? They had plenty of time to shake out the particulars of making decisions together.

ॐ

"So he would stay up nights, I'd read to him and he would memorize Scriptures," said Angel. "He couldn't read a lick when I met him. A real outlaw."

"You're making this up," said Mrs. Abercrombie, "but I like it, I do!"

"It's not made up," said Angel.

"And what'd you say his name was?" asked Mrs. Abercrombie. She was crocheting.

"Jeb Nubey." Angel kept her threads straight and spooling out of her bag.

Mrs. Abercrombie laughed. "So the two of you pulled the wool over a whole town, making them think this Jeb was a real preacher."

Angel remembered. "I was trying to feed my brother, Willie, and my sister Ida May is all, ma'am. I wouldn't do that again. Jeb, he is a real preacher now."

"Mended his ways, did he?"

"He did, ma'am."

"So he's looked out for you all along, all this time, since your momma got put in the nervous hospital?"

"Like a daddy to me and my brother and sister. Him and his fiancée, Fern. She's a teacher."

"Why'd they send you here?"

Angel pressed her fingers together over a knot, smoothing the thread. "We found Claudia. She's who I was looking for when I met Jeb."

"Sounds like you had a better deal back in Nazareth." Mrs. Abercrombie put down her crocheting. "I can't see any more. These glasses don't help."

"I know the stitches you're doing, ma'am. My granny taught me back in Snow Hill. Want me to finish your row?"

"You are a lamb, aren't you? Tell you what, I've got to run an errand. You finish where I left off, wash down the pork belly. You'll find it in the icebox. You'll find some salt and fennel in a dish. Rub it on the pork and let it set. When I get back tonight, we'll make cracklins." Her hat was already on the table, so she put it on.

"If John and Thorne wake up from their naps, I may have to bring them over, if that's all right," said Angel. Mrs. Abercrombie had taken to calling her over after she got them down for the afternoon. The adult chat was welcome company.

"You make them wipe their feet. Their momma hasn't taught them any manners."

"I will." Angel picked up her needles. "Not my business, ma'am, but can I ask who your gentleman caller is? If you'd rather not say, I understand."

Mrs. Abercrombie dug through her pocketbook. She

pulled out two coins and laid them on the table. "Those are for keeping things to yourself."

"You don't have to pay me to shut my mouth."

"Then take it for the help you give me. You're smart, I can tell." She left out the front door. Angel waited until she thought she had crossed the front lawn. She ran to Mrs. Abercrombie's bedroom window. Sure enough, the man in the black car waited a few yards up the pasture on the side of the road. She got in the car and they drove down Meloncamp Lane.

The pork fat was, as Mrs. Abercrombie said, in the icebox. Angel got the dish out. She rinsed the slab under the sink pump in case that had not yet been done. Mrs. Abercrombie had ground up salt and fennel with a mortar and pestle. Angel scored the pork skin and rubbed the seasoning into it. She washed her hands clean and dried them so she could return to the crochet work in the parlor.

The front door slammed. Mrs. Abercrombie had gone off and forgotten a handkerchief or maybe her brooch. Angel smiled and walked into the parlor, drying her hands.

"Look who's made herself at home," said Edwin. His trousers were stained with grease, as if he had been under a half dozen cars.

Angel folded up the towel. "I'm on my way out. Got to take your mother's crocheting with me, though." The sofa was between them, Edwin standing in the doorway behind it.

"No hurry, Angel." He walked around the couch, closed the gap between them. "Was that name a joke? Did your momma know how you'd turn out?"

Angel wound up the spool and tucked it with the needles into the sewing bag.

"Claudia home?" he asked.

She didn't answer.

"Stay a spell. Make me some coffee, why don't you. Momma pays you. You may as well earn your keep."

The telephone rang.

Angel was standing between Edwin and the telephone. After a third ring, she said, "I'll get it."

"Stay put," he said. He walked past her.

It was no matter. She could go out the front door as easily as the back. The sewing bag hung nicely over her shoulder. She nearly made it out the front door when Edwin said, "It's for you."

She didn't believe him for a second.

He returned the receiver to his ear. "Who is this?" he asked. "Nash. He says it's Nash."

She thought it best to continue on her way out the front door. But it could send the wrong idea to Nash. He might never call back again. She reached for the telephone. He touched her hand. She jerked away and then put the receiver to her ear. When she said, "Hello," Nash wanted to know who had answered the telephone. "No one important," said Angel. Nash thought her voice sounded different. "I have chores," was all she could think to say. When Nash asked if she could talk, she only said, "Not a good time." Finally Nash told her, "I'm coming to Norman Friday night. There's a place in town, The Diner, you know it?" She said she did. "If you're there, say around eight, we'll see where it takes us. If not, I'll take it as a no," he said.

"Probably not," said Angel. "There's things I have to do." The first time Nash called, she lay awake, imagining Claudia waking up to find her gone, no place to leave John and Thorne.

"I'm only showing up for the enchiladas, Angel. If you're there, we'll see. If not, then it's a no. Easy."

"Fine, then," said Angel.

"Are you all right? You don't sound all right," said Nash.

Edwin had not backed away, not even a step, from the time she had answered the telephone until now. "I'm fine," she said. "I'll be fine. I have to go." She hung up.

"Boyfriend calling. Does Momma know?" asked Edwin. "Or sister?"

"My family is all," said Angel.

"I thought Claudia was your only family."

"You don't know nothing about me, Edwin." She pulled out a crochet needle, pointed at him. "I'm leaving now."

Edwin was upset about that. He took it from her, let it drop. She backed up until her hips pressed against Mrs. Abercrombie's counter. Edwin blew out a breath. "You irritate, girl, when you ought to be grateful."

"Claudia likes you, Edwin. She won't if you touch me," said Angel.

"How you know she likes me?"

"She said."

Edwin laughed. "Who says I can't have you both?"

"She wouldn't go for that. I know her better than that." She knelt without taking her eyes off him and picked up the crochet needle. "You ought to know too, your momma listens to me."

"She's a lonely old woman. You're company is all. Don't mean she'd believe you over me. You go ahead and try, say Edwin is bothering you, see if she don't throw you out and Claudia too. I'm all she's got left."

Angel was to the end of the counter by now. Edwin's hand reached gently toward her. He stroked her cheek, saying, "Soft as a doe." She slipped past and ran out the back door. Out front, the squeaking brakes from the laborers' truck sent Thorne squealing from the back, "Momma's home!"

Angel ran and scooped her up and met Claudia out by the road. Her dogs were tired, she said, no mood for chitchat. Angel followed her back inside the shack without looking across her shoulder and over the picket fence.

Fern set up the kitchen like a regular kitchen cook, the spatulas in their places, forks, knives, what have you, in a drawer. She lined the insides of the drawers, cutting out newspapers to make a nice smooth fit. The white curtains were yellowed, she said, so she set them to soak, wrung them to death, and put them out to dry. The kitchen smelled like bleach and rising dough. A pot jingled cheerfully on the burner. No surface escaped her sponge. Two framed art pictures of Christ hung slightly cattywampus on the two walls jutting out from the window. They could not stay and wound up in a closet. She washed down the excessively painted white cabinet doors, left them open, airing out the bare shelves. A cockroach retreated. She ended it with a cookbook.

There was a thermometer in a drawer. She hung it outside the kitchen window to be seen on cold mornings, Jeb thought. A man ought to get out of the way of such goings-on, make tracks to a waiting chair until the dinner bell clanged, the butter out, the vegetables tender in the soup. "There's a book on my desk calling my name," he said. He took refuge in the living room, retreating into a passage he read thrice.

Willie and Ida May played down the street. He hardly knew what to do about the silence. Two car doors slammed. He took off his glasses, put them on the open book. "I'll get the door," he said.

Two women holding covered dishes greeted him. "We're from the church," said one. She might have been Fern's age, if not a bit older. Her complexion was sanguine, her hair light and cropped. "I'm Sybil and this is Jolene," she said.

Jeb had them come inside. They brought him dinner, Sybil said. "Smells like someone's beat us to the punch."

"My fiancée, Fern Coulter," said Jeb.

Jolene said, "I hope we get to meet her."

Jeb yelled for Fern. There was not a lack of interest when she came into the living room. Sybil and Jolene seemed genuinely glad to meet her.

"I'm Fern," she said. The women made their introductions. "Good, you brought food by. Jeb's pantry is bare, I'm afraid."

Fern engaged them in talk about Oklahoma City, the best downtown stores and the like.

"So you'll marry in December, I heard," said Sybil. "We've not had a big wedding in a while. This Depression has sent so many to the justice of the peace."

"My mother wants the ceremony in our church back in Ardmore. I'm keeping it modest," said Fern. "As you say, there is this Depression."

"Abigail's sons have married ahead of her girls," said Jeb. "She's got wedding fever."

Fern was holding a mitt. "Want me to take your dishes to the kitchen?" she asked.

Sybil gave her the dish. Jolene offered to follow with hers.

Jeb invited Sybil to sit on the only furniture in the room, the old sofa he brought from Nazareth. "We've not had time to fix it up," he said. He brought his chair over from the desk and sat across from her.

"You don't have to explain. Lots of families have sold down to the bare necessities. Our last minister and his wife were given some good practical pieces. Not knowing what you-all needed, they were stored outside in the shed. I know there's a nice bedroom set, a few more chairs for this room."

He liked that news.

"Is your fiancée staying in town?" she asked.

"In Ardmore, at her mother's place."

She seemed to mull that over. "Must be a chore, her driving back and forth. It's a good piece from Ardmore to here."

"Truth be told, I wish Abigail would relinquish this whole wedding scheme of hers. I need Fern close by. Just having her here today is a weight off. I'm not much good in the kitchen."

"Sounds like my husband."

Fern came back talking to Jolene.

Sybil lit up. "Miss Coulter, I hear you're driving back and forth from Ardmore. Would you be open to a better offer?"

Fern joined Sybil on the sofa. "I might have, but I've taken a teaching position for the next few weeks. It's not permanent."

"That's too bad."

Jeb wanted Sybil to finish. "Tell us your idea."

"My husband and I have an extra bedroom. Since we live in the same town as our folks, that room stays empty most of the time. It's only about a five-minute ride from here."

"I couldn't put you out," said Fern. She shot Jeb a look.

He had known her long enough to know when she had had her say, said her piece. She was good to hold it in when in front of others, only to let it out once the coast was clear, like the tide letting go, until every bit of her case was made. She was being good for now, playing the part so well of the minister's wife, and her on the cusp of making her vows. But she needed prodding. Sybil's offer was plainly heaven-sent and she ought not to let it go. "Should we drive to Sybil's house and give the room a look?" he asked.

"We can go now if you want," said Sybil.

"She's sewn new curtains that you'll have to see, a

sight to behold!" said Jolene. "Didn't know you could sew, actually, did you, Sybil?" The women headed for the door.

Jeb picked up his hat. Fern remained on the sofa. She was biting her lip, staring down at the bare, rugless floor. "You've left the soup on the stove, is that it, love?" he asked.

"I have," said Fern. She got up to head for the kitchen. "I'll need your help for a moment, Jeb. You will excuse us," she said to Sybil and Jolene.

Jeb followed her dutifully, but his ire was up already. She ought to have asked him first about the teaching position. Look how things worked out if patience was exercised. Fern was smart as a whip. She would learn.

She turned off the soup. "You ought to ask these things of me privately, Jeb. I can't take that room."

"I agree we need to discuss matters first. Like you taking that teaching job without asking me."

"I won't be dependent on my mother, Jeb."

"I need you here, Fern. I've been in this house two days, but here you've come in and in an hour everything has its place. The whole house smells like hot bread. Ida May and Willie need you."

"You're learning to get along without Angel. I understand that. But I can't be in two places, Jeb. Let's both go out and tell Sybil I can't take the room."

"Why is it that things that seem plain to me are hard for you?"

"You don't know what you're asking. Anything forced comes with a price tag, Jeb. I'm not the one that's blind." She removed the soup pot lid and stirred the red broth.

Jeb lowered his voice. "At least go and see the room.

Go back and work for a week, two at the most, but then move closer. I can't stand this distance, Fern. We ought not to have put the wedding date off so far."

"Maybe we needed that time, Jeb."

"For what? To argue and squabble when we could be living here together in marital bliss?"

"Or living under the same roof at war?"

Her words stunned him. "Let's drop the whole room business. I'll go and tell Sybil that you need time to think it over." He left her standing in the kitchen. The door closed behind him, but there was a gasp and that odd noise she made when she was crying. He wouldn't want Sybil and Jolene to hear her crying. He went back and found her bent over the sink, a towel to her eyes. "I don't know what to say, Fern. I try to make life better, it falls apart. Tell me what I've done to make you so angry."

Fern dabbed her eyes. "Why is it I seem to be disappointing you all of the time now?"

"Fern, no."

"Maybe I'm the last thing you need right now."

"What are you saying?"

"They say a pearl is made by a little grain of sand irritating the oyster. Maybe this distance between us is making a pearl."

"Or a boulder."

Her face was red now from staring into the soup pot.

"Will you at least look at the room?"

"You want me to stay at Sybil Oakley Bloom's?"

Why did the name sound familiar?

"If you insist, I'll move up next Friday. I at least want that teacher to have time to find a replacement."

The Oakley name kept running through his mind. "I think it's best," he said.

"There's no need for me to drive and see the room then. Tell her I'll take it," said Fern.

He put his arms around her. The wedding was two months away. They'd get through.

⌗

The smell of pork cracklings was all over the house. Angel shook the second batch into Mrs. Abercrombie's big green bowl and then broke them up with her potato masher. After the sun went down, Mrs. Abercrombie made a fire of logs out back in the same hole where Edwin had smoked a hog. The logs smoldered red as embers. Angel shoved another batch of pork into the oven and then went outside onto the porch. Mrs. Abercrombie lifted a cast-iron skillet and tossed it onto the embers. She took a shovel and covered the pan with the embers. The second pan went in next and she performed the same ritual.

"You burning your skillets, ma'am?"

"Got to. Only way to clean them." Angel stood by her side, watching the handles turn red as pokers. Thorne and John sat passively on their mother's porch. Claudia had gone into town with Edwin for a beer. "I'll have to leave them to cool until morning."

A light moved slowly across the distant pasture like an ant moving a bread crumb. A figure walked through the pasture, holding a lantern. "You expecting company?" asked Angel.

"Oh, that's Loretta, you know, one of those girls that walks past every morning to school. She sneaks out of her daddy's house to meet boys, thinks I don't know she uses my barn. They park near the far gate, do some sparking, then head into town for a bite to eat."

Angel remembered her. She wasn't interested in school. "How you know it's her?"

"Edwin got messed up with her. Big mistake. She made all kinds of claims, lies. But everyone in town knew the truth. She got what she asked for."

The air cooled. Smoke was filtering up from under the pans, white, noxious. There was a cold moon overhead, a drafty wind blowing against the coals, driving the smoke into their faces. Her summer sleeves could not keep her warm. She excused herself to go inside.

13

Mrs. Abercrombie's curiosity about Jeb grew. If Angel didn't know better, she'd believe she was asking her over to hear her tell another story about the outlaw turned preacher. She relived the stories and Mrs. Abercrombie asked her to put out the checkerboard on the kitchen table while she poured the coffee. Angel gave her red and she took the black. "Jeb kept that Negro baby a good six months or so," said Angel. "He couldn't put her out."

"I wouldn't think so," said Mrs. Abercrombie. "He's been good to you then, it sounds like."

"He took us in after Claudia disappeared and has had us ever since."

"Claudia. Was she living in Nazareth?"

Angel did not mean to spill out yet another reason for Mrs. Abercrombie not to like Claudia. "Bo made her leave."

"He was a hooligan from the get-go."

Angel did not remember him so poorly, but she was young when Claudia left. "Granny didn't care for him. Daddy and Momma liked him." It was one less mouth to feed when he took her away from Snow Hill. She remembered more about Claudia each day. She shirked her chores. Sewing was her interest, that and cross-stitch and getting into cars with boys easily.

"Claudia, now she's not one you can count on, is she?" Angel shrugged.

"If she needs you, that's a whole 'nother story. I know her type. But once a man enters the picture, she's done with you. Sorry to say, dear, but that's why you got left in Nazareth." She said one thing as easily as another. "Edwin, he's cut from the same cloth. Claudia's an amusement, that's all. Are you hearing what I'm saying?" asked Mrs. Abercrombie.

Angel opened her mouth to state her piece about Edwin, but changed her mind.

"Edwin's good when the liquor and the sex is free. But that isn't life, is it, girl?"

"I guess not, ma'am."

"Women lose their positions. We get pregnant. Babies get fevers." She was looking at the photograph on the kitchen counter of her husband and herself. "There's no luxury of time for us."

"How about Mr. Abercrombie, did he stick around when the baby got a fever?"

"If he'd been around, he'd have stuck. James was as good a man as they make. Edwin was not his boy. But he did best he could by him. Edwin had already taken on too much of his daddy's ways when I met James." She rested her hands in her lap and looked straight at her. "You didn't finish my crocheting night before last."

Angel shook her head. Her new habit was staying at Claudia's mornings until Edwin took off for the shop. If Mrs. Abercrombie left to meet the man in the black car, she left too. Unless she had Thorne or John by the hand, she stayed out of the yard. Edwin kept his distance better with too many little eyes and ears underfoot. Claudia told her she was starting to act as bad-tempered as Granny. There was good reason. She slept on the floor, staring at the front door that had no keyhole because it had no lock. She was tired of losing sleep over Edwin, the way he showed up when she was alone, was always trying to touch her. Mrs. Abercrombie was wise to Edwin, it seemed. Whenever her grandmother nosed around to know things, like how she felt about her momma being taken to the sanitorium, she would fish. It was a kind of game Angel and her grandmother played. She would ask if she was sleeping nights. Angel would say no, she wasn't. Then Angel could tell Granny things that her daddy had forbidden them to discuss. Maybe Mrs. Abercrombie had seen the way Edwin watched her when she crossed the pasture to milk the cow. She was a smart woman who had birthed a lunatic. It happened to good people, same as bad. Maybe the woman was fishing to find out things. If anyone could head off Edwin before he fell into trouble, it was his own mother. Angel played the next checker. "Your boy ever live off on his own?"

"He did. But after James passed, it was hard going on without him. It was me asked him to stay on after the funeral."

"Where did he live before?"

"Oklahoma City. They got jobs in that place when no place else does."

"He ever been married?"

"Not even engaged."

"He comes around when you're not here." It was as casual as jumping Mrs. Abercrombie's corner checker.

"It's his place too. Why wouldn't he?" It was the first time since she had first walked into the yard with Claudia that Mrs. Abercrombie sounded unsettled. Angel thought she'd want to know what her boy was up to. At times, she had her temperance ways, but others not. Mrs. Abercrombie's eyes bore the same pale blue color as her son's. Edwin had said she'd throw her out if she told on him.

"He's not perfect, but he is my son."

Angel was finished with checkers.

☙

Ida May ran through the house in nothing but a pair of cotton panties. "We're going to see Angel tonight, bringing her home, bringing her home!" She hopped on the hardwood floor from the living room into the kitchen.

Jeb was weary of telling her any differently. "Willie,

I've got business at the church. You keep an eye on Ida May. We'll head for Norman this afternoon. There's food in the icebox." A pair of churchwomen showed up each day, including this morning. They brought simple food, but better than the tasteless dishes Jeb would cook up. Another reason Willie and Ida May ought to join Angel. She cooked.

Willie surprised him by asking, "Are we going to start school?"

"We'll see what your sister has to say about it. If she feels settled in her school there, we'll go and see about getting you and Ida May enrolled."

"You ever been to Norman?"

"Don't expect I ever have, Willie. It's close by, though. Won't take more than an hour, and Fern and I will be knocking at your door at all hours, in your business, same as always."

"Should I bag up my things then? Is this it?" His voice was tense.

"It's only a visit. I want to know first that Claudia is settled in her job and can handle all you varmints." He wanted Angel to look at him and tell him she was happy under Claudia's roof.

Willie stared vacantly at the floor.

Jeb was annoyed that Fern was not here fielding Willie's questions. She was better at settling the waters, so to speak. Each day closer to her moving in with Sybil was one less day of feeling frustrated with her. It was fifteen until eight. He had time for one more swallow of coffee before meeting the deacon board.

"Are you and Miss Coulter all right?" asked Willie.

"Good as gold. Why wouldn't we be?"

"I don't know nothing about women, Jeb."

"Makes two of us."

"But she's not acting the same as usual."

"She was happy in her job, Willie. Fern's given up a lot to come and be with me."

"They gave her a big send-off at Stanton School. Gave her an award, called her the world's best teacher."

She hadn't told him that.

"Some of the girls cried. Even Ida May cried until I poked her and told her she was leaving too." Willie laughed and made Jeb laugh.

Jeb downed the last sip of coffee. He asked Willie, "Did Fern cry too?"

Willie bit his lip, staring at the floor.

"You don't have to answer. Women do those things."

"It was more like she was apologizing to all of the teachers for leaving, like she was deserting them."

Ida May ran back through the kitchen, Jeb's shirt for a hat.

"Go and get dressed, Ida May!" said Jeb. It was time to go, to get back to the real world. He could not explain it, but this bigger congregation made him feel needed, and as though he could make a difference. He cut his teeth on Nazareth, coddling old ladies and taking chickens for pay. God's genuine work could now commence.

꙳

The deacon board was easy to find. Jeb followed the men's laughter into a small room not far from what would be his pastor's study. Henry Oakley was the first to stand from the wooden table, where the men were gathered. "Welcome, Brother Nubey!"

The deacons all got up from their chairs to meet Jeb and shake his hand. He recognized most of their faces from the dinner that followed his sermon that Sunday.

Henry made the introductions. First an elderly man called Everett Bishop shook his hand. Then, "Fred Sellers, Joe Gallagher, and Sam Baer."

The names were familiar. All of the men came dressed from their respective places of business. The coats and ties were a nice change from Church in the Dell's deacon meetings in overalls. Henry gave Jeb the chair at the head of the table.

A boy poked his head in the door, a youth actually of about sixteen, the same boy who poured him water before his sermon. "Rowan, is it?" asked Jeb.

"Your water boy." Rowan grinned.

"Rowan was Brother Miller's apprentice," said Henry "He's been useful during our hiatus, so we decided to keep him around."

Jeb was glad for Rowan's enthusiasm. He was wearing a suit cut out of older cloth, borrowed possibly. The arms hung long over his hands. "I'm glad to know you," said Jeb. "You training for the pulpit?"

"I hope I am," said Rowan. He carried in the water tray and left it for the men. He closed the door as he left.

"First order of business, financial report," said Henry.

Jeb smiled. Will Honeysack would have prayed. "May I ask you-all about your families?" asked Jeb.

"You'll have to pardon me, Jeb," said Henry. "I may be a little overzealous, since we've gone so long without a preacher."

Each of the men told a little about their wives and the number of children they each had.

"Our daughter-in-law is ill," said Sam.

"You remember us talking about her, don't you, Jeb?" asked Henry. "Over dinner at the Skirvin? Her name is Anna."

Jeb recalled dinner at the Skirvin. Fern had been in a foul mood after meeting an old beau, the senator. There was a pause as Henry politely waited for Jeb's reply. Marion talked about a girl named Anna. He was sure he remembered.

"Senator Walton Baer, you remember, left our party early to see to his wife. She's Anna," said Henry.

Jeb shifted uncomfortably in his chair. "Anna is Sam's daughter-in-law?"

"And Walton is my son," said Sam.

"My daughter, Sybil, you've met. Your fiancée, Fern, is going to stay with her until your nuptials. That's Syb all over. Anna has been her best friend since college. She has tended to Anna like a mother hen."

Perhaps Fern had tried to tell him. But he wasn't certain of it or if she was trying to tell him that Sybil was Anna's friend, Anna the wife of Walton Baer. Fern's old beau. "I may have pushed my fiancée into that matter without meaning to," said Jeb. "Fern is worried it would be an imposition."

"Nonsense, no imposition. She and her husband have never had children and that room sits empty reminding her of that. Sybil will love having Fern around. The three of them will get along so well and make your fiancée the center of attention. I know women like that."

❧

The postman came early. Mrs. Abercrombie accepted the mail on the front porch and she was in an unusually optimistic frame of mind, so much so that she hummed to herself. She tucked the mail under her arm. "I'm off for a bit," she told Angel. "There's a stew on to boil. After it simmers, turn it down, will you, Angel?"

Angel already had her hand on the back doorknob. "I was leaving, ma'am. Edwin comes home early of late. He'll see to it, won't he?"

"Dear, don't balk. Edwin's never home early and he's a mess in the kitchen. Am I paying you too little?" she asked.

"It's enough," said Angel. "I have to keep watch for Thorne. She's young yet and can't be left alone or she'll get into the waste bucket." Thorne and John would sleep another hour, but she needed the alibi.

"You know those children can play out on my porch, long as they want."

"I know."

Mrs. Abercrombie laughed and put on a woolen hat,

pulling knitted flaps over her ears to keep them warm. "He's taking me to a cockfight. Ever heard of that?"

She never said who the mister was, but Angel told her, "Where people place bets on roosters that peck one another to death?"

That surprised her, as if she really didn't know. Then she laughed again. "Learn something new every day. You must think I was born yesterday."

Angel liked watching her leave through Mrs. Abercrombie's own bedroom window. Her linens crisp and clean across the bed, not a ripple. This man of hers had never rumpled the sheets. He hadn't set foot on the lawn, let alone Mrs. Abercrombie's bedroom. The music box on the vanity closed shut, the lamps all turned out but one on the nightstand, as if waiting for her return. The black car rolled away in a veil of dust.

She rocked on the back porch, sunning, watching the house in case Thorne or John got up from their nap; also the front door for Edwin. The pot lid commenced to jingling. She ran in and turned down the fire and stirred the bottom of the pot, using a long-handled wooden spoon. She resumed sunning. The days were shorter and colder, so the sun beating down through the screen warmed her bones. She had not planned to drift off. Nothing so gentle and calming as the afternoon nap, the rhythm of the rocker, the lulling away. The tiny screen holes acted as a strainer for the October wind, mingling into the sunny rays, summer and fall reconciling. A clock on the stove chimed, three slipping away, four slipping away, five. The sun moved farther away, a kite let go. Cold seeped in, afternoon fell away. Fingers touched her skin. Her eyes opened. Edwin crouched in front of her watching her sleep.

⤳

Ida May had no coat, and the evening would be cold. Night was falling and the first frost whitened the grass that morning. Jeb told her to put a blanket in the car. Willie's coat from the previous winter was long in the sleeves. He had grown into it now, had not used it for hunting, saved it for school and church. Angel had a coat too. Fern boxed the things she left behind in Nazareth, one personal item being a pale blue coat. Jeb laid it on the passenger seat.

The motorists thinned out beyond the city limits. The deacons were a chatty bunch, holding over at least two hours longer than expected. He didn't mean to get out of town so late. It would be supper time, at least. Angel would have a meal on. Jolene brought by a cake, one he salvaged for Claudia and Angel. It was covered and on the floorboard. Cinnamon, it smelled like, and vanilla.

He drove through Del City and on into Moore, a highway, mostly, dotted by older houses, laundry on the brew in one front yard, a hunting dog in hot pursuit of a fox squirrel. The road was bumpy in places.

Henry Oakley's voice yet rattled around his thoughts. He was long on exposition, but it was smart of him to lay out the figures and facts, a man who kept the books right on the money. Sam Baer was the lawyer in the bunch, first one he ever had the chance to know. He was a ruddy-faced gentleman, a white shock of hair, his face chiseled out like the side of a mountain. He and Henry worked side by side like brothers, or like men who had gone to sea together. But it was a Baer Fern had known, shared a past with. That was all no more, she said. Still, the Baers and all of their acquaintances unconsciously tortured her, not that she said it exactly that way.

Sam supplied a pencil-drawn map to Norman.

"Remember to tell Claudia that Angel has to come home. She can't stay at Claudia's anymore," said Ida May.

Willie asked for cake.

"When we get there," said Jeb. Sybil Bloom, he liked. She was a confident young woman, not ever having used her education like Fern, at least not in the traditional sense of female graduates. Pregnancy dodged the Bloom household. So she devoted herself wholly to sick Anna, whom Jeb had not yet met, nor had he met Sybil's husband, Rodney, only Anna's husband had he encountered. Walton Baer. Their family ties extended to the state capitol.

Anna has a tumor, Sam said. Where, Jeb didn't know, only that she grew weaker by the day. If it had not been for Sybil, she'd have been lost for certain. Little was said about Walton.

"Norman, straight ahead!" Willie came out of his seat, pointing to the town sign.

Highway 9 angled straight into downtown. Most of the lights were out on the shops. The Diner on East Main was still lit. Jeb parked, pulling out the address that Claudia scribbled down. A waitress cleaning the counter smiled at him, asked if he'd like a cup of coffee. Jeb showed her the address.

"Take East Main two more blocks up, make a left.

Stay on that road until you run out of pavement." She pointed out to Jeb the twists and turns, landmarks like a big oak, a small grove, and a cornfield picked over.

Jeb wrote down her directions the best he could and thanked her. The sun was gone entirely.

⤳

Angel lost track of time knowing that with nightfall the only thing illuminating the pasture was the moon. It had not taken long to shove a few clothes into a small bag. The big suitcase she lugged from Ardmore to Claudia's was too big to haul on foot. Claudia's small bag was nice and light for traveling in a hurry. If she followed the fence line, eventually she would make it to the road without crossing Mrs. Abercrombie's yard.

Claudia fell asleep listening to a news drama. Thorne and John played quietly at her feet.

A light flickered behind the barn and the back pasture fence. Angel crouched. Edwin could be out looking. A female giggle, the muted thump of running feet made her freeze. Two figures ran in the shadows and hopped inside a sedan. A young male voice spoke. Angel ran for the sedan. The engine cranked. "Wait, wait up!" she yelled.

"Who's there?" said the male. "I got a gun."

Taking a chance, Angel called, "Loretta, it's me, Angel. Your neighbor."

First silence and then muttering. The boy spoke again. "What do you want?"

"Is it you, Loretta?" she asked.

"What's it to you?" Loretta answered.

Angel made it to the driver's side of the sedan. She could not breathe, bending over, clamping her hands on her knees. "I got to get a ride into town. Have to meet someone."

"A boy?" asked Loretta.

The story seemed the best to tell. "Yes, a boy." She straightened.

"Can't help you out," said Loretta's beau. He put the car in gear.

"Please, Loretta, you have to get me out of here!"

"Let her talk, Joe. What's wrong?" asked Loretta.

"Edwin. He . . . he came after me." A tear streamed down Angel's face. She locked eyes with Loretta. Angel hiked her skirt up past her knee. "He hurt me."

"Hurt you, how?" asked Loretta.

"Tried to hurt me like he hurt you."

"Loretta, what's she talking about?" asked Joe.

"Give her a ride," said Loretta. She opened her door.

Angel ran around to the other side of the car and climbed inside. Loretta pushed her seat back in place, but was turned so she could see Angel. "Gun it into town, Joe. Edwin Abercrombie will burn in hell!"

Angel wiped her eyes.

"That momma of his, she's no help either, is she?" asked Loretta.

"She's mad, like I was the one done something wrong."

"What happened?" asked Loretta. "You can tell us."

"I fell asleep on Mrs. Abercrombie's back porch. When I woke up, Edwin had me by both arms. I slapped Edwin, kicked at him, and ran hard back through the house. It was Mrs. Abercrombie coming into the house right about then. I ran straight into her. When I told her how Edwin had grabbed my arm, tried to take me down on my knees, she called me 'liar' and 'hussy.' "

Edwin had stared at them both from the front door, gawking, raking his hair out of his face.

"You got away, right, Angel?" asked Loretta. "I mean before he did something bad."

"He hurt my arm. My leg is bruised, but I got away. I got someone meeting me in town for a lift."

"Where you going?"

"Away from here." She thought it best not to say.

"Where's your family?"

"That was my family, my sister Claudia."

"She blind or something?"

The waitress insisted on giving Jeb fresh hot French-cut potatoes. They would at least keep Willie out of the cake. Willie took them gratefully.

"You think Angel will look different? It's been so long since I seen her," said Ida May.

Jeb turned around in the car seat and said, "Ida May, you need to listen. We're paying Angel a visit. If she says that it's time for you and Willie to join her, then we'll see about getting you down here next week. She thinks you-all ought to be with family now and I have to let her decide those things. Claudia is family."

"For a visit. We're going to come visit Claudia, is that what you mean?" asked Ida May.

"For good!" said Willie.

Jeb cut his eyes at Willie.

Ida May wailed.

"Not like that," said Jeb. "You don't unload on your sister like that!"

Jeb drove them through the downtown sector past a drugstore, a dry-goods store, and a barbecue joint. "That's a hopping place," he said. The parking lot was full. He turned left and headed down the road, away from town.

The thought of how Fern looked when he insisted she live with Sybil was haunting him. She was coming up Sunday for the church service, she said. He wanted to sit down with her, talk over the matter about the Baers. Tell her he was having second thoughts.

He followed the directions, drove too far, as she said he might if he came to a sign advertising a dairy farm. He turned the car around, headed back up, finally saw an arrow-shaped sign in the weeds pointing him down Arrowroot Road. He pulled aside at a house painted a dark color. But what color he could not tell by night. The farmer inside was helpful and knew the address. "Go past this next house and you'll see a white house, a pretty white fence. That ought to be the place," he said.

Jeb did as he said. Ida May was clambering over the seat by now, squealing. Jeb told her to watch for Angel's coat. She spotted the fence and he had to grab her to keep her from opening the door before he pulled to a stop. She ran out of the car, cutting across the dark yard, and beat him to the front porch. Before he could reach her, she was pounding the door.

A woman answered. She pulled her spectacles up onto her forehead and asked what they wanted.

"I'm sorry, ma'am. We're looking for Ida May's sister Angel. She's a little anxious to see her."

The woman did not answer right away. Finally she said, "Is she expecting you?"

"Ought to be," said Jeb.

"I'm Claudia Drake's landlady. If you're family, she got a piece of mail today." She got it from the radio top and gave it to him. "You'll see she gets it?" she said.

Jeb accepted the letter. He recognized his own hand-writing and the postmark from Nazareth.

"She lives out back, the house directly behind this one, with her sister."

Ida May and Willie raced around the house. A cat streaked in front of them. Willie opened the rear gate.

Jeb stared at the shack. There was a dim light burning inside. He came up onto the porch. Before he could knock, the door opened. Claudia was surprised to see him. "Preacher Nubey, we was wondering when you might come." She stretched. "I fell asleep, listening to the radio. John, go and fetch your aunt."

John looked up from his trucks on the floor. "She left," he said.

Claudia said, "What do you mean, 'she left'?"

"I thought she was going to Mrs. Abercrombie's barn to milk," he said.

Claudia told Jeb, "She never milks this late, not after dark." She pulled on her shoes and a jacket and a promise to return with Angel. Ida May and Willie sat down to play alongside Claudia's two.

A half hour passed. Jeb got up and changed the radio dial. Finally he heard footsteps on the porch. Claudia came in, her temple wet from sweat. She panted as if she had been running. She walked past Jeb and into another room. Out she came in a minute. "Her suitcase is here, but mine is gone."

Jeb told Ida May to put her shoes back on. "Might she have a friend she's off visiting?" he asked.

She shrugged.

"She was mad at Edwin," said John.

"Shut your mouth!" said Claudia.

"Who is Edwin?" Jeb asked.

"Momma's boyfriend," said John.

"I said shut up, John!" Claudia plopped down in a chair. She put her head in her hands.

Jeb kept his voice low, trying not to spook her. "Can I speak with this Edwin?"

"I don't know, I really don't know nothing. Edwin and her got into it. She hates him. Maybe she took off, I don't know."

John eased up beside Jeb. Jeb knelt and put his arms around him. "John, can you remember anything your aunt Angel said?"

"He don't know nothing," said Claudia.

Jeb kept looking into the boy's eyes.

John cupped his hand to Jeb's ear, ignoring Claudia's threatening look, and whispered, "She ran away. Edwin hurt her."

"Willie, take your sister to the car," said Jeb.

"That boy is a liar!" Claudia shrieked.

Jeb walked Willie and Ida May through the dark and back to the car. He cranked the engine and turned the car around in the road.

"Where we going?" Willie asked.

"To find your sister," said Jeb.

Ida May sniffed.

"Don't cry, Ida May. Not now," said Jeb.

14

IF WE DON'T EAT HERE, WE DON'T EAT UNTIL morning. Can you make it that long?" asked Nash.

"That is what I want," said Angel, for it was the only way to get away from Edwin. Claudia would come looking for her and she would ask him to drive her. He was a thug. His touch was like bumping up against a form in the dark. Nash drove away from The Diner onto the highway.

"Can we go south?" she asked.

"I have a job. We can go south in three days."

All right, then, she thought. He was giving her a free ride out of Norman. Nazareth could wait. A car passed. The headlights blinded her, made her head hurt. Ida May was in her thoughts, though, and Willie too. Now, because of Claudia, Thorne and John too. They were like Willie and Ida May, in need of a better mother. "Where's your Studebaker?" she asked.

"Told you. It wasn't mine. How south?" he asked.

"Nazareth, Arkansas. Is that all right?"

"You scared? You look it, girlie."

"How do I?"

"You haven't let go of that door handle since you got in the car," said Nash.

"Where are we going?"

"A friend's place. You look like you need a decent bed and a hot meal."

She rested her head, closed her eyes.

"Who were those two back at the diner? Friends of yours?"

"A neighbor. I don't really know her," said Angel.

"Did you give out my name?"

Angel lifted her head off the seat. "Does that matter?"

"It appears that you are running away, girlie. People you don't know, they snitch."

"She won't snitch." She was wrong about everything else, joining Claudia, leaving Nazareth. But she was right about Loretta. Had she said Nash's name? No use trying to remember. She told Loretta and her boyfriend how she knew that she would mess up Claudia's position, what with no one to watch Thorne and John. Loretta said, "You got to do for yourself. Who'd blame you, who'd blame you?" The boyfriend, Joe was it? Was that it? He didn't say much. He kept asking Loretta about Edwin Abercrombie. She didn't answer, but looked back at Angel, like the two of them knew more than was being said.

The moon was out, but the rest of the sky was a black blanket, not a star in sight. But it was early evening. A fire could be seen burning in the woods, migrants keeping warm, most likely. The car smelled faintly like rotting fruit. Angel rubbed her arms. She rifled through Claudia's few belongings looking for something to keep her warm. She owned so little and she was in a hurry to get out before Edwin came back to argue his defense. Claudia didn't believe her anyway. Whatever happened, she brought it on, according to her sister. Had she baited Edwin? Was there something about her that invited him to press himself against her, smelling like the insides of a car? Her arms were cold as ice.

"Don't they wear coats in Arkansas?" Edwin had asked. When she didn't answer, he said, "I know a place, they got good women's things. We got to get you some good clothes, girlie. No one's taking care of you, and you're too pretty to be let go like that."

"My better things are all back in Nazareth." She didn't like that he implied she walked around in rags. "It all happened fast, me moving in with Claudia. Jeb, he was supposed to bring me my things. I don't know what happened." The weather had turned cold and still no Jeb.

"Who is Jeb again? You told me once before, but I forget."

"I guess he's really like my daddy. He's looked after us, me, my sister Ida May, my brother Willie. It's a long story."

"So he's back in Nazareth."

"He was."

"You depend on others too much, girlie."

She knew he was right. Here she was headed back to Nazareth to live with whom? Will and Freda Honeysack? Fern Coulter? She needed more time to think things through. "Not south. I was wrong about that. Anywhere but south." Her bottom lip trembled and that troubled her. She didn't want to cry in front of him. She would get him talking about himself. Men liked that, she knew. "Tell me about Boston." She closed her eyes and let go of the door handle.

꒰꒱

There was only one place left open in the whole town. Jeb pulled back into The Diner parking lot. Ida May opened the car door before he could react. "Ida May, get back inside!" he told her, but she didn't listen. By the time he and Willie walked into The Diner, Ida May was running and stopping, looking over the counter and staring into booths.

The waitress recognized him and pushed a cup at him. "Fill 'er up?"

"I'm looking for a girl, she's seventeen, brown hair," he told her.

"What's she wearing?" the waitress asked.

Jeb had not asked Claudia, mostly because he wanted to get away from her before he throttled her. "She's about this high." He made a knifing motion at his chest.

Ida May came from the rear of the diner, tears welling, her dam about to break loose for the tenth time all day.

A youth swiveled around on his bar stool. "How tall?"

Jeb showed him.

"Girl seventeen, brown hair. I gave her a ride, not ten minutes ago," the teen said.

A girl sitting next to him gave him a punch and told him, "Shut up, Joe!"

"Can you tell me where she went next?" Jeb asked him.

"Don't know. She was meeting a boy, that I do know," he said.

"Know his name?" Jeb asked.

The girl huffed.

"Please, she might be in trouble," said Jeb.

The girl turned her back to them both.

"She give me a name. Nash Foster. He drove a light-colored car. Two-door Ford sedan. That's all I know."

Jeb wrote down the name on a napkin. "Which way did they head?"

Joe's girlfriend sighed. "I'll show you." She walked Jeb outside and pointed. "That way. She was good to get out when she did. The Abercrombies, they're no good."

"Who? Claudia's landlady?" asked Jeb.

"Edwin and his mother. That woman, she means well, but she's let that boy go too long. Is Angel your girl?"

Jeb thought a moment. "Yes, she is."

"She was scared, I think. Not a lot of what she said made sense, but I don't think she knew the fella too well she left with."

Jeb and Willie and Ida May climbed back into the automobile and headed back up Highway 9.

The inside of Nash's car warmed her. She might have fallen asleep had Nash not talked so much. He told her about the North End of Boston, the Italians who lived there, a place called Paul Revere Mall, which she could not picture, but it sounded like a pleasant place. He said it was pretty in the snow. His uncle owned a shop that made men's clothes, but it had all but gone belly-up after the stock market crash. After he mentioned the cemetery twice, Angel asked him about it. "My mother was buried there" was all that he said, so she left it at that. "What brought you to Oklahoma?" she asked.

"My father worked for the railroad and was gone all the time. He didn't leave me much reason to stay. When my mother was alive, things were different. She loved looking good, told my brother and me that all we needed to succeed was a good suit. Her brother, my uncle Fred, he kept us all looking good. My mother worked for him, so she sewed real good. The rich ladies in town, they'd hire her to make their clothes. They could bring her a picture out of a magazine, and she'd make it right out of the magazine, just like the duds out of Hollywood." He did not sound as lively as earlier, but it was getting late. "Then the Depression hit. Uncle Fred's business got into trouble and my mother got sick. After she died, my father started selling off our things. I hated it, maybe I hated him. He sold my brother's suits and mine. I had nothing left, and Dad was gone all the time. So I hooked up with my poor relations here in Oklahoma. Only I get here, and they're doing better than the Boston Fosters."

"Is that who answered the telephone, your relative?"

"My uncle," he said.

"Where do you live?"

"Wherever the wind takes me. Tonight it took me to Norman to rescue a pretty girl from, where did you say, Nazareth?"

"Nazareth. You like moving around? Not staying put in one place?"

"I get to see a lot of places. My mother used to talk— it was talk, but she wanted my brother and me to see Europe. She talked about the clothes there, how she could rack up the dough in a place like Europe. Maybe it was all talk." Nash slipped off his shoes and drove in his sock feet.

"Your shoes look new," she said. "You like clothes, shoes, talking about nice things."

"I'm going to own my own suit shop, like my Boston uncle's, when this Depression turns around."

"Where are we going tonight?"

"The big city of Edmond. You ever been there?"

"I've been to Oklahoma City." They passed the Oklahoma City town limits a mile back. "Is it close to here?"

"It isn't far. My job doesn't always keep me in the same place. Edmond is where I'm staying for now. There's two beds in the room. I'm by myself." He got quiet. "I hate traveling alone. That's why I called you. You're easy to talk to."

She thought he was too. "What kind of work do you do, I mean, it must be good work. You can afford new shoes." And he had offered to buy her clothes.

"I thought I told you. I'm a chauffeur."

"For who?"

"Different people. I'm getting my name spread all over the place as the best driver around."

She finally got up the nerve to say, "A car kind of like the Studebaker you were driving back in Ardmore, it was seen during a bank holdup."

"Did you tell anyone?"

"There wasn't anything to tell."

"I knew that about you when I met you, that you weren't a snitch."

"So it was you. You held up a bank, Nash."

"Are you kidding, girlie? I couldn't shoot a deer at close range. My fingers shake so hard I can't put in a bullet. I just do what I'm asked, show up when I'm told, get paid, go find a new town to lay low."

"What if you got shot?"

"My head's so low behind the wheel, the cops all think a ghost is driving." He took a sharp right onto a dark road. There were tents set up alongside the road, men seated in circles around small fires, coffeepots on the brew. "See those men? They're all making do with what they got. Most of them, they left behind their wives and kids. Some of them are so far from home, they can't remember their own addresses anymore. When I pass one of those tent cities, I imagine my old man sitting there in the cold. It's not for me. Ah! I thought I remembered right." A sign flashed in a café window, HOT COFFEE. "Best tamales in town. You had a good tamale lately?"

"I've never had a tamale," said Angel.

"We got to get you out of the house more. Good food, good clothes."

Behind them, the fires from the migrant tents were enveloped by the dark and many miles. Nash got out of the car and opened her door. He gave her his jacket. Angel followed him inside, glad they had the place to themselves. The waitress said, "All we have left is tamales and beans."

Nash gave a war whoop and ordered two. He led them to a booth, one of those red and white shiny vinyl seats, only the white was dingy.

"Has your daddy always worked the railroads?" she asked.

"Started out, he wanted to be a cop. His pop, my granddad, he was a cop. Lost his badge during the strike of 1919. Still, it was always in him to go to police school. His old man wouldn't hear of it. Bad blood between him and the Boston police. What about your father?"

"Two tamale specials," said the waitress. Two white plates, two tamales each, and a spoonful of beans. She set their plates in front of them and left.

"My father took work where he found it," said Angel. "The coal mine, the cotton field. Now I don't know where he is. He sent us to live with our sister Claudia, that was back in '31. But things went wrong. The woman taking us, her name was Lana, she ditched us. That's when we met up with Jeb Nubey." For the moment, she felt Jeb so far away. She could not recall exactly how his voice sounded. She could only hear the inflection and the way he cleared his throat before reading from the Scriptures.

"You said your mother was in the hospital, didn't you, back in Ardmore?"

"I don't know if she's still there. Her sister, my aunt

Kate, she may have taken her in. Momma didn't have no money, so she may have lost her room. You ever heard of a nervous hospital?"

Nash nearly ate a tamale whole. "The loony bin."

"Don't call it that."

"Sorry, sweet cakes. It is what it is," he said. "For you, I'll call it a palace if that makes it better."

"I like these tamales," she said. "They're not bad."

. ⟩

Willie called out the sign for the Oklahoma City border. He rode shotgun, sitting watch for any sign of a two-door, light-colored sedan.

Jeb stared into the dark, certain he had gone blind. Ida May was falling asleep. Willie's interest in gawking at every passing car was waning fast. Ida May took Angel's coat into the backseat for warmth. He was so certain he would be sitting with Angel at this hour, listening to how she was sending the boys into a spiral, beating out the other girls in the spelling bee, wrestling against arithmetic, that the emptiness left him sick at his stomach. He took the letter off the dashboard, the one he mailed to Angel. He tore it in two.

Willie didn't say anything, but stared at Jeb like he might.

If Fern had come . . . he kept thinking, and then he'd dismiss the thought. For if she had come, she would have, like he had, found Angel run off. But she might not have tolerated the late hour when he took off, might have gotten them all to Norman sooner. Had he not said that to her, that he managed poorly without her? Angel would have been at Claudia's still, not having been attacked, and by whom? Who was Edwin Abercrombie and how did he gain access to her? How badly was she hurt? This woman at The Diner, she hadn't asked enough questions, or else he hadn't. Again, Fern was better at thinking of all the things a girl might think.

Willie's belly rumbled.

"Are you hungry?" asked Jeb.

"Of course, ain't you?" Willie sure sounded surprised.

"You ate your supper," said Jeb.

Willie laughed. "We ain't had our supper, Jeb. Ever since leaving Oklahoma City, we been doing nothing but hunting down Angel."

Supper came and went, with no thought for it. "I'm sorry, Willie." He was surprised Ida May dozed off rather than worrying him about a missed meal. "I'll try and find a place." He slowed the car. There was a sharp turn right or he could continue straight ahead. A group of migrant tents were camped up the side road. He could stop and ask one of them to recommend a place still serving supper.

"What about cake?" asked Willie. He picked it up from the floorboard.

"It's good enough for me," said Jeb. He continued up the highway. Willie passed him a handful.

⁊

Nash fell quiet on the drive from the café toward Edmond. Angel dug through Claudia's bag. She left in too big a hurry and only brought half of what she brought to Claudia's. But Claudia's bag was lighter for fast traveling. And, of course, most of her things hung in a parsonage closet back in Nazareth, so she didn't need the larger suitcase in the first place.

Nash had called Mrs. Abercrombie's house, so that meant he had a telephone. By morning, she would be rested and in a better frame of mind. She would call again, this time for Miss Coulter. The youth at Will Honeysack's grocery had it wrong. Jeb leaving Church in the Dell was nonsense. He had his worries, but leaving had not been on his mind. Of course, he and Fern had not gotten on well in Ardmore, even putting off their wedding date. But that was Abigail's doing, not Jeb's. If anything, he wanted the wedding date moved up, not back. Even though Miss Coulter was nervous on the trip, that was a bride's privilege.

"We're not far now," said Nash.

Worry took over Angel's thoughts. John and Thorne had it bad all over again. Claudia would find the note on her pillow tonight when she pulled back the covers. On it would be Aunt Kate's address in case she had lost it and five dollars for traveling money, saved from the chores she did for Mrs. Abercrombie. If she wouldn't smoke it up, and would take that and this week's pay, she could make it back to Little Rock. Aunt Kate might help her find work. She could see to Momma. "I need to find work," said Angel. "I gave most of my money to my sister to get home on."

"Nazareth?"

"Home to our mother and aunt Kate. Little Rock."

"Is that where you plan to go to?"

"No, I'm like you. My family takes all I have, all I make. It's time for me to do for myself."

"I'm staying in a house where you might get work for a few days. Would that tide you over? Making beds, washing dishes."

"I can do that, Nash. Then what?"

"How about a steak dinner at the best little place this side of the Mason-Dixon Line?"

He made her laugh.

15

REPORT PROVES 250,000 HOMELESS YOUTHS roam the country. Jeb folded up the *Oklahoman* to take inside and put away. He knew every crack and brick at the top of the church landing. He had paced it since two hours after sunrise, taking the walk from his study to the landing, back inside, repeat.

The world aged as he waited for the squad car to pull up and park near the church steps, for the deputy to get out, fetch his pad of paper. From Thursday night until Friday midafternoon gave a girl hours to be lost. "Is there a Reverend Nubey here, sir?" he asked standing down on the street.

"I'm Nubey," he said.

"You have a missing child, I hear, Reverend." He had

to move the bulk of his weight from the first step, straining to the twelfth, but reached it at last. His face was slick and pink.

"Angel Welby." Jeb helped him spell it.

"Shame. So many kids out on the streets now. You hear of one that has left behind a good home and you shake your head. So many others got it so much worse. Welby, you say? I thought it was Nubey."

"Welby. I'm Nubey."

"Is she yours, Reverend? By that, I mean are you blood related?"

"Angel has lived with me a long time. I'm what you'd call her guardian. Her brother and sister live with me too."

"Are her parents alive?"

"She was abandoned."

"But you're the one looking out for her?"

"Of course. Could we go inside?" A cup of Rowan's coffee might help calm the waters, he thought. He took the cop to his study, pulled out a chair. Jeb leaned against his desk. "Angel and her brother and sister, Willie and Ida May, they've lived with me since 1931. We recently found some of Angel's kin in Norman."

"Good town."

"It is, but this sister of hers, she didn't look after Angel in the right way. Claudia let . . . she was seeing a man. He might have hurt Angel. She ran off."

The deputy wrote each letter block-fashion.

"But I have a name and a car model."

The deputy lifted his pen. "We don't normally take

down information from a person outside family. It's not what you call protocol."

Jeb went around his desk and sat where he could look into his eyes. "Angel is like my own daughter. I never should have let her go to her sister's. It was my mistake." He couldn't say whether or not the deputy understood him. "I'm worried."

"How old is she?"

"Seventeen."

"When does the girl turn eighteen?"

"March fourteenth."

The officer kept writing.

There was a knock at the study door. Rowan stuck in his head. "Your fiancée, Reverend," he said.

Jeb was relieved. Rowan opened the door and in walked Fern. "Rowan said we've lost Angel," she said. "I'm sick to death, Jeb. Is this Claudia's doing?"

"Officer, my fiancée, Fern Coulter."

Fern said, "I came the second I could get away from the school. What do we do now?"

The deputy scribbled down a few more notes. "Lots of missing children nowadays. You have a telephone?"

"We do, here at the church, but she doesn't know," said Jeb. "She never got our letter saying where we moved."

The deputy stared thoughtfully at the floor. "You say you have a name of who she might be with?"

"Nash Foster, we think," said Jeb. He gave him the car's description.

The officer flipped his notepad back a few pages. He

pulled out his pen and said, "Mind saying that name one more time?"

"Nash Foster."

"Where was this automobile last seen?" he asked.

"The Diner, in Norman."

"The girl's description."

Jeb told him. He was glad to see the officer finally taking an interest. He told him what few facts Joe gave him about this Nash fellow.

"Reverend, did he say what direction this driver was headed?"

"North on Highway nine, out of Norman, last night. I drove up and down the highway, looking myself, but I never found the car," said Jeb.

"Do you know how Miss Welby came to know this Nash Foster character?"

Jeb admitted he didn't. "What can you tell me?"

"This name came up once before, tied in with a gangster out of Boston name of Bill Foster. They've been hitting banks from here all the way down to Texas. This Nash fellow, he was questioned, though, and let go. He claimed he was related to Bill Foster, but not tied into his crimes."

"Wasn't there a gang robbery in Ardmore?" said Fern.

"Was the girl in your care then?" asked the deputy.

Jeb hesitated.

"She was out shopping," said Fern. "Not always with us."

"Your girl could be in a world of hurt, Reverend, or completely fine, never know." He closed up his book and asked for the telephone number of First Community Church.

Jeb gave it to him, but asked, "What do we do now?"

"What you do best, sir. Pray for your little girl." The deputy left.

"My head is swimming," he told Fern. "This can't be true, not of Angel. She'd never follow after that kind, not her."

"Maybe she doesn't know."

"What if she does?" Had she slipped completely away this time?

"What happened at Claudia's place?" asked Fern.

Jeb helped Fern to a chair. "I learned this from little John, mind you, not Claudia. Claudia was dating some hoodlum. He tried to make a move on Angel and she took off. How she hooked up with this Foster fellow, I can't say. Claudia has no telephone, and little of anything else to keep together body and soul."

"I'm staying at Sybil's this weekend," said Fern.

Jeb nodded. He didn't know what else to say.

⌇

Nash stayed in a boardinghouse, a brick two-story surrounded by a dying garden. The interior was sectioned off by a staircase, a maze of halls, and many rooms, all rentable on either a long-term or a short-term lease. His room, as he said, offered two clean beds, one against one wall, the second near the window; there were stiff, crisp linens, white from thorough bluing. Angel slept near the window, at times startling awake to see Nash sleeping as he had promised, not finding his way into her bed. When she roused at dawn, Nash was already gone. The proprietor, he said was a woman named Ruth Levy. Don't let her know, he told her, that you slept here, only that you know me and I said she might give you some work. He left an uncle's address on the nightstand for her use. The plumbing was often warmed up by sunup, was another thing she ought to know, since the guests were early risers. Nash got the lucky draw. His room had its own private toilet and bath. Angel slid into the warm tub, water up to her chin. She pulled up her knees and there was the bruise on her thigh. It was deep purple, a crescent moon yellowing on one side. She borrowed the bar soap left on the sink, soft and white and smelling of lilac. The lathering felt good, a coarse cloth rubbing her torso and legs, washing away yesterday.

A key rattled in the outside latch. She rinsed quickly and yanked the stopper. A white towel, thick and soft, hung on a hook on the bathroom door. She wrapped up in it. A young woman's voice called out, "Anyone here?" The voice was expectant, familiar. The bathroom door opened. An Asian girl stood holding a stack of towels. Angel surprised her.

"I sorry, I sorry," she kept saying, a trite curtsy, her knees slightly bending.

"It's fine, it's fine," said Angel, keeping the towel around her, the water dripping from the strands of her hair onto her shoulders. "You brought those for Nash. I'll take them." She held out her hands, but the girl wouldn't let go of the towels. "I put away. My job, not your job," she said.

Her words spilled out rhythmically, coming out from between her throat and nose, ringing almost. Nearly fearful.

Angel stepped around her, into the bedroom. She asked the girl her name.

"Guan-yin. And you are?"

"Angel."

"Where is the young man?" Guan-yin asked.

"Gone to work."

She backed toward the door. Her body was thin, moving like silk, nearly weightless, so that she slipped out of the room more quietly than breath.

Angel hung up the towel to dry and dressed. Her hair was damp at the ends, so she combed it off her face. She would need Nash's notes, the proprietor's name, and Uncle Bill, was it? She'd need his address and the room key. All lay on the nightstand.

The doors in the hallway had all been painted black, a white number nailed into the wood. Nash's was an upside-down 4. The wainscoting in the staircase, the banister, the curving balustrade, were white, but the steps were black like the doors. A man passed her as she descended, but he did not speak, even after she said, "Good morning." The smell of fried eggs lured her into the room to the right of the staircase. Two men sat at a long dining table, the remaining chairs either vacated already or not yet claimed. A maid gave them their utensils and a napkin each. Angel's belly rumbled. Mrs. Levy was easy to pick out. She poured coffee for the two guests, but where the serving maid wore a dark short-sleeved dress and white apron, Mrs. Levy sported a long-sleeved dress and a necklace string of large red beads. No apron. She was short and thick, her sleeves barely containing her arms. She gave the maid the coffeepot and then crossed the room the minute she laid eyes on Angel. "You looking for someone?"

"Mrs. Ruth Levy," said Angel. "I'm Nash's friend."

She was unmoved upon hearing Nash's name. The guests were given sausage with their eggs and a red sauce made up of tomatoes and something green.

"He said I might find work here."

"Already hired a girl two days ago. Chinese. If she doesn't work out, who knows, maybe."

A cold draft seeped in. Nash had not left her a note telling her to put breakfast on his tab. Angel had Mrs. Abercrombie's last two bits upstairs in her pocketbook. Enough, she thought, for a breakfast.

"Someone must have left the back door open," said Mrs. Levy. "Thanks for coming by. If I need you, how can I reach you?"

Angel said, "I'll stay in touch." Biscuits were set out.

Mrs. Levy left, heading for the back of the house beyond the staircase. When she was out of sight, Angel headed back up the stairs to dig out her money. Guan-yin passed her coming down the hall and scowled. "You Mr. Nash's girlfriend?" she asked.

Angel shook her head.

Guan-yin smiled.

The door was standing open at room number 4. Nash was filling his open suitcase, thrown on the bed near the wall. "Come in, fast," he said. "And then shut the door."

"Mrs. Levy has no work for me, Nash," she said. "Have you eaten?"

"Pack up. We're moving out," he said.

There was a faint rap at the door.

Nash told her, "Ask who it is."

"Who's there?" asked Angel.

"It's me, Nash, Guan-yin."

Nash closed up the suitcase. He opened the door. "Guan-yin, what do you want?"

"Are you mad at me?" the maid asked.

"What are you pulling? For crying out loud! I don't have time," he said.

"Is she why you not talking to me?" She pointed to Angel.

"Angel's a friend, Guan-yin. That's all. I don't live here. You know I can't stay."

Her cry was like a small bird's. Nash put his arms around her and said, "I'm sorry. I have to leave. You go. And stay away from room seven." He wiped her face. Guan-yin left.

Angel shoved her clothes into her bag. Nash led her out of the house, out the back way.

༄

Jeb gave Rowan a folder of invoices and instructed him to prepare pay envelopes for them. "I'm leaving early," he said. Fern waited in her car. He would follow her to Sybil's house.

The Blooms, both Sybil and her doctor husband, Rodney, came from Ardmore, like Fern, but unlike her, settled in Oklahoma City, Fern said. The bungalow, spread low and wide over the neatly trimmed lawn, had a sleepy look.

Sybil met Fern on the porch. She held open the door after Fern passed inside, waiting for Jeb to make it to the door. "Nice of you to drop by, Reverend," she said. She apologized to Fern for the way she looked. There was no color to her face and her hair was pulled back into a scarf. Fern kept apologizing for dropping in unexpectedly.

"Sybil, can Fern stay here the weekend?" he asked.

"You don't even have to ask," she said. "Fern, you have your things?"

She did.

It was settled then. "I'll come after supper, though," said Fern.

"There's extra for dinner. Both of you join Rodney and me. We love company," she said.

"Jeb has to get home to see about Willie and Ida May, and I ought to cook them something," said Fern.

"How old are the children?" asked Sybil.

"Willie's eleven and Ida May's nearly nine, old enough. But Jeb still keeps watch over them."

"How about you eating here and then I'll fix two plates to take home?" asked Sybil.

She was so insistent, Jeb finally told her they would stay. "You've kept body and soul together for us since we got here," he said. Half-meals sat in the parsonage icebox.

Sybil instructed the Latino woman that helped around the house to stay over to help fry up catfish. Jeb invited Fern back out to the porch. "There's a swing," he told her.

"You warm up the swing," she said. "I'll check to see if Sybil needs kitchen help."

He left her jacket on the sofa back. Chilly air moved in over Oklahoma City. The clouds partially overtook the sun cooling the air even more than the morning. Jeb swung, closing his eyes, listening to the women laughing over the stove, dipping fish into egg, and then cornmeal, as they schemed in the absence of men. Sybil's voice rose higher, the longer she spoke. Fern was a good listener, adding to Sybil's prattle, tossing in a "sure" or a "you don't say" between her tightly packed content.

"Have you met my friend Anna Baer?" she asked.

His toe dropped, stopping the swing's movement.

"She's Senator Baer's wife. I haven't had the pleasure," said Fern.

"We both attended the university in Oklahoma together, in Norman. That's where she met Walt. He actually introduced Rodney and me."

Jeb kept the swing perfectly still to quiet the rusted chain.

"We were silly back then. But when Walt set up his law practice and Rodney his doctor's office here in the same city, well, you can imagine. We were like sisters. Still are."

"She's sick, I hear," said Fern.

"I take her a meal every night. Walt's so busy at the capitol. She lives two blocks from here."

"How sick is she?" asked Fern.

"Cancer."

There was no noise at all, only the knifing sound the Latino cook made chopping potatoes.

"Sybil, I'll go with you tonight," said Fern. "I'm not doing anything else and I need to make myself useful. Between this wedding and this girl of ours gone missing, I'm a mess."

"What girl, Fern?"

Jeb came up off the porch swing. Surely, Fern did not mean that she would go to Walton Baer's home. He was not principled. If he were, he'd be seeing to his wife and not so dependent on Sybil. He wouldn't have followed Fern up on the roof of the Skirvin Hotel. He was not a man to be trusted. Jeb went inside. He found the women still talking about Angel.

"I'm sorry, Jeb," said Fern, her tone light and rather cheerful. She told Sybil, "I was supposed to meet him out on the porch swing." She and Sybil giggled.

Jeb said, "Fern, I'm starting to worry about Ida May. You know she's distraught over her sister and I'm thinking you and I ought to go home and see to her."

"Angel is Ida May and Willie's sister. I understand now," said Sybil.

"We've already got supper started, Jeb," said Fern. "Willie is plenty old enough to look after her anyway. She'll be fine." Fern dried her hands. She walked Jeb back into the living room out of Sybil's hearing. "Are you all right? You wanted me to be here tonight, didn't you?" She was smiling at him, tugging at the apron Sybil gave to her.

"Of course I want you here," he lied.

"I think it's getting too cold out for porch swinging. Why don't you take a seat by Sybil's fireplace? I'll bring you coffee, you'll relax. You look tired."

He sat near the fireplace. Fern joined Sybil back in the kitchen. She was making do the best she could, he thought, and he wasn't making it any easier. The thought came to him that he had called this arrangement heaven-sent.

16

Nash brought two dresses from the rack, holding one in front of Angel as she looked into a mirror. After they checked out of the motel across the street, he stopped to fuel up. Inside the filling station was a ladies' dress shop, "Madam's Bouteek" by name. The outdoor sign overhead read MISTER'S FUEL.

A husband and wife sat behind a short counter, sharing a smoke. She gave the fag back to him and got off her stool. "I got a room in the back, miss, if you'd like to try on a few outfits."

Nash handed her the dresses.

Angel followed the proprietor to the back of the store. She pulled back a curtain that hung over a broom closet and turned on a naked bulb overhead by a string. "If you need another size, let me know. I'm Sue."

Angel slipped out of her skirt. Her stomach was still growling. She had worn the skirt for two days, saving the better clothes in her bag for better days. The new cloth was thin as silk, smooth and blue. It fell over her bust and hips, the skirt long and touching her calves. She buttoned it up the front and then stepped out to see herself again in the mirror.

Nash whistled. "That's a different woman than the girl that went in."

"Honey, it's made for you," said Sue. "Raglan sleeves, blue crepe, the length is perfect for your height."

"We'll take it," said Nash.

Angel checked the price tag. "It's four dollars," she said.

"Special sale today, three-fifty," said Sue.

"Can she wear it out of here?" asked Nash.

"Not with those shoes," said Sue. "Come see."

She called two shelves near the storefront window the shoe shop, one row of black, one of white. She gave Angel a chair handing her one shoe after another until she found a fit. "You're a size five," said Sue. "Stand up, so your mister can get the full effect."

Angel had not seen herself quite so fully grown before. "I like how the fabric feels against me, kind of soft." She felt older after seeing herself.

"You got any ladies' coats?" asked Nash.

She showed Angel three on a rack of otherwise empty clothes hangers. The first one, she held in front of Angel.

"Gray-and-blue plaid, all the rage. The other two have a fox collar, pricey."

"The plaid is fine," said Angel. Before she could slip it on, Nash was holding out the fox collar coat.

"That's thirty-nine-fifty, hon," said Sue.

"Try it on, girlie," said Nash.

"I like the plaid," said Angel.

"Have you ever tried on fur?" he asked.

"I don't need it," said Angel. She buttoned up the plaid.

"For fun. Just try it," he said.

The clerk backed away.

Angel put the plaid coat back on the hanger. "I don't want fur, Nash." She'd feel a fool, like she was playacting.

He stood between Angel and the clerk. He mouthed, "Don't say my name." He was pushy and getting on her nerves. She extended her arms behind her. Nash slid the fox coat over her arms. She turned and looked in the mirror. It was Fern all over.

"Hotsytotsy, babe," said Nash. "We'll take the fox, there, Sue, is it?"

Angel handed the coat to Sue and trudged back to the changing room.

Sue boxed up the coat and her old clothes. Nash paid out.

Angel ran out into the cold and climbed into the car. She was quiet as they drove away. Nash was even more talkative than he was the first night. Spending money was his whiskey.

"I noticed you had a roll of bills in your pocket," she said. "Was that your pay from the 'job' this morning?"

"Money well-earned. You got to learn to look out for yourself, Angel. First off, don't be saying my name all over the place. You didn't hear me blabbing yours. Second, you want respect, you got to dress respectable." He pulled into a restaurant parking lot, a mom-and-pop steakhouse. The window sign advertised choice cuts. Nash got a hat out of the car trunk and placed it at an angle. The air was brisk. He pulled out the new coat while he was at it, holding it open. She met him at the rear of the car and he slipped the coat sleeves over her arms. "I laid out the dough, may as well put it on, babe. Look at you, very chic, very chic." He said it like the bird. He was making her blush, though, making over her. The collar rose to her neck. Nash gave her a lesson on how to make the fox bite its tail to hold the collar closed. There was a handgun in the trunk. He closed it.

A hostess met them at the door. "Two for lunch?"

Nash held up two fingers, handed her a bill, and said, "See that my friend here is taken care of. She's had a hard day."

The woman told Angel to follow her. She offered her a chair near a window, a table decorated with a rose in a vase, two glasses on the table, one placed in front of Angel, crystal was it? It looked like some of Abigail's things. A waiter filled the water glass. Nash sat next to her. He pulled out a cigar. The waiter gave her a menu. Nash winked and mouthed, "Respect."

Angel wanted everything, the steak cut-to-perfection, the potatoes seasoned in butter, the fresh greens. "I need something now," she told the waiter. "Is that possible?"

"Calm yourself, they're not going to run out of food, girlie."

"I'll bring you some bread, miss," said the waiter. He disappeared into the kitchen.

"You ever been hungry, Nash? I mean, where you don't know if you'll get to eat again?"

"You're not the only one that's seen hard times, Angel."

"It scares me. To this day, I get so scared like I'm afraid I'll die of hunger. Except that's not what I'm really afraid of."

"What scares you?"

"Everybody knowing that I starved to death."

The waiter appeared. Nash ordered them two steak dinners. A bread plate was set in front of her. She bowed her head, a habit.

"Let us pray," said Nash. He bowed his head.

"Don't poke fun," she said, the right side of her mouth lifting.

"I'm respecting you, that's all." He closed his eyes.

"God, thank you for the food we're about to eat. Please keep Ida May and Willie safe and be sure Willie keeps up with his arithmetic. Help Ida May not to cry. Amen."

꘏

GANGLAND STYLE ROBBERY
RACKS SMALL-TOWN BANK!
GET YOUR *OKLAHOMAN*, READ ALL ABOUT IT!

Jeb dropped a dime in the newspaper boy's hand. The kid sold papers on the street corner Saturdays, a block up from the parsonage. A couple walked past, out for a stroll. One delivery boy rode his bike past, a sack of groceries in his bicycle basket. Jeb snapped open the newspaper. A bank in Yukon had been robbed. A neighbor was raking leaves out front. Jeb asked him, "You know anything about Yukon?"

"Small town, west of here. Nice place."

"You know anything about the robbery?" he asked.

"Some guy trying to take Dillinger's place, I'll grant you."

"Doesn't say who," said Jeb.

"One day, the FBI'll catch them. They'll get what's coming to them."

"Shame these small towns are getting hit," said Jeb.

"Oklahoma City's been hit too. No one's safe anymore."

Fern pulled up, parking out front. Jeb did not know what happened last night after he left, after she joined Sybil to visit Anna.

"You were right," she said. "About staying too far away. I've missed you."

He felt her skin, her cheek. "You're cold. Let's go inside."

She kissed him the instant the door closed.

"Whoo!" said Ida May. She was holding a doll, standing in the hall outside the kitchen. "Jeb and Miss Fern is sparking, Willie. Come see!"

Jeb told her to go back in the kitchen and finish her

grits. He kissed Fern again. "I've missed you too. Tell me again why the wedding's in December."

"Abigail needs time."

"To invite all of the relations, I know. You taste good." He caught his reflection in the mirror. His eyes had dark circles beneath them. "You always look good in the morning. I look lousy. You sure you want to wake up to this mug every morning?"

"Every day except the eighth."

"How was Anna?"

"Thin, weak. I've never seen a woman as sick as her."

"Was her husband around?"

She looked toward the kitchen, took off her jacket. She wanted to sit down, she said, so Jeb sat next to her on the sofa. "Walt came in after we gave Anna a bath."

"You bathed her?"

"She was so grateful. People walk on eggshells around her. She was grateful for not just our company, but the attention."

"Did Walton, did he say much?"

"Why you want to keep bringing up Walt?"

"No reason."

"I've never met a woman with so much humility," said Fern.

"Anna, you mean?"

"Yes, and she is so sad she's never had a baby. Said Walt wanted a big family. We let her cry a good while."

"Does Anna know that you and Walt, you know, once dated?"

"You can't ever say that to anyone, Jeb. Ever."

"People date, Fern. Who doesn't have an old flame they run into at some time in life? I don't see what it matters."

"Promise you'll not bring it up, not to anyone in that family, in that church. Anna says her father-in-law is one of your deacons. Especially not to him."

"Want to tell me why?"

She was looking around her, not straight at him.

Ida May was finished with her breakfast, wanting Fern to comb out her braids. Fern took her into her arms. "You're old enough to fix your own hair, Ida May. Your brother has already outgrown Angel, now look at you. You're about to do the same." Her voice had only a slight nervous tremor.

"Angel is gone," said Ida May.

"We're going to find her," said Fern. "Don't you cry now. You're getting so old, you don't have to cry about every little thing."

"I won't. I cried last night. I'm finished with that," said Ida May.

Fern had the girl rest her shoulders against her knees. She was going to fix her hair. "And then we'll get dressed for a burger, down at one of those city cafés," she said.

Jeb had not seen his first pay yet. "We have some food in the icebox," he said.

"My treat," said Fern. She smiled, walking across the sparse living room, not a care for things like money or last-minute trips to the diner. At least it was a hint of a smile, for Ida May's sake, it seemed.

࿈

"Can I ask you about Guan-yin?" asked Angel.

Nash was driving, not saying where they were going, but checking a handwritten note on occasion. "Guan-yin is no one. She changes bedsheets at a boardinghouse."

"She sure liked you."

"I'm a likeable guy, don't you know."

"Did you sack her?"

"Watch your tongue, girlie. Didn't your mother teach you better?"

"She acted funny around you, don't you think? Like she was expecting something from you? I'm wrong, maybe."

"She was fresh off the boat, overly dependent on the kindness of strangers. Angel, you can't be dependent on others. One way to wind up, as you say, starving to death. And the whole world doesn't care, it doesn't care. Who cares about Guan-yin? Not anyone, not a soul."

"Were you kind to her?"

"She only wanted a silk pillowcase. So I bought her one. Reminded her of home."

"That's all? You bought her a silk pillowcase, no roll in the sack required."

"Would you look at that face, you're jealous."

"I'm not. I'm asking you if you slept with her. Did you?"

He let out a breath. Then he took his arm and put it around Angel's shoulder. He pulled her close to him. "You think I'm going to make you pay for that steak dinner?"

"And the fox coat and the dress, yes, I do." She laughed. "There's no free rides."

"I'm Nash Foster, future brilliant businessman, chauffeur to Angel Welby. All I want from you is company. I mean, look at me, do I look like a guy who has trouble getting dates? I can get a roll in the sack anytime, anywhere. But someone I can talk to, harder to find."

"I'm not like Guan-yin. I'm not gullible."

"That's why I like you. But you are like her."

"In what way?"

"Dependent on the kindness of strangers." He did not sound as though he were trying to be cruel.

"Not for long. I'm going to be a schoolteacher."

"I think those people have to go to school."

"I'm going to get back in school. Miss Fern, she's marrying Jeb, she went to a teachers college. It's not far from Mrs. Levy's house, as a matter of fact."

"We're driving farther and farther from that place. How you going to get back?"

"I'll work, get a job. Make my own way. Come March, I'll be eighteen."

"How much you figure a schoolteacher makes?"

"Over a thousand a year. More than my daddy ever made," she said.

"Chicken scratch."

"How much you make knocking off banks?"

"Hold your tongue, princess, I'm no thug. I'm only a chauffeur. I don't know nothing about no holdups." He had an easy smile.

A squad car passed them. Angel watched the cop

drive past, turn on his lights, and pull a motorist over. "How do you know no one is looking for this car?"

"The people I work for, they are, what is the word, resourceful. My car is out of the picture, I drive the boss's car. Guys like him, they like the limelight. They're not looking for me or my car."

"How much you going to make selling suits then? Not too many people buying suits nowadays."

"This Depression, it won't last. Maybe another year. Then I'll take the money I make off the suit store, buy up shares in the railroad. Trains, they're here to stay. Now you take your average railroad executive, young, industrious as I am. I'll make five times what you'll see as a teacher."

"Where you want to live?"

"Maybe Chicago, not sure I've found my city. My feeling is that if you look hard enough, your city will find you."

He sure liked to talk. "You ever kill anyone? I saw your gun."

"That's only window dressing. I didn't mean for you to see it. My uncle, he gave it to me, was afraid I'd need it. But so far, nope."

"I've been afraid enough to kill someone. Not hungry enough, though," she said.

"You want to know the truth?"

"Nothing but."

"I don't even know how that thing works. I've never loaded it." He drove onto a country lane off the highway.

"Where are we?" she asked.

"You ever been to a football game?"

Stanton School never got big enough for a team. "Not ever," she said.

"Cops don't look in places like that. I'll take you to your first game."

"Are the cops coming after you?"

"No reason. I'm a lowly chauffeur."

17

First Community's Sunday crowd was up in number, according to Henry Oakley. He paced in front of Jeb. They waited in the study for the other deacons to come, as Jeb requested, and pray. "We ought to have been doing this a long time ago," said Henry. "Reverend Miller, he gently asked these things, but, well, it's hard to get men to come and pray."

Jeb went through his notes once more. The nervous jitters subsided. It was easier preaching to a large crowd. He never knew that until now. Fred Sellers and Joe Gallagher walked in next, laughing and talking about Joe's son who played ball for his high school. Jeb shook hands with each deacon. Everett Bishop and Sam Baer stood outside the doorway, chatting with people as they passed through the lobby. Henry invited them inside and closed the door.

Before Jeb could say a word, there was a knock at the door. Henry opened it. "You looking for your daddy?" he asked.

Sam said, "Morning, son. Anna with you?"

Walton stopped in the doorway.

Each of the men greeted Walt, shaking his hand, calling him Senator, even though they all had watched him grow up.

"Anna stayed home," said Walton. "Mother's gone to see about her."

Jeb wondered why everyone except Walton Baer looked after his sick wife.

"I hadn't had the chance to properly welcome our new preacher, so welcome," said Walton. He reached toward Jeb. Jeb shook his hand, thanked him. "I wanted you to know what a help your wife was to Anna the other night. Anna must think me useless. But Fern, she comes in and takes over," he said.

Jeb stared stoically at the senator.

Walton looked at his daddy. "Fern gave Anna a bath, washed and fixed her hair. Time I got home, they had her looking like a movie star."

"Fern's going to make quite a preacher's wife, isn't she?" Sam put his hand out to his son. "Reverend's called us in to pray, so I expect we ought to get to it."

Jeb thanked him for dropping by.

The sermon was not exactly as he planned. The opening was better than he practiced, but he got into the sermon and wished he had developed it more deeply. He normally had his Saturdays free, but the day was eaten away running Fern and the kids all over town. Ida May finally got a coat, Willie a pair of socks, and Fern, of course, a hat. She paid for all of it, but he was going to have to get used to Coulter money, she told him. That was awkward. And his private study had not been either private or a study all week, but a revolving door of people, deacons' wives chattering about committees, orphan funds, widows, and the like. More than anything, he needed to lay eyes on Fern and see her smiling and agreeing as he spoke. Finally he saw her seated next to Sybil and Rodney Bloom. Walton Baer sat on her other side. His arm was up, not exactly behind her, but near her. That wouldn't do at all. He looked straight at Walton's husky hand, as if by an invisible thread, he could lift the hairy thing up and away from Fern.

The second point came to him more smoothly. There was this funny story about Angel he told, and since she was not here, he could get away with telling it. But as he described her to the sea of faces, he saw that none of them could imagine her, not like the neighbors at Church in the Dell, not see her bouncy step, the annoying way that she could get under his skin, and no matter how often she had her sleep interrupted, she always got up pretty as a little bird. "Truth be told, our girl is not with us and we are in need of your prayers to find her." He didn't mean to tell his personal business. There was a ripple of muttering, concern he took it, rolling like a morning tide through the members. There was a catch in his throat, not as if he were about to shed a tear, but a woman in the front row took it that way, and let out a sort of woeful moan. Other women were pulling out their handkerchiefs and it was all so godawful emotional. Gracie would accuse him of stirring up sentiment.

He moved on to point three. Walton's arm stretched across the pew back. It was behind Fern. He surely knew that she could hardly stand the sight of him, had even tried to talk them out of coming to First Community because of him. He was smug, a bore, and so full of himself he thought that he could move in on Fern before the December "I do's." It was that sick wife of his that got him thinking. That she was dying and here was Fern. She was the next in line, pretty enough to be a senator's wife. How dare he! He could see it all, the way he schemed, the scoundrel! What an idiot! "There is a payday for deceivers!" he said.

The woman in the front row pulled out a second handkerchief.

An usher opened the back door and let in the deputy. He did take a seat, but it was the end of the message. Jeb was closing in prayer.

⌇

There was a single church bell ringing, a low booming chime, sounding from across the street, tolling through the windows of the inn where Angel was waking. The bedsprings popped under her every time she moved. The tip of her nose was cold and her feet stuck out of the sheets. She tucked them back under the linens and the thin blanket, wanting to warm up once, as she had been cold most of the night. There was no clock on the nightstand. Nash left a note. She was angry to find him gone and a note left in place of him. She sighed, and when she picked up the note, some bills dropped onto the table. He left her some cash. "I'll be back soon. Breakfast downstairs." His handwriting was plain.

Since it was Sunday, she put on her fancy filling-station dress, as Nash called it, not knowing how the guests of the inn might dress for the morning. She found the inn when they got out from the football game, the roadside sign flashing in the headlights of a passing motorist. She begged Nash to turn around, not wanting to be on the road all night, to chance him growing sleepy and some curious cop pulling him over.

The morning lady innkeeper was not a happy sort, not as jovial as the man who let them in Saturday night. She may have been his wife, not that Angel knew. Talking to strangers every day, not knowing who she'd meet next, bored Angel.

"If you're looking for your boyfriend, he was on the telephone all morning. Took off with some man in a big car not fifteen minutes ago," said the innkeeper.

"May I use the telephone?"

Mrs. Pierce held out her hand. She wanted fifty cents. Angel paid her and she led her to a booth near the inn's entry. She showed her how to crank the machine, to connect the operator. Angel got the hang of it and thanked her. She told the operator Will Honeysack's number. The phone rang six or seven times and the operator asked if she'd like to continue ringing. Yes, she did. The operator asked if it was a business and that was when she reminded her that no one was open on Sunday and that was the last straw. Angel hung up.

"You want breakfast, you got ten minutes," said the innkeeper.

The church bell tolled again.

Angel ate the breakfast: some apple slices, eggs, and grits. The hot bread was good and the butter as good as Abigail's. Angel paid her for the breakfast and asked, "You ever go across the street to that church?"

"I got to keep the inn running. It's a colored church, but anyone can go. I seen all kinds coming and going."

There were some cars in the dirt lot, but most of the members were on foot, walking to church up the partly paved streets that crossed the highway near Mt. Zion Church. There weren't any whites going in, as the innkeeper might have said in a roundabout way. A side door opened. It was a choir, men and women dressed in gray-and-red robes, filing out onto the dirt lot. A woman stepped out and faced them. She led them in a song. They were holding rehearsal, it seemed to Angel, out on the parking lot. The building was nothing more than a square framed by a gabled roof, so they practiced, she guessed, wherever it suited them. What she couldn't figure out was what drew her to cross the street.

When the preacher shook her hand, he seemed glad to see her, like she was a novelty. She sat in the back, same as when she first started going to Church in the Dell. The back row was the place where people who either did not know anyone or were trying to figure out why they came, liked to hide. Whether or not that was true of Mt. Zion, she couldn't say. Several teen girls filed into the same pew, three older women, one smelling of snuff, and two ushers.

She had heard one of the songs before. The minister wore a robe the same as the choir, maybe slightly different. His collar was gold. But he stretched out his arms and not once did he have to sing from the hymnal. He knew the words, and when he didn't, he echoed. Easy enough. Angel put down the hymnal and echoed too. Not hard to do.

The three women took hands next to her. It was the thing they did each week, obviously, for they only did it on certain songs, like the marching kind. But they all knew when it was time to take hands. It was a mystery. They were wearing gloves and white hats and the songs were their language as much as the white hats and gloves. There was a lot of freedom music. One set free, and I'll see you in the morning over there, and words that were about leaving the earth behind. She thought, if the whites knew what they were singing about, would they mind?

She shed a tear. That was not expected. But she had not slept well. Ida May was in church somewhere and, she was pretty certain, had missed the top button of her dress. If she remembered to tie up her braids, well, then, the ribbons most likely didn't match. It was hard to breathe now. The church was full, more women filing into her row. And where, pray tell, had Jeb gone off to and why had he not written? Ida May and Willie were her responsibility. It was like him to go off and not think through what needed to be thought through, not a care for how she would find him. He had done stupid things in the past, but it was, as her

granny once told her, the way of a man. She did not care
that the tears dripped onto her new dress.

The preacher shouted, as he had been shouting, "I see
those tears you cry."

She accepted a handkerchief from one of the white-
hatted women.

"Is it," he asked, "because you've lost your way?"

Angel nodded.

"Are you tired of being a stranger on life's journey?"

There were a lot of amens. Angel shrugged.

"Do you feel as if you have no home?" he asked the
flock.

"I don't," Angel whispered.

"There is a reason you feel this way. I tell you, friend,
this world is not your home."

A few women came to their feet.

Angel was sobbing into her handkerchief.

"That's it, girl, let it out." The stranger took hold of
her arm. Angel wrapped her arms around her. She let her
cry it out.

℘

"Deputy, glad to see you," Jeb said, even though seeing him
walking through the back of the church had unnerved him.
He asked his name.

"Deputy Abner Faulk," he said. He took off his hat.

Rowan brought a pitcher of water into the study and
was gone.

Jeb had not noticed during his first visit the red mark

on Abner's bald pink scalp. It was not a wound, but a sort of birthmark. It was in the shape of the country of Italy.

"I'm here on business, I guess you know, Reverend." He turned down the water. "I'm working with the deputy up at Yukon. You read about the bank heist in yesterday's paper, I guess."

Jeb let out a sigh. He poured himself some water.

"This is the third bank robbery this month. I don't have to tell you, the FBI is all over this thing. I had to give them your daughter's name."

Jeb didn't correct his calling her his daughter. "She would never rob a bank."

"That doesn't mean she's a suspect. At this point, it could be she's entirely innocent. But this fellow, Nash Foster, he's wanted for questioning. If she's with him, she'll be questioned too."

Jeb rubbed his temple. Walt Baer gabbed outside the door and Fern responded. "Angel needs to be brought home. She has a loving family, her little sister is sick with worry. So am I," he said. "Deputy Faulk, you've got to promise to make sure everyone on this case knows that she is not a bank robber. Keep this girl safe."

"I wish I could say that the FBI cares a hill of beans about what I say. I did tell them, but they want this string of robberies solved. If they tie them to Charley Foster, Nash's uncle, they'll be after the whole gang. They get who they're going after, starting at the top, and work their way down."

Faulk's words seemed distant, as though he were in a different room.

"I did tell them the circumstances surrounding her running away. But they frown on young girls who run with getaway men."

"What does that mean?"

"One of the witnesses in Yukon got a description of the driver. It matches the description we have of Nash Foster."

There came a pounding on Jeb's door. It was Fern. She let herself in. "Deputy, have you found Angel? I'm sorry, Jeb. I saw you go in with him. I couldn't wait."

"Not yet, ma'am," said Faulk. It was time, he said, to go. He told Fern, "You try not to worry. If I hear that Angel's been brought in alongside this Nash fella, I'll do everything in my power to see she's returned." He said to Jeb, "Pray I get to her first."

Fern was ashen. Faulk saw himself out.

Jeb did not want to add to the weight. "He'll do what he can do."

"I know, I know," she said. "We're invited to Sunday dinner. Sam and Anita Baer."

Jeb saw that she was staring down. "Not today," he told her. Constantly comporting himself through all of the church circles had worn him out.

"They assumed we'd come to dinner. You know what that's like. What am I supposed to say?"

Jeb assumed that Walton would come. "Can't you get us out of it?"

The door opened. A woman said, "Hello, Reverend, I'm Anita. You've met my son, Senator Baer, and my husband, Sam, one of your deacons." She was absolutely pink with satisfaction. "You can't get away without trying some of my chicken-fried steak. No one cooks it like me, I don't care what you've heard. I told Fern how to find our house." She closed the door.

Fern looked at him. She didn't answer his last question.

✻

Angel did not eat that night. The innkeeper closed up her kitchen since only one room was rented out, theirs. She fell asleep twice. The sky darkened a little more each time she opened her eyes, until finally the room was black except for a wedge of electric light seeping under the door. The room bill lay on the floor partially under the door.

She put out her hand to brace herself and her fingertips slid across the cold window glass.

Nash had not come back. But his car was still parked in an alley behind the inn.

A food smell was coming from outside the room. They weren't to cook, the innkeeper said, no cooking at all. She thought it was beef, onion, green pepper. A guest must have checked in late, or else the innkeeper was fixing her own dinner. There was no sound of feet, so it must have been the second thing.

She walked across the mattress on her knees, the mattress springs squeaking like an old man's jaw. The lamp string was gone when she reached for it. She would open the door, she decided, to let in some light and find the lamp. Also missing were her socks, and since the rug was undersized, her feet hit cold, hard flooring. She found the doorknob. Like the window glass, it was cold and an October draft blew under the door, pricking her bare toes. She opened the door. Nash caught her by surprise. He took one step into the room, but then staggered. She couldn't say how long he had been standing outside the door. She tried to hold him up. He muttered something unintelligible. He was heavy, like her brother Willie. He held out one arm and dropped a bag inside the room onto the cold floor. Angel instructed him to take a step, leaning against her, until finally he dropped onto the bed. There was the lamp. She got turned around in the dark. It was near the window, not the door. She turned it on.

Checking the hall, no one had seen him like that. She shut the door.

Nash was muttering and holding his side. He kept saying he was fine, even though she was too shocked to ask. He rolled off his side, bloodying the linens.

"I'm going for help," said Angel.

"Sweet cakes, you got to come here," he said.

Angel sat on the side of the bed.

"What I tell you about depending on the kindness of strangers? We got to take care of our own worries."

"You're shot, Nash."

"It's a scratch. Go down and ask Mrs. What's-her-name for some liniment and some rags. Tell her I fell hunting."

"She'll know, Nash."

"She won't ask you a thing. It's supper time. She won't want to be bothered."

Why was he so sure of things? "I'll be right back then," she said. The CLOSED sign was hung out on the office door.

Angel knocked lightly. The "in" innkeeper, Mr. Pierce, answered. "Evening," he said. He was still chewing his supper.

Angel used marriage as a front. "My husband was out deer hunting. He fell and he . . . he got this gash."

"Don't look so worried. We get that all the time. Got just the thing."

She could not believe that he bought the story. Even she did not think herself believable.

He came back. "Here's a box of some bandages and some of the wife's medicinals. If it's deep, now you know he'll need a doctor, don't you?"

She took the box and thanked him.

Nash was passed out. She kept checking his pulse to be sure he was breathing. Her touch on his side was making him groan. She was worried he'd draw one of the proprietors up the staircase. She gave him a rag and told him to bite down. "I can feel something, Nash." She didn't know how to tell if she had found a bullet. He was expecting her to take it out. She stood up and went to the window, where she rested her forehead against the cold glass.

ॐ

Anita did cook the chicken-fried steak, but left the rest of the meal to her domestic help. The meal stretched into the afternoon, until the black cook, who had cleared away the noonday dishes, was back setting places again. Fern told her not to set service for them, but not even Fern could stop Anita, who told her cook, "Sandra, I'll help out. We can make sandwiches out of the leftovers."

Anita wanted Fern to see her new radio. "The music

sounds so alive, you'd swear the drummer was here in the living room."

Henry and Walton got up and headed for the porch out back. Henry stepped back inside. "I'm going for my sweater. You need a sweater, Reverend?"

Jeb took that to mean he was expecting him out on the porch. "I've got a jacket," he said. Walton stared up at him through the screen.

The Baers' backyard was a good two acres back. White wicker furniture was left scattered across the porch, exactly as the last partiers had left things. The porch ran nearly the width of the house. Jeb sat two chairs away, to leave space for Henry and to put some distance between him and Walton. Sandra filled his cup again, struck a match, then lit the candles on the table right in front of Jeb; she went inside complaining it was too cold for the porch.

"I envy you, Reverend," said Walton.

Jeb didn't know what to expect, so he sipped his coffee.

"You got what you need, don't you? Seem content in your work, helping people."

"Senators help people, don't they?" Fern wasn't within earshot, so he didn't temper his tone. He didn't feel much like talking to the man.

Walton finally looked at him. "We might, if we didn't have to spend so much time helping ourselves. First you think you have to get in office so you can make a difference. Then once you're in office, you got to do the things it takes to stay in office."

Jeb put his hand near the candle and felt the heat.

"The public never stops needing, this I know. The more time I spend fighting all of these government wars, the less my wife sees of me."

Jeb closed his eyes. The man needed to talk, it seemed.

"I'd like to know if you, as a minister, ever think a man can find contentment."

Senator Baer was asking him for counsel. Jeb let out a sigh, and then realized Walton was waiting for an answer. "If by contentment, you mean will you ever get to the end of your work; no, I don't."

"Now why is that?"

"Work is, well, work, and it's always there. Will be, even after we die. But you have to get to the end of something, that I know."

"What else is there to get to the end of?"

"Yourself," said Jeb.

"You getting philosophical on me now, Preacher?" Walton's face was pale, his eyes pensive. Not once had he taken his eyes from Jeb. He was leaning forward, his hands clasped somberly in his lap.

He didn't want to help Walton, he wanted him to leave and go home to his wife. But he looked as though he had lost his way and Jeb knew that lost place and the end of it. "You think you know what you want when you're a young man. You can name it and it has work attached to it, so you see that as your purpose," said Jeb. "Then other things attach to you, like people. But you don't mind, because it seems to come with the territory." Walton had a blank look about him, so Jeb filled in the blank. "Women."

"Oh, that, I get that. They're needy."

"Like us."

Walton nodded, a weak attempt to affirm.

"Then we start to lose sight of one or the other, either what we thought was our purpose or else our family. We don't juggle as well as women," said Jeb.

"That's the honest truth."

"The truth is, if there's nothing left but the people who've decided for some insane reason to love us, then that is when we know that we've gotten to the end of ourselves." Jeb sipped some of Sandra's coffee. "So in spite of what we lose, we still have a mysterious satisfaction because of who we've held near."

"And if we've kept all else, but lose the one we love?"

He seemed to be getting the idea. Still, for a man who went to law school, he was a little slow on the uptake. Jeb wondered what was keeping Henry.

Anita's radio was blaring so loud, Walton got up and shut the house door. Instead of taking his chair, he stood his carcass in front of Jeb. "There's a chance I may have lost my way," he said.

This was one for Gracie, not him, for crying out loud! If he stared long enough at the candle burning next to his coffee, maybe Walton would take his chair. But he kept standing, looking down at him, a big dumb kid. "I know the feeling," said Jeb. "Have a seat, Senator."

"Walt is fine."

Jeb pushed aside the candle and the coffee. "Anna is sick, Walt. But she's still here."

"Fern said that."

She hadn't told him that. "There's no perfect love, except God's love."

"What makes Him so special?"

Walt was being serious, not making light, Jeb told himself. "He doesn't change like us. So we have to work at love, and, as men, it drives us nuts because we think we have a grip on it, and then the landscape changes."

"God changes the landscape?"

"And life, life changes." He did believe God was that involved, but as to how much theology Walt could soak up, he didn't know. "The fact is, as Fern said, Anna is still here. There are things about her, all women actually, I mean, that take a long time to find out. We have to go after knowing those puzzling things with the same zeal we did when we were young and chasing after work. And it seems to be in the cards that they won't tell us everything at once. You wish they would."

"But they don't. Now why is that?"

"Trust."

"I don't follow."

"We have to earn their trust. When they open up, you know, give us a bit of themselves that we hadn't known before, then they wait."

"What are they waiting for?"

"To see how we react."

"There's a problem. I don't know the right questions to ask."

"I know. I know."

18

FERN WORKED ONE MORE DAY AT THE
school in Ardmore. The Blooms insisted she move
on in and she was too worried sick about Angel to teach,
she said. Jeb took Monday afternoon off and helped her
move some of her clothes into Sybil's guest room. The rest
of her belongings she wanted moved into the parsonage.
There were some linens Abigail bought, she said, for their
wedding. But no need to leave good linens in Ardmore.

Jeb kept saying, "Of course" and "Why not?"

The hall closet was empty, so she folded and snapped
linens until she filled the shelves with towels and sheets.
She made a list of things they would need, like an ironing
board. He used the bed. It seemed fine. But he had also

hung the picture of Jesus in the hall and she took it back down, promising to find a good place for it.

The picture of Jesus could go. What he wanted was the sound of her rattling around the parsonage, her bare feet next to his, small blond strands of hair left in the bathroom sink.

There was another box she opened. It was full of small cloth bears. They made a row across the fireplace mantel, some arms crossed in front, or looking down.

"I'm trying to decide where all my bookcases will go," she said. Those she left at Abigail's. She invited him to the sofa, to help her plan the room. "You've put your study desk in a dark corner."

He saw the small nook as the perfect fit for the desk, as though one had been made for the other.

"You want your desk near the window." Light, of course, he hadn't thought of, no more than the ironing board. Her hand was soft, but for the small calluses on the inside of her thumb and forefinger, her golfing calluses. He liked running his fingers over even the calluses.

"We have to talk, you know," she said. That was the way it was, when things were changing. She had those things that she had to say, like he told Walton. He knew not to say anything, so he sat back, waiting.

"Willie and Ida May," she said.

He waited a bit more.

"They can't run around all day like wild kittens, Jeb. Why aren't they in school?"

He had forgotten. "School here?"

She sighed.

"They can't live with Claudia. You want them here with us, Fern?"

"You're the one that has been trying to get rid of the Welbys, not me."

"For you."

She removed her hand from his, clasping and unclasping her fingers. "I've never asked for that."

He tried to remember. If he was wrong, she'd tell him. Back at the bus depot, when Angel was put on the bus with Claudia, wasn't she relieved? There was the time when he was going to take Angel to live with her mother in Little Rock. "You've never . . ."

She shook her head. "I've known since I first laid eyes on you."

Even he had not known. "How did you know?"

"Women know."

Of course it was like what he was telling Walton. Fern had not been asked. "I want Angel home," he said. "Do you?"

"I've been crying my eyes out since she left."

He took her hand again. "I think the bookcases need to go against that wall in the hall. They'll be between the living room and the bedroom, nice and easy to get to," he said.

"I like to read in the bedroom. It's quieter."

"Bookcases in the bedroom then. Ironing board in the closet. Picture of Jesus out in the storage shed," he said.

꒰

The sun was taking forever to come up. A couple of cars had pulled in, guests checking in early. She unstuck the window shade darkening the room. Nash was still sleeping, not even flickering a lash. Breakfast was going to be served, what with the arrival of more guests. She couldn't leave him, though, not until she was certain he was going to keep drawing another breath. He moaned softly.

She took the chair next to him, bending over him, and then saying his name.

"I hurt," he said.

"I did the best I could, Nash. You need a doctor."

"Not going to happen, sweet cakes." He couldn't get up.

He was going to have to stay in the bed for days, she thought. There was the bullet on the nightstand, red like a trophy, but a hole in his side. "I'll go down and buy a breakfast, bring it back up."

"Don't leave. I'm not myself."

"What happened? I want you to tell me."

He made a hissing noise, grimacing. "I called Uncle Bill yesterday morning." She knew that. Mrs. Pierce told her.

"He was hot on busting into a bank up the road, called it a pushover. It was Sunday. I kept telling him that . . . that we didn't know enough about it. It was in a quiet part of town, like everything around here, all of these bumpkins. What do they know? Nothing, they just let things be taken and they're sleeping and letting it happen."

"Was there a guard?"

"A yokel. Couldn't hold his gun right. We had the loot in Charley's car. Piece of cake, it was so easy that I could have done it in my sleep. We're climbing in the car and out runs this guy, he thinks he's a cowboy. He takes aim. I see Charley pulling out his revolver, like he's going to blow him away. 'No!' I think I screamed. I can't remember. I'm so thirsty. The guy's gun goes off. The last thing I see is this surprised look, like he can't believe he hit me. Charley runs around and fires on the guy. I can't see too good. If the guy got away, I couldn't tell you. But Charley pitches me into the car. His car is hot, we hear sirens. He has to drop me off, we have to separate. I'm blood, he says, and he don't want me in jail, doesn't want my father to know what he's gotten me into."

Angel said, "That bag. Is that the money?"

Nash laughed. "He knew the heat was on him. Wanted me to stash it. We could hide out here for weeks with the loot in that bag."

She made him roll on his side, to have another look at the bandage. It was blood soaked, like the one she changed at four o'clock. "What if we get you out of here, not now, but tonight. We drive far away, find some country doctor."

Nash closed his eyes. "Better look out. You're starting to think like a gangster's wife."

She applied a fresh bandage. He closed his eyes and took it, not complaining or saying anything. "Can I know something?" she asked.

"Anything, just don't touch me again with Mrs. Pierce's antiseptic."

"Was I another Guan-yin to you?"

"You mean, was I going to sack you, leave you?"

"I'd like to know."

"It's sappy, but I'm not in my right mind. I never knew

about love, so I was afraid that when it hit me, I'd miss it. When I met you, even back in that hayseed town where you rooked me out of a soda, I felt something different. Maybe I wanted to see if you were the one."

She had not noticed his eyes until now or the way his small finger crooked when he waved his hand. He was telling her the truth. "I'm getting you to a doctor."

Mr. Pierce knocked at the door. She had not taken him the bill or tried to pay it. She opened the door a crack to apologize. "Morning, Mr. Pierce. I was about to come down and pay you."

"The wife, she wants to know if you want breakfast."

"Two, and I'll bring them up to the room if that's all right."

"She'll go for that, what with your husband's situation," he said. "I'll wait for you downstairs."

Nash came up onto his elbows. "I'm glad to say I've known you, sweet cakes."

"I'll be right back with breakfast. You stay in bed." She was backing out of the room and he watched her go, the smile back and his eyes dark and blue.

The guests must have stayed downstairs for breakfast. Two of the doors were standing open, the linens taken off. Mrs. Pierce hadn't made it upstairs to change out the rooms. There was a skylight over the staircase and sunlight poured straight down through the glass. The staircase was white, washed in the overhead light. She would open the shades and let Nash see out, that the day was nice and not so cold as last night. Reaching the bottom step, she remembered that she was supposed to pay Mr. Pierce for the room and, of course, ask to stay another day or two. She turned to go back up the stairs and would have, but a man standing at the bottom of the stairs, she thought waiting for Mrs. Pierce to make eggs, said her name. She wasn't sure, so she waited until he said it again. "Angel Welby?"

Nash said she ought to watch her back, to not give out names, but this man knew it. Her heel lifted, taking the step backward.

"Mrs. Pierce has your breakfast ready. I'm starved myself," he said. "I'll join you, if you don't mind."

He walked Angel to the dining room, even had a chair waiting for her. There were no other guests in the dining room, and as she looked around for Mr. and Mrs. Pierce, she could not find them. "I was supposed to pay for the room," she said.

"Mrs. Pierce left our breakfast here. You look hungry. Have you eaten?"

She asked his name. He was more interested in the plate of eggs and sat down and commenced eating. She sat across from him. Since her belly was hurting, she thought it best to eat too. "Are you a cop?" she asked.

"Your daddy said you was a smart girl."

He startled her. "You know my daddy?"

His cup was empty. He tapped it against the tabletop and then went searching until he found Mrs. Pierce's coffeepot. She had left it on the sill of the kitchen passthrough. "He's been looking for you."

It was hard to believe after all this time. Even Claudia didn't know where he was. "Where is he?"

"Oklahoma City."

"How did you find me?"

"It was your daddy who helped. I don't think he meant to be so much help. Knew more than he gave himself credit. I'd say he's got a lot of humility. Loves you."

He was talking too fast and none of it was making any sense. "You talking about my father, Lemuel Welby?" She hadn't said his name in three or four years.

"Jeb Nubey."

"Did you find him? I mean, I lost him and Ida May." A tear trickled down her face. "Miss Coulter, did you find her? I been sick with worry, no place to go back to."

The front door opened. A cop dressed in blues poked his head into the dining room. "We can't hold them off any longer, Deputy. You going to get this girl out, or aren't you?"

"Girl's got to eat," he said. He offered Angel his hand. "I'm Deputy Abner Faulk. I promised Reverend Nubey I'd find you and bring you back."

"You can't let them take Nash, Deputy. He's not bad."

"I got a bank guard in the hospital says otherwise."

"Nash keeps his gun in the trunk. He doesn't load it, because he never wanted to use it."

"He's upstairs, I take it," he said.

"Can I go to him, be the one to tell him? He's in the bed and he needs a doctor."

"I promised to take you out of here and that's what I have to do," he said. "The whole FBI's out there, Angel, and you don't want none of that."

She stared up the stairwell as the deputy walked her out of the house. She told the cop on the porch, "He isn't armed. He's in the bed, shot in the side. He can't hurt any-

one." She was led out to Faulk's car, parked under the upstairs window.

⤳

"I'm going to see about Anna," said Fern. "Willie, you and
Ida May can go ahead and take your bed linens upstairs."

Ida May kissed Fern for the gift of the linens. Willie
took an apple out of the fruit bowl left behind by the
churchwomen. "I hope your friend gets better, Miss Fern,"
he said. He chased Ida May up the stairs.

"If you have to go," said Jeb, "I want to go with you."

"I'll be fine. Better you stay with the kids and get
them in bed early."

Anna had been well the night before. Jeb wanted to
coax her into staying. "Stay and let's make the first fire in
that old fireplace," he said.

She rubbed her arms. "It has gotten cool, hasn't it? If
you saw her this morning, you'd go too, Jeb. Sybil says she
hasn't been this bad until now."

"Willie and Ida May will be fine."

"I knew you'd want to go. But Anna is my project. I've
been doing nothing but chasing after students all these
years. Anna needs me in a different way."

"I'm glad Sybil has you. She'll appreciate your showing up."

"If you could see the way Sybil hovers over her, like
she's breathing life back into her."

"I guess you'll go back to Sybil's place tonight, then."

"Guess so. You can still make a fire."

"Not a chance." The last thing he wanted was to sit alone, stoking a fire.

Fern sat back down. "We got to bring some more furniture up. It's a big old house, isn't it? This place looks so empty."

"It did," he said. He pulled her close. Maybe a fire was a good idea.

"I want to tell you about Walt and me," she said.

There it was. "I don't want you to," he said.

"For just this moment, Jeb, don't look at me or I'll never get this all out," she said. "There's a lot to be said for everyone knowing about your past. I know you think it's been hard trying to convince people in Nazareth that you are a legitimate minister. But you worked at it until you finally earned everyone's respect. You're like the woman in the Bible with the bad past. Jesus is scribbling in the sand, and then in plain sight of everyone, she was absolved. It was like that for you."

Jeb got the box of matches off the table. "I'm going to light this," he said. The wood and kindling were already stacked inside the fireplace.

"Before I came to Nazareth, I got into some trouble. I met a lawyer at Dornick Hills during a tournament. He was alone and seemed lonely. I was a kid. But I imagined myself some sort of sophisticate. I had a drink with him and we talked until closing time."

"Walton Baer."

"I shouldn't have left with him. He took me to a hotel in Oklahoma City."

Jeb removed his jacket. He kept stoking the fire, his

back to her. He did not ask until now for that reason. He had grown accustomed to the Fern Coulter of Nazareth. The Ardmore Fern was more complicated. The fire was taking too long to ignite.

"He never said a word about Anna. I imagined I'd be his wife. He never said I would. I made it all up and thought that by wishing, I could make it happen."

His neck felt as if it would snap. He looked up the hallway. Willie and Ida May had gone upstairs. Their quiet banter was muffled by a closed door. "Until now, had you met her?"

"I never met her."

The late-afternoon sun was behind the large tree, the shadows stretching. There was a breeze and the sunlight. The movement of light on the old birdbath reflected against the trunk of the tree outside the window, the flickering showing through in places and hidden in others. Jeb came back to the sofa.

"It wasn't a one-night stand."

He kept listening. She was dabbing her eyes. He touched the place left on her skin by the tear. "Don't cry, Fern," he whispered.

"It went on for that entire spring. I was a senior. He came to my college graduation. Mother thought it was sweet. Walton brought a buddy and she thought he was a friend of Daddy's come to see Francis's daughter graduate. That friend took me aside, told me Walton was married."

"What did your father think?"

"I was sick to death from what happened. I told Walt to leave, to go back to Anna. Daddy kept asking me where he had gone. Finally I asked him to take a walk with me. There was a cigar stand on a terrace and I knew he'd like lighting his cigar at the lighter. I told him straight out about Walt. He went back into the restaurant and left me standing alone on the patio. I've never seen him so disappointed. I had to sit through dinner that night, seeing the look on his face, like he was doing anything to avoid looking at me."

The fire started to crackle.

"Daddy gave me a bear every year that I finished another year of school." She pointed to the white bear on the end of the mantel. "That one sat on the restaurant table that night. I knew he had brought it for me, but he never did muster up the words to give me his usual speech. He left it on the table. The note on it said, 'This one's for my angel, my Fern.'"

"You didn't move back home then," he said.

"When Daddy and Mother left for home, I was supposed to come home the next week, to talk to the school in Ardmore about a teaching position. I got in my car and drove to Oklahoma City. I knew where to find Walton. It was a Saturday night. He always took me dancing," she said. "I saw him through the window of the club. He was in the usual spot, corner booth, always surrounded by other lawyers. They each had a woman, none of them wives. At first, I was almost afraid I'd find him with Anna. Then I wished that I had."

"So that is why Walton wanted to see you at the Skirvin."

She swallowed.

"The jeweled bracelet, you said your father gave that to you," said Jeb. He turned his hand up and opened his fingers so that she would lay her hand in his. "Was that true?"

"I wasn't lying." She clasped his hand. "Daddy had given it to me. But I left it behind one night in Walton's car. He left it dangling on the mirror. Anna got in his car and saw it, thinking it was for her. She must be thinking by now that she's lost it."

"Nice of him to return it. Is that all? Is there anything else?"

She shook her head. The sun was gone.

His usual custom was to comfort her when she was upset. But now all that he could think to do was try and imagine the way they were before now, before he drove her to Oklahoma City. "I'm sorry I made you come here, Fern."

"I wanted to be like you, to face up to the past."

19

FERN PROMISED TO MEET JEB BY NOON IN his office at the church. By twelve-thirty, she was a half hour late, and then by one, it seemed not showing at all. If her time spent with Anna was pleasant or if Walt showed up, he did not know.

Rowan came in bearing letters for Jeb. There were quite a few cards welcoming him, so many that he had Rowan keep them in a separate stack for later. He had the morning free of deacons and women's committees, a relief. After he got a couple of letters off, he'd start his Sunday sermon early, get ahead of the week. There was one difference only between Church in the Dell and First Community, he thought. More people. People that needed advice or wanted to talk, needed to be made to feel better about

themselves. "Rowan, you're going to be a busy young man."
He gave him the job of opening all of the mail.

"I like that, Reverend," he said. He said he'd take out
the mail and bring it back, but he surprised Jeb when he returned five minutes later. "Someone to see you."

"Is it in the book?" he asked.

"No. Unexpected. I think you ought to see, sir."

After, he would take Rowan aside and give him a talk.
"Are you going to tell me who it is?"

"Just me, Reverend, Deputy Faulk." The deputy stuck
his head in.

He wearied Jeb the last time and upset Fern. He
stood up and extended his hand. Faulk shook it. "The last
time we met, we forgot something," said Faulk.

Jeb couldn't imagine what he forgot.

"Your home address. My missus had to sit up half the
night with an anxious teenage girl because we didn't know
where to take her. Poor girl doesn't know her own address,"
said Faulk.

Jeb was broken in two. He came around the desk.
"Don't tell me if it's not true," he said.

Angel walked into Jeb's office, her eyes taking in the
new space, nearly overcome, yet a funny giggle coming out
of her. "Jeb! I thought you were gone for good!" She threw
her arms around him.

His heart was thumping.

The deputy backed away. He bowed his head.

"I'm sorry." Jeb kept saying it until he was sobbing.

Angel commenced crying too.

He held her out at arm's length to look at her. Her

dress made her look grown-up. He was overjoyed and sad. Sad she had changed in his absence.

"I can't believe it!" said Angel. For an instant, she was thirteen again. But then he pulled back and she was seventeen, tired around the eyes, but pretty as always. Her smile faded and she looked sullen. "You moved away."

"Mrs. Abercrombie forgot to give you the letter."

"So you did write! I knew something was bad wrong. I'd never believe you'd leave me like that."

The dam broke loose again.

"You're crying, Jeb. I'm sorry. I didn't mean to pain you," she said. She kept throwing her arms around him, squeezing him.

Fern came up behind the deputy. "What's going on? Angel!"

Jeb didn't want to let her go. "Our girl is back, Fern." The women hugged. He liked the look of Fern and Angel crying and holding on to one another.

The deputy backed out into the hall. "I owe you, sir," said Jeb. He followed him and kept shaking his hand. "How did you find her?"

"You gave us the lead, the name, the description of the young man's car."

"So it was him. Jail?"

"I expect so, sir." He kept inching toward the front door. "I could still use that address. Your daughter is a witness for a high-crime case."

"You're right. She is my daughter," said Jeb.

Rowan stuck his head around the corner, still holding the mail.

"Rowan, my man! Take this deputy for coffee," said Jeb. "And give him whatever facts he needs about us."

✌

Jeb was glad that Fern took Angel home for a hot bath and to sleep. He managed to get out the letters. The sermon for next Sunday would not settle down in his thoughts. He was thankful to God for bringing Angel home, but also upset she went through so much. He could do battle with life's monsters, but hated to see a girl so young exposed to such seedy elements. It wasn't right. He got up to take a walk. He wanted the chance to be alone in the sanctuary. The afternoon sun poured through the stained glass. All the lights were off, so the natural light exploited the cathedral's tranquility. He was going to kneel and pray. But it seemed a shame to turn his back on the light. He lifted his hands.

"Thanksgiving, Reverend?"

The voice completely startled him.

A woman wheeled out of the shadows. She was in a wheelchair, but it moved along well under her hands. He had not seen her before. That was not a surprise. He knew that he wouldn't know all of the members right off. "If we've met, I'm sorry."

She rolled into the light. Her face was round and encircled with a tangle of brown and silver curls. "Not officially, we haven't met."

Jeb didn't know what to say. "I never get to appreciate the windows. My last church didn't have stained glass."

"They're kind of ostentatious, aren't they?"

He might have thought that once. "It's what they do for the room and my soul," he said.

"What do you see?"

He studied the glass. "The Passion. Is that what you mean?"

She kept smiling up at him.

"What do you see?" he asked.

"The beauty of suffering." She rolled back into the center aisle. The sun hit right at the exact spot where she stopped. She looked bronzed. "Don't be impressed," she said. "I've done this before."

She was a funny woman. "I have a question," he said.

"I got nothing but time, Reverend."

"Henry Oakley told me a story about a young artist who made these windows. It wasn't you, was it?"

She rested her arms palms up. Henry also told him how the artist's arms and neck ached as she colored and assembled each pane.

"Can't put nothing past you, Preacher." A covering of clouds crossed the sun. The light dimmed. "I'm done. Enjoy your prayers." She rolled out of the sanctuary and was gone.

He had not knelt or spoken a word in prayer. Yet, there it was, a message for Sunday. He hoped she would return to hear the sermon Sunday. He'd like to know her name.

❧

Angel sat on the sofa, wearing Jeb's robe, her eyes closed. Fern stayed to make a meal. "I'm glad you're here," said Jeb.

"I'm grateful," said Angel. She looked it.

Ida May kept running back into the room to make sure she was really back.

"I'm sorry for what happened to you at Claudia's," said Jeb. "I wasn't paying close enough attention to you."

"I wasn't either, that is, paying you enough mind. But if I never went, I'd not know."

"Know what?"

"My family is here," she said.

Ida May slumped onto the sofa, tossing her legs across Angel's lap. "Miss Coulter wants to know if you want tea," she said.

"Big glass," said Angel.

"That boy, Nash, Deputy Faulk says he'll go to jail," said Jeb.

"I know." Angel shoved Ida May's long legs off her lap.

"Did you care about him?"

"I felt sorry for him. I think he needed me."

"He didn't hurt you?"

"Not once, Jeb. I'd tell you. Before, maybe not. But it feels good to lay it all out."

"Agreed. From now on, we all lay it all out. Nothing kept back."

Fern stood in the hallway. "Don't give up every secret, Angel," she said. "We need to keep a few between ourselves, us women."

"Don't listen to her," said Jeb.

"Supper's ready," said Fern.

20

*A*HARD FREEZE HIT ARDMORE, BUT NOT cold enough to put a damper on a December wedding. Jeb almost talked Fern into eloping, but now seeing the holly in the arbor, he saw what Abigail wanted to see. Coulters were spilling into the reception hall, the nuptials having been said. The deacons from First Community drove down together. Henry passed Jeb an envelope. "For the honeymoon, from all of us," he said.

Will Honeysack walked right up to him, holding a slice of wedding cake. "Beautiful ceremony. Not so modest as Fern said, though."

"You'd have to know Abigail," said Jeb. He was glad for some of the frivolous touches following a long dry spell in Oklahoma.

Donna Faye and Angel were in blue dresses; Ida May was given a white dress like the bride's, being one of the flower girls. Fern's other sister, Ruby, came and served as a bridesmaid too. All of Fern's family, including Buddy and Lewis, kept toasting the couple. Fern finally came into the hall. She had changed out of her wedding dress into a nice outfit for the trip.

"Where's the honeymoon?" asked Will.

"A place in the Poconos. You ever heard of it?"

Will hadn't.

"Someplace where Abigail and Francis stayed when they were married. She insisted."

"I hear you're flying, Jeb," said Will.

"I hear that too." He had never flown before, not anywhere at any time. But it was time to enjoy a first with his bride. Walton walked in, a woman on his arm. Jeb excused himself. "Will, I need to meet someone," he said.

Anna was gracious, her face a vigorous pink. "I'm glad to see you," Fern said, and then handed Anna a glass of punch.

Anna took the glass, a bracelet jingling at her wrist.

Jeb saw the sapphires and emeralds in the silver setting. "That's a lovely piece," he said it to Anna, but he was looking at Fern.

"I thought it was lost. But it showed up. I'm so glad to have it back," said Anna.

Walton kissed the top of her head.

"We learn what's important, don't we?" asked Fern. "How to appreciate what we've got while we can."

There wasn't a person there who did not agree.

ABOUT THE AUTHOR

PATRICIA HICKMAN is an award-winning author whose work has been praised by critics and readers alike. Her writing has been hailed by peers as the "new and lyrical voice of the South," and described in such glowing terms as quirky, beautiful, a triumph, humorous, intimate, deep, and a virtual feast for the senses. Patty earned an MFA degree in writing from Queens University of Charlotte. She loves experiencing life to the fullest and can sometimes be found exploring the salt marshes of North Carolina's Outer Banks or river tubing down Deep Creek with her handsome boys. She and her husband have founded two churches in North Carolina, the second of which her husband is the senior pastor. They have three children, two on earth and one angel in heaven. You may correspond with the author at www.patriciahickman.com.

1. Jeb is not completely honest with Fern in the beginning about the full purpose of their trip to Ardmore. He justifies his lack of full disclosure by rationalizing that if the new pulpit position might be a chance occurrence, why trouble her? Does this indicate that he might secretly fear she will protest? Was he being dishonest or protective?

2. Angel finally seems to be more accepting of Jeb and Fern's union. She begins to see herself as a member of a real family, her unspoken desire throughout the series. But when her sister Claudia is finally discovered to be living near Oklahoma City, she suddenly has to prepare herself for the inevitable—that after all these years, she will be reunited with her true family. Have

you ever had to move away from your family and then be reliant on others to serve as your surrogate family? Was that a positive experience?

3. First Community Church in Oklahoma City welcomes Jeb with a sense of serving him as he serves others. With all of the problems he has faced as pastor of Church in the Dell, the sudden presence of a strong infrastructure and support are a huge temptation for Jeb. He has had to serve without pay at times, occasionally without support, and suffered self-doubt when some of his wise decisions faced criticism. Our loyalties tend to root for the home team—in this case the families of Church in the Dell—but, like Jeb, our human nature tends to seek out havens of support over nests of conflict. Have you had to make a difficult life-change decision and worry that you were looking for an easier life? What did you learn through the process?

4. When Jeb finds Fern and Walton Baer on the roof garden of the Skirvin, he is alarmed by the past intimacy they seem to have shared. Like Fern, we may avoid discussions about certain aspects of our past with our spouse. Prior to marriage, how much should be divulged and what should remain hidden?

5. If you've read the first books in the Millwood Hollow series, what was your impression of Fern? How did it change? Do you feel others know you because you have been authentic? Do you suffer from trying to present your life as perfect in every way? How do you feel when you are loved in spite of your flaws?

6. Angel prepares to leave with Claudia but Willie and

Ida May will remain under Jeb's care until she has had the chance to scope out what a life with Claudia might be like. In spite of her flaws, Angel has always made the responsible decision when it comes to her siblings. This was a common thread among people I interviewed who have lived through hard times. How might sibling relationships vary today as compared to families who lived through the Great Depression? What can we learn about relationships by studying lives lived in adversity?

7. Fern wants nothing to do with Walt Baer until she finds out his wife has a terminal illness. She accepts the volunteer assignment of taking time to care for her. Did she do this out of an ulterior motive or was she motivated by compassion?

8. Even though Angel and Claudia have come from the same parents, distance and a dissimilar set of learning tools have shaped their lives differently. How has Angel's character changed since she last saw Claudia? What were the factors in her life that served as a change agent?

9. Nash serves as get-away man for a gangster relative. But he paints himself as a chauffeur to Angel and seems to believe his own fictions—that clothes make the man, that a wad of cash in his pocket makes him a winner. He even compares himself to the men who sit along the roads in migrant camps, believing he has found success while they have succumbed to the wound of national failure. Have you gone through hard times? Did a new set of clothes help your sense of

self-worth? Improve your circumstances? How did hard times help shape your views of personal success or failure?

10. An artist in a wheelchair symbolizes hope for Jeb and his acquired belief that adversity and pain create beauty and a window to the soul. Because God has given us all the gift of free will, He may use adversity to open our hearts to Him, or provide a window into our souls. Has life taught you any similar lessons?

11. Angel has a different view of family and home at the end of the story than the opinion she touted at the beginning of the series. What has she learned about what makes up a family? Have you or someone you know had to create a family out of a patchwork of lives? What was learned from it?

Sadly, we have to say farewell to the Nubeys and the Welbys, but not to one another. I hope that you have enjoyed your visit and that you have found a connection of friendship in sharing this series with others. If you have not yet considered a life of faith in Jesus Christ, please know that He loves you and has a plan for your life. You can pray right now and know the transformation that comes when you embark on the great journey of faith. Please write and let me know how faith came alive to you through the reading of this series.

Your friend and sojourner,
Patricia Hickman
www.patriciahickman.com

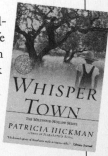